T0171635

Book 1

The Talent Sucker

The Jethro Sirius Experiment

Trevor Mason

iUniverse, Inc.
New York Bloomington

The Jethro Sirius Experiment
Book 1: The Talent Sucker

iUniverse books may be ordered through booksellers or by contacting:

iUniverse
1663 Liberty Drive
Bloomington, IN 47403
www.iuniverse.com
1-800-Authors (1-800-288-4677)

ISBN: 978-1-4502-7291-9 (sc)
ISBN: 978-1-4502-7292-6 (ebook)

Printed in the United States of America

iUniverse rev. date: 01/14/2011

For Alexandrea
Because you were the first to read it and the first to like it.
Thank you for believing in me.

PROLOGUE

The ship hung in mid space, dented and worn in a way that made it look as if it had been abandoned for scrap. It rested some two miles above the asteroid field that moved steadily below it. Those on board watched silently, scanning the massive grouping of space rock for signs of intelligence.

"Anything," said a harsh whispery voice.

"Nothing, General Carb, sir," came the reply.

"All eyes open, I know it's in there somewhere. They've been stunned, but that shouldn't disable their shield. Their shield is still up, right? I don't want them getting crushed between the rocks."

"Sensors are reading positive, sir. Their shield is definitely still up. We'll catch them."

"I know, Doil, but it's been almost a week since our last catch. Totally unacceptable. How does one build an empire on the slim pickings of this pathetic universe?"

"Things will pick up, sir. It's just a slow time of year. It's the meteor shower season, and you know how tourists are." Doil continued to scan the rocks below.

"Yes, yes, I know. All plugged in at home, surfing the...Net!"

"Of course, sir."

"No, I mean net, initiate the net! Initiate the net! Do you see them?"

"Hoser, stimulate the transit fusion particles," hollered Doil.

Suddenly, from beneath the rusty belly of the ship, a large and bright, laser netting, the size of the ship itself, dropped down in front of the asteroid field. The ship lurched as giant boulders began to gather in the net. A few smaller rocks bounced off the huge, exterior, neon strands and careened off to rejoin their brothers and sisters in space.

"We've got them, sir," said Hoser.

"Good. Pull up."

The ship began to rise. When it had reached an appropriate level, General Carb gave the order to stop.

"And now Mr. Doil, I would appreciate it if you and your crew would go salvage my prize from that giant cereal box of asteroids."

"Yes sir." Doil exited the main cockpit to go round up his team.

General Carb remained, sitting silently, nursing the evil grin that was splitting, end-to-end, across his forehead.

CHAPTER 1

THE OZZBOURN SIRIUS EXPERIMENT DISAPPEARS

Jethro Sirius had spent the last ten years of his life growing up as slowly as he possibly could. Being a kid on board an intergalactic tour bus was about as good a life a Sirian kid could ask for. You see Jethro's father, Ozzbourn Sirius, was one of the biggest rock-stars in the entire universe, and had been on an intergalactic tour for the past eight and a half years.

The inside of the tour bus was all Jethro knew for a home, and he figured it was the most fun place to be this side of Sirius. He had every cool toy you could possibly imagine, ate the tastiest food money could buy, and enjoyed the kind of freedom that every kid dreams of.

He wasn't the only under-age Sirian on board either. Three of his best friends lived on the bus as well and each of them enjoyed all the same benefits. One of these friends was Seth Tron, whom Jethro was on his way to visit.

Seth's father was Rolando Tron, Ozzbourn's drummer, and was well known for his brilliant mind and technical abilities. Seth had inherited his father's brains and was constantly inventing musical instruments for his dad's band. It was these inventions that led Jethro and Seth to forming their own band – *The Jethro Sirius Experiment.*

Though only eleven years old, the boys were creating music that could fool even the most critical listener into thinking that their songs were written by musically brilliant adults. This was something the boys knew and it definitely contributed to both of their all ready, over-inflated egos.

Jethro arrived at Seth's quarters and walked in. As usual, Seth was working on a project in his shop. Jethro found him immediately and began waving his friend away from the distracting work.

"C'mon Seth," he said. "Let's go jam man."

"Jethro," his friend replied, "in case you haven't noticed, I'm not a man. And besides, I'm busy." Seth didn't even look up at the source of the potential irritation.

Jethro rolled his eyes. "Oh brother, what are you working on now?"

"Do you really want to know?" asked Seth, smirking slightly.

"Not really."

"It's a beat box."

"What in Sirius is a beat box?"

"Well, I got in a bit of an argument with my dad the other night."

"Ya, so," replied Jethro, feigning slight interest.

"We were arguing about the importance of his job in your dad's band. He was arguing that he's not replaceable. I was arguing that he is."

"Is what?"

"Replaceable," Seth repeated irritably.

"So who won the argument?"

"Neither of us, yet. But I'm about to, just as soon as I finish building my beat box." He said this with confidence as he tinkered around some more with his invention.

Jethro looked slightly annoyed that Seth would ditch jamming for inventing but he couldn't conceal the fact that he wasn't surprised. Seth was famous for immersing himself in his projects for days at a time and there wasn't much that could pull him out of it other than the allure of another challenging project.

"Well, I'm gonna go find Val and Quasar," Jethro said. "I think they mentioned something about going down to the water park for the day."

At the mention of the girls, Seth looked up, unable to conceal the only other thing in life that could effectively and without fail, drag him away from his work. "Actually, now that you mention it, I could use a dip. I've been at this all morning."

Jethro rolled his eyes, again. "Oh, sure. You won't ditch your little project for jamming, but you will for girls."

"Not for girls. For a dip, I said." Seth stood up and walked toward the door, then turned back to his friend. "You comin'?"

Jethro let out a frustrated sigh before choosing to follow his friend out into the corridor.

The reason Jethro loved the water so much was because he was Sirian, an amphibious race from the planet Nommo. A lumpy rock shaped head provided a surface for his shaggy blond hair to swell upon. His two antennas shot straight out of the top of his head, capped with little pink balls of skin. He was a typical looking Sirian, with his big, pancake like eyes that sat like two mounds upon his face, and he felt quite comfortable knowing that Sirians were considered to be some of the most attractive aliens in the known universe.

He admired himself in the corridor mirrors as he and his friend walked through the bus corridors on their way to the water park.

Now, you're probably wondering what the intergalactic tour bus looked like. It was nothing short of amazing. Only the biggest stars could afford the best tour vehicles and Ozzbourn Sirius definitely traveled in style. On the outside, it was sleek and shaped like a bullet with one giant propulsion unit attached to its back end. It was dark green, but if seen in the proper starlight, it could appear to change colours. Its bullet-like shape was partially responsible for the speeds at which it could travel. It was the fastest of its kind. It needed to be, in order for the band to make it to its shows on time.

Inside, it consisted of four separate floors. The top floor contained the main cockpit, where the pilot and crew controlled and operated the ship. At the back of the ship resided the engine and propulsion unit. The service workers pretty much lived in this area, desperately trying to look busy all the time, due to the fact that the engine, although quite complicated, pretty much ran automatically with little need for service, other than that provided by the ship's central computer. The next level down contained the living quarters of the band, their families, and the crew. Of course, the band enjoyed much more grandiose quarters than the crew, which made sense for you see, the musicians only worked about four hours a day: two hours for rehearsal and two for performing. Their argument for enjoying nicer digs was that they spent much more time in their quarters than their 'fourteen hour a day' working shipmates. The crew, of course, argued that if they were paid more they'd be living in quarters fit for kings, too. Jethro and the other kids, who spend much of their free time exploring the ship, often eavesdropped on the conversations of disgruntled crewmembers.

Third floor was devoted to entertainment and exercise. It contained parks, mazes, tunnels and gyms for both adults and kids. Jethro and his friends spent much of their time on this floor, as it was the most kid friendly. The bottom floor was where the educational departments were located. It also shared space with the Galactic Research Department, an area that was full of laboratories run by a handful of Sirian scientists and explorers. The Ozzbourn Sirius Experiment was actually partially funded by the G.R.D., which was interested in the scientific research of the galaxy. By sharing the same ship, both the band and research company were able to enjoy the mutual financial benefits of sharing the immense cost of the tour. Due to the size of the ship, they were able to pretty much stay out of each other's antennas, which was just fine by them. As far as both parties were concerned, music and science just didn't mix.

Jethro and Seth arrived at the third floor and made a bee-line for the water park. When they entered, they saw that their other two companions were already in the water. The park, itself, was a spectacle to be admired. A rather gigantic wave pool provided a destination for a vast array of slides and diving boards. Quasar Ion was presently marching her way out of the water when, seemingly from out of nowhere, Val Netatious came swinging out on a rope and dropped into the middle of the pool. If there had been judges present, she would have gotten ten points for style. She broke the surface a few seconds later and waded out of the water to greet her friends.

Seth gave her a 'thumbs up'. "Nice jump," he said.

"Thanks," she replied, grinning. "You guys comin' in?"

"Yep," he said, turning to Jethro. "C'mon, let's go get suited up, man."

"All right."

Quasar hollered at them as they headed for the change rooms. "Don't ride the 'Black Hole' today guys. For some reason, it's not getting any water. You'll be scootchin' yer butts down the whole slide."

Jethro turned. "Thanks for the tip."

The boys disappeared inside the dressing rooms and the two girls headed back towards the drive lifter that would take them back to the upper area of the slides. They reached the top within moments and stepped out onto the platform.

They eyed their choices up and down. Val turned to Quasar. "So, what's it gonna be?"

"How about the Zornado?"

"Cool. Let's do it, dawg."

Val hit the slide like a bad case of diarrhea – fast, wet and unpredictable. Quasar wasn't too far behind her, though she exhibited a little more caution before jumping on. About halfway down the slide, Val let out a loud battle cry, and Quasar soon added her own voice to the sonic cheer of pleasure. Their voices were cut short when a thunderous rumbling suddenly broke the din of rushing water. It was soon accompanied by an uncontrollable shaking of the entire water park. Val and Quasar were now three quarters of the way down the slide and had to sit up in order to slow themselves down.

Val hollered over her shoulder. "What's goin' on Quas?"

Her friend either didn't hear her or was too afraid to answer, because Val received no reply. The shaking of the slides almost sent Val sailing over the edge, but she was able to throw her hands out to stabilize herself and prevent a premature end to her ride. She finally hit the water with a loud smack. The water, itself, was tumultuous and the waves were five times their normal height. Val had no problem staying afloat, though, and watched the end of the slide for the appearance of her friend. Quasar soon came shooting out and landed in the water next to her.

"What in Sirius is goin' on," she demanded, between breaths.

"I have no idea. I think we better swim for shore and make sure Seth and Jethro are okay."

They both swam for the edge of the pool. Though the waves were high and continued to crash down on top of them, they had no problem reaching their destination. Due to their amphibious nature, Sirians are very much at home in the water. They reached the shallow end within moments and began marching out of the pool. The ground was still shaking, though considerably less than the slides had been. Jethro and Seth were running towards them, feet smaking the wet surface of the water park floor.

"You two okay?" Jethro yelled.

"Ya'," replied Quasar. "You?"

"We're okay. What in Sirius is goin' on?"

"No idea."

The ground had now stopped shaking, and the loud rumbling they had heard earlier had dissipated substantially.

"Libby, what's going on?" Jethro shouted at the walls.

Libby was the ship's central computer. Basically, she was its brain, heart and vital organs all rolled into one. She controlled all its functions and knew everything there was to know about its operations, particularly its tour schedule.

"Libby!" Jethro shouted once more.

Libby's voice came, as usual, from out of nowhere. It echoed, loudly, in the large chamber. "Sorry, Junior. It took me a moment to calculate an answer to your question."

"And?"

"And what?"

"And what in Sirius is goin' on?"

Before Libby had a chance to respond, a brilliant flash of orange, neon light swept through the park, passing through the kids' bodies like smoke through an open window.

They all felt as if they'd just been put through a scanner and quickly patted themselves down to ensure all their body parts were still present. "Libby, what was that?" Asked Seth.

"Okay, so here's the deal kids," said Libby, "I need you to stay put. The bus has been in an accident. We've been stunned and caught in an asteroid net of some sort, and are about to be boarded. That orange light that just passed through you was a life form scanner. I'll get back to you as soon as I know more."

"Libby," shouted Seth.

The computer didn't answer and the kids all looked at each other. Ignoring Libby's instructions to stay put they all, immediately, ran for the door. Jethro keyed in the access code, but the door wouldn't open.

"Libby, open the door," he yelled.

Again, the ship's computer did not answer however, at that moment, they suddenly heard voices on the other side of the door-unfamiliar voices. They all pressed their ears up to the cold metal surface in an effort to hear what was being said.

"...better keep your mouths shut," said one voice.

"General Carb wants you all loaded and ready for transport within the hour."

"Where are you taking us," said a voice that sounded vaguely familiar.

"You were told to keep your mouth shut. Now move it."

"What about the children sir. Scanner picked up six life forms on board."

"Our instructions are to get them later. They ain't goin' nowhere. General wants all the adults geared up and ready for shipping first. He hasn't decided what to do with the kids yet. Now let's get movin'."

The voices soon disappeared and the kids exchanged a set of fearful looks they'd never had to use before.

"Something really bad is happening, isn't it," said Val.

"Ya," said Seth. "This is not good. What are we gonna do?"

Jethro shook his head. "I don't know. They said they're coming back for us right?"

Quasar nodded. "Ya, but they also said that the scanner picked up six life form readings of kids. There's only the four of us on this bus."

"Must be some sort of computer error, or something," said Seth.

"Well, what are we gonna do," demanded Val. "Just stand here and wait for them to come get us?"

She was answered, but not by any of her friends. Libby's voice, once again, rang out in their ears. "Okay kids, I'm back. If you want to get out of this alive, I have a few ideas. Do you want to hear them?"

"No, Libby, we'd rather just stand here and do nothing," said Jethro.

"Okey doke."

"Libby! I was being sarcastic. Tell us what to do."

"All right. All the adults have been taken off the bus. I need you not to panic. The ones who took them are coming back for you, but not right away. If we don't make an effort to escape, they'll disconnect me, take you hostage, and salvage the bus for their own needs."

"Who will, Libby," asked Jethro.

"I don't know who they are Jethro, but they've assumed that I'm not tactically programmed to operate on my own. I'm pretty sure I can get us out of here, but I need you kids to pay attention. Do you understand?"

"Just tell us what to do," said Seth.

"Sorry I had to lock you in, but I didn't want you wandering the corridors while they were still on board. The door is unlocked now and the bus is empty, but not for long. Get up to the cockpit as fast as you can. Go, now."

The kids did as they were told and, still in their swim suits, opened the door, ran through, and headed straight for the drive lifters. They all boarded and shot straight up to the cockpit level. They stumbled out into the main compartment, quickly grabbed a seat, and belted themselves in.

"Okay, Libby," said Jethro. "What now?"

"Hold on."

An awful creaking and grinding noise was heard throughout and, looking out of the windshield, the kids could see nothing but grey caverns of rock.

"What is that," said Val.

"Asteroid," answered Seth. "Libby said we'd been caught in an asteroid net. I'm assuming she's presently getting us out of here."

The bus quickly turned and rose up, breaching the apex of the topmost asteroid. Soon the kids were no longer looking at rock, but at a rather large, beat up looking ship. Two ship pods had ejected out of it and were now heading straight for them.

"Libby!" hollered the kids all at once.

"I see them. Like I said, hold on! 'Cause we're outta here."

The bus suddenly shot out into space, the two pods speeding after it. Laser fire shot forth from their pursuers and the bus shook under the force of the attacks.

"What now Libby," screamed Val.

"Don't worry, I've plotted a course and found a way out. The likelihood of them following is slim but I can't make any guarantees."

Through the windshield the kids could see that they were now approaching a large blue neon tube of light. They were heading straight for it.

"What is that Libby?" asked Quasar.

"Not sure, but I know it'll get us outta here. Now hold on. We're goin' in."

The bus shot straight into the end of the blue light, and just as Libby had predicted, the two pursuing pods did not follow.

The blinding blue light suddenly engulfed the entire tour bus and the cockpit lit up like a siri-tanning bed, forcing the young banditos to cover their eyes.

Jethro cautiously peeled open his eyelids, just enough to get a small glimpse of the blue light. It was all around them now and it felt as if the bus was being jettisoned down some sort of space tunnel. It was more like a roller coaster ride. The bus zoomed sharply down, arced to the right, danced to the left and then shot off in a direction that felt like 'up' at a speed that Jethro didn't even want to think about.

It was now obvious that the bus was shooting straight up the dazzling blue fluorescent tube and the children all held on tightly to the edges of their seats. They soon noticed that a tiny black pinprick had opened up in the end of the space tube. It felt like they were being pushed rather than pulled and their faces began to peel back across their bone structure in reaction to the incredible speed the bus had reached.

The black hole, which clearly marked the end of the tunnel, was getting wider and wider and the youngsters all felt pangs of relief as the twinkling of stars appeared in the opening. No sooner had they realized this was the end of the ride when they shot out of the tube like a spitball through a straw. The expectation of landing safely in outer space was immediately quashed when the bus, having reached the pinnacle of its ascent, began to drop as if succumbing to the will of some unknown gravitational pull. The blue light hadn't yet disappeared though and was still all around them.

The bus had resumed its horizontal posture and Seth jumped up and ran to the front windshield of the bus. He looked out and what he saw caused his jaw to drop immediately.

"This blue stuff ain't light you guys." His comment caused the rest of the crew to run up to the front to join him. "It's some sort of space gel."

Before anyone had a chance to question their observant friend's judgment, the bus lurched once more and they all felt the undeniable sensation of rising.

"Libby, what in Sirius is going on now," demanded Seth.

"Unfortunately, this substance is driving my sensors all haywire. I don't have an answer for you. My independent decision mode has gone totally loco."

"Well, that's just fantastic." He paused and drummed his index finger against his lip. "What about our external camera probes? Are they still functional?"

"One moment Seth," came the computer's reply. After a short pause she responded. "Affirmative Seth man. All external camera probes are fully operational at this moment."

"Great. Launch one out port side about two miles, aim it back at the bus, and bring it up on monitor."

"Gotcha Eggman. No problem."

A monitor screen directly above the front windshield suddenly came on.

"What are you thinking Seth?" asked Jethro.

Seth ran over to the starboard side of the bus and slammed his hand down on a small purple button. A piece of the wall suddenly lifted up to reveal another window.

All Sirian eyes turned starboard to see what was on the other side of the window. It appeared to be some sort of giant green waterfall and Val was the first to comment on this.

"What is that, a giant green space fall?" she asked.

"That ain't no space fall," said Seth. "Libby is that camera probe ready?"

"Affirmative Seth."

The monitor screen above the front windshield shimmered and suddenly displayed an image. They were all viewing a giant Slimacular space slug floating in space.

Now, perhaps you're wondering what a Slimacular space slug looks like. Throughout the known universe, there is a saying common to all races and it is this: beauty is in the eye of the beholder. Unfortunately for the self-confidence of the Slimacular space slug, history has not recorded a single race that did not describe the space slug as a giant, floating, green, space turd with arms.

It is the arms of this particular Slimacular space slug that the children were presently focusing on. They all stared at the picture on the screen.

"That's one giant space slug," said Quasar.

"What's it holding in its hand," asked Val. She was referring to the long thin rock-like utensil that the slug was raising up toward its face. On the end closest to the monster's mouth, was a large grouping of white asteroid trees whose tops were layered with a thick, blue, gel-like substance. In this blue substance was a small green speck of colour. As the giant utensil rose slowly toward the space slug's gaping maw, Val made an observation.

"That's a giant space tooth brush."

Quasar cocked her head to the left. "You're right," she said. "It looks like the handle was carved from a meteor or something. And that blue stuff must be the space paste."

"Oh, I see," said Jethro. "But…what's the green fleck in the middle of it?"

"That would be us," stated Seth.

CHAPTER 2

IN THE MOUTH OF THE SLIMACULAR SPACE SLUG

Dental hygienically speaking, the Slimacular space slugs have some of the best sets of teeth the universe has to offer. Some intellectuals like to argue that the universal agreement of the space slug looking like a giant turd has contributed to the species' low self esteem issues and therefore the slugs have been overcompensating by maintaining outstanding oral hygiene.

Whichever argument one may subscribe to, the bottom line was that Jethro and his friends were about to run buff and polish control on the largest space calcium deposits they had ever seen.

Inside the cockpit all but Seth were beginning to panic as the gargantuan wall of pearly whites lowered down to confront their field of vision.

"We're gonna die. We're actually going..to...diiiee," ranted Val, in her usual fashion.

Jethro was gripping Seth's shoulder tightly with his left hand. "Now would be a good time to venture forth a bright idea, my friend."

Seth flinched under the pain of his friend's unusually strong grip before answering. "I'm thinking, I'm thinking."

Tooth caverns lowered into view as the kids all waited on a brilliant idea from Seth. Fortunately for all of them, though the space slug is famous for it's great oral hygiene, it has never won a medal for the speed at which it accomplishes this. Raising its hand up to its mouth could often take up to ten minutes. The kids, of course, didn't know this but it was a fact of the universe that granted Seth enough time to come up with one of his brilliant plans.

He began talking to no one in particular and turned his back to the windshield. "Okay, so first we escaped that net, then we got shot through the tube with all this space paste, and now we're stuck in the paste with...Libby?"

"Yes?"

"Are we still powered up?"

"Yes we are," said Libby.

"Uh Seth," came Jethro's voice again.

"Is there any way out of here?"

"We're too close to the teeth Seth. By the time we're able to get out of this blue muck, it'll be too late. In fact...."

"Uh Seth..." Jethro yelled this time.

"What?" Seth demanded irritably.

"Too late," was all Jethro managed to say as the bus slammed into the mountain of glistening teeth.

An ear-piercing shriek of metal against bone rang out through the entire bus as the space slug began dragging the brush across the length of its mouth. The young Sirians all covered their ears, squinted their eyes, and gritted their teeth, hoping that somehow the unbearable noise would stop. Seth stared intently out the starboard window, while his friends stared intently at him, hoping he would do something. The giant wall of white that was moving past the window suddenly turned black and the shrieking sound stopped abruptly.

"Libby," he shouted suddenly. "Turn us ninety degrees to the right and accelerate full speed. Now!"

"I see where you're going with this. Gotcha," came the metallic reply.

A loud slurping sound soon replaced the shrieking noise as the bus shot out of the space paste and straight into a rather large cave of darkness.

"Okay Libby, hold us here if you can." Seth continued to stare out the starboard window and his friends soon followed suit. Blue fluorescent space paste was shooting past them on both sides and started to drip down the front windshield. Seth ran to the front panel and pushed an orange button. A pair of wiper blades the size of water skis flipped up and began forcing the paste off the glass. The bus itself, however, did not appear to be moving anymore.

Jethro looked around nervously. "Seth, where exactly are we?"

Seth looked at his friend and smirked. "Let me put it this way. Let's all pray this space slug doesn't have a giant string of cosmic floss."

"We're between its teeth," said Val.

"Yes Val, we're between its teeth."

"I thought you were gonna get us out of this mess Seth. Now we're stuck in this thing's mouth. I wouldn't exactly call that a brilliant plan."

Seth cast Val an angry look of defense. "Since when did we vote that I was in charge of getting us out of trouble. Jethro's the one who ought to be in charge. It's his dad's band."

"Jethro's in charge of thinking he's in charge," said Val.

"Hey," cut in Jethro.

Val continued. "But we all know you're the brains in this bunch and we all expect a little more from you."

The young Sirians had to raise their voices as the overpowering din of the space slug's circular brushing motion threatened to drown them out.

"Oh and what's your job Val? Complaining and whining and making sure your antennas are perfectly straight?"

"I do not."

"Oh come on. I've seen you in the vanity centers, singing away in front of the mirrors with your stupid toothbrush microphone..."

"Shut up Seth."

"Why don't you both shut up," interjected Quasar. "We're still stuck in space slug mandibles with space paste flowing all around us. Arguing about who's smarter and who's prettier isn't going to prevent us from being dissolved by this thing's saliva, so if you two love-birds wouldn't mind, we'd all appreciate it if you'd knock it off."

Both Seth and Val seemed a little put-off by the 'love-birds' comment, but any Sirian with even half a working set of eyes could tell that both of them were blushing.

"Umm, can I say something?"

All eyes turned to the unfamiliar voice that had just spoken. Two young Sirians were standing in front of the drive lift doors and staring, intently, at the arguing kids. They were obviously twins and appeared to be about five years old. One was a girl, the other a boy. It was the girl who had spoken.

"Who're you?" Demanded Val.

"Umm, my name's Bobbee and this is my brother Bettee, but he doesn't speak."

The older Sirians looked completely confused.

"Where did you come from?" asked Seth.

"Ummm...downstairs."

"What do you mean, 'downstairs'?" said Jethro. "We've been on this bus for eight years. We've never seen you before. You're lying."

"I am not lying," insisted Bobbee, hostility entering her voice. "Our parents got hired by your dad two years ago, but they were told 'no kids allowed'. They're the best sound company in Sirius and really wanted the job, so they snuck me and my brother on board and have been hiding us ever since."

"That's a crazy story, and I don't believe it for a second. Libby would have known about you. Right Libby?" said Val.

"Well, actually," said Libby, "they were never registered as boarded. I do have the ability to detect unregistered beings on board but, for some reason, these two have never showed up on my sensors."

"That's because of these," said Bobbee, holding up her arm and displaying a bracelet that was clasped securely around her wrist. Her brother did the same.

"What's that," said Seth.

"Concealment bracelet," answered Bobbee. "It causes computers to read our life forms as common scrats."

"So you're the two scrats," said Libby. "I've been trying to convince everyone that we have a scrat problem on board, but Ozzbourn kept telling me that until someone actually sees a scrat, that it's not a problem. This explains everything."

"So, let me get this straight," said Jethro. "You two have been stowaways on this bus for two years?"

"Yep," said Bobbee.

Bettee nodded his head.

"Unbelievable. What can I say? I guess, welcome aboard...or...something like that."

"We came upstairs 'cause we don't know where our parents are. We were hiding in the storage compartments in our quarters and someone took them away."

"All the adults are gone," said Seth. "But we heard someone mention six kid life forms. How come they knew there were six instead of four and two scrats?"

"Because their life scanner would have been highly advanced," answered Libby. "It would have detected the fact that these were kids right away. It actually scans right through the body, where as mine just scans for the existence of life. My programming is not that advanced because there's really no need for it."

"Does anyone know what happened to our parents?" asked Bobbee.

"Sorry, kid," said Quasar. "We just barely escaped with our lives. We haven't had a chance to discuss what we're going to do next."

Bettee suddenly started pointing over Quasar's shoulder towards the front windshield.

"What's he doing?" asked Quasar, looking over her shoulder.

"That space paste stuff seems to be all gone and I just saw something go past that window," said Bobbee. "My brother just saw it too."

"What do you mean, 'something'?" said Jethro.

"Well it looked like some kinda creature riding some other kinda creature."

Everyone, at once, ran up to the window and peered out into the darkness, hoping to see nothing so that they could all tell young Bobbee and Bettee that they were imagining things. They soon realized that the youngsters' imaginations were not presently engaged. There were creatures out there in the darkness: red, hooded creatures partially lit up by bits of dripping fluorescent goo. They were riding about on ugly, red, fleshy steeds that seemed to float and move through the air effortlessly.

"What are those things," asked Val.

Seth turned on her with an instant comeback. "Do I look like I'm carrying a guide to the galaxy Val?"

Val opened her mouth but found it immediately clamped shut by Quasar's hand.

"Don't even bother," said Quasar, giving Val the 'I mean business' look.

The kids continued to peer out into the darkness as the fleshy creatures rode around on their steeds. Most of them appeared to be wearing thick pink hoods that covered their faces, revealing nothing but a set of glowing, blue eyes. Each of them carried a weapon and, after a short time, they began picking and scraping away at the mountains of teeth.

"Okay," said Val, "whatever they are, they're starting to freak me out."

Almost as if it heard her, one of the creatures spun around, rode up to the window and peered menacingly at the gang of quivering kids.

"Thank Sirius my dad got the windows tinted. We can see it, but it can't see us. I think."

Everyone looked at Jethro and, for a moment, he thought they might demand he shut the Sirius up, but no one said anything. The creature began tapping on the glass with the rather sharp looking pick it was carrying. It was at this point that Seth decided to make an observation.

"You know, this thing looks like it's made entirely out of flesh. I don't think that's a hood. I think that's its head."

Closer inspection by the rest of the gang confirmed Seth's suspicion. Blue and green pulsing veins were throbbing all over the creature's body including its head, and the glowing eyes appeared to be sunk deep into the fleshy face. It began tapping the glass much more aggressively causing the kids to all back up a few feet.

"Okay, so what happens if this thing breaks through the glass?" ventured Val.

"We're not going to let it break through the glass, Val, 'cause Seth's gonna get us out of here, right Seth?" said Jethro.

Seth just simply glared at Jethro then turned to Val. "You know, flying a space bus isn't exactly my specialty. Solving problems isn't exactly my specialty either. Having to be an adult when I never asked to be one in the first place isn't exactly my specialty. I build things. I'm an inventor. I wish you'd all stop puttin' all the pressure on me. You guys gotta accept some responsibility too ya' know."

"Seth, just chill man. We all just figured you'd like taking care of the technical stuff," said Jethro.

"Look, you guys. It's not exactly like we've had much time to discuss our predicament. You know, since we discovered our parents were missing, we've been shot through a galactic size tube of space paste and nearly had a brush with death against the unstained wall of teeth of a giant Slimacular space slug. Now we're stuck between the thing's chompers and there's flesh creatures on the outside of the bus threatening to bust their way in. And to top it all off, the space goo has messed with Libby, and for some reason, she requires us to come up with all the solutions. I would have to say that that's just a slight bit of pressure for an eleven year old to have to deal with in a ten minute period of time. Thank you very much."

The flesh creature, in the meantime, was still banging away on the window. It didn't appear to be having much luck with breaking the glass, but this piece of reality did nothing to eliminate the nervous tension floating around the cockpit. The fluorescent space paste had indeed stopped flowing around them and with the exception of a few remaining globules dripping from the slug's teeth, it was actually quite dark on the outside of the bus.

Quasar was the first to notice this. "Hey Libby?"

"Yo sista Quasar, watchoo need girl?"

"Can you turn us around 180 degrees?"

"No problemo."

The bus slowly turned around until it was facing the opposite direction and everyone stared out the front windshield.

"How come I can't see any stars?" questioned Val with a slightly worried tone in her voice.

"I'll tell you why," blurted Quasar. "While we were all arguing about whether or not Seth ought to be more responsible, the stupid slug closed its mouth. Now we're gonna have to sit here and wait for it to open. Man, you guys are so lame."

"Okay, can we all just make a little more effort to get along?" said Jethro looking around pleadingly at his friends. "We're all stuck on this bus until we find a way off it. And I, for one, ain't getting off until we find our parents. So I say we stop bickering about every single problem we encounter, and start putting our antennas together and come up with some solutions. In my opinion, right now, at this point in time, waiting sounds pretty good to me. Anyone else got a better idea?"

No one responded, so Jethro continued. "Good. Libby?"

"Yo Jeth. Can I call you Jeth?"

"Fine. The moment this thing opens its mouth, I want you to fly us outta here, okay."

"You got it."

"And keep flyin' us until we're far out of this slug's reach. I don't want it thinkin' we're a vitamin pill or somethin' and swallow us back up."

"No problem Jeth. I'll fly us so far outta here that this space slug'll be nothin' but a distant memory; a picture in a photo album; a brief moment of history caught on film; a grand and epic..."

"Libby! Enough already." Jethro looked at his friends. "Well you guys may as well get comfortable. It could be a long wait."

"What about Mr. Flesh Geek tapping on the glass Jethro? Are we just gonna sit here until he breaks through?" Val had her arms crossed against her chest, an eyebrow raised, and a foot tapping, irritably, on the floor.

Jethro sneered at her, but decided not to say anything. He wasn't about to get sucked into another argument.

"Anyone got any ideas about the angel of flesh out there," he asked.

"Oh great," exclaimed Quasar. "There's two of 'em now."

She was right. Another flesh creature had arrived at the window and was beginning to tap on the glass alongside its counterpart.

“Okay Mr. Space Slug,” Val said, “time to open your mouth now. C’mon ya’ big ole salt-a-phobic. Open yer big fat mouth.”

The space slug did not comply with Val’s request and immediately following her verbal outburst, four more flesh creatures flew up to the front windshield and began tapping on the glass with their weapons.

“Open yer mouth ya’ stupid slug,” they all hollered at the same time, but the slug, of course, could not hear them and there were about ten flesh creatures banging away on the glass now, making it nearly impossible for the young Sirians to hear themselves think.

Once again a young voice cut through the din of excitement and fear.

“Has anyone seen my brother?” asked Bobbee.

Half forgetting that the two young twins had joined their group the rest of the gang began looking around the cockpit. Little Bettee was nowhere to be seen.

“Yo Libby,” said Jethro.

“Yes?”

“Can you locate...umm...uhh...” He looked over at Bobbee. “What’s your brother’s name again?”

“Bettee”

“Right...and you are...”

“Bobbee,” came the frustrated reply.

“Libby, can you locate Bettee for us please.”

“I would if I could Jeth bro, but I’m afraid Bettee is not on the bus.”

“What! Well where is he?”

“There he is,” shouted Val, pointing out the windshield.

Young Bettee was indeed on the outside of the bus, flying around in an egg shaped, two-seater ship. He was piloting the small vessel straight toward the backs of the flesh creatures that were still engaged in the monotonous activity of tapping on the windshield.

“What in Sirius is he flying in?” asked Quasar.

“A bus pod,” Seth stated simply.

“What’s a bus pod?”

“That is,” he retorted, pointing at the small flying egg.

The pod quickly approached the flesh creatures and two mechanical arms extended from its sides. Each arm had three metal fingers attached to it and the artificial hands were soon grabbing hold of flesh creatures, steeds and all and tossing them over the back of the pod.

“Way to go Bettee,” shouted Bobbee, shooting her fists into the air. “Get ‘em.”

“Not bad for a little guy,” noted Jethro.

Bobbee looked over to him and replied, “We may be little, but we’re not useless. We spend all of our time hiding in our quarters and Bettee’s a pro on the pod simulator game that our parents got us.”

"Apparently."

The mechanical hands continued to grab hold of creatures and toss them back, but each time ten more would zoom in to take the other ones' places. Bettee soon became over powered and his bus pod disappeared under a mound of flesh, which dragged him off into the darkness.

"Bettee!" screamed Bobbee, reaching out and sticking her hands on the windshield. She looked around at the older kids, a pleading look on her face. "Someone's gotta do something." She began tugging nervously at her antennas.

"Hey little sister," Val exclaimed, "we didn't ask your little bro to fly out there and act all macho."

"Why don't you just stuff it you big ugly, big ugly, big ugly..."

"Big ugly what?" Val challenged.

Bobbee slapped her arms down stiffly at her side, bulged her cheeks out and began to hold her breath.

Val crossed her arms across her chest and shook her head. "Oh ya right. Like I'm gonna fall for that old trick."

Bobbee continued to hold her breath.

"It's not gonna work girl so don't waste your breath."

"Well, technically," interjected Seth, "she's not actually wasting breath, she's saving it."

"Shut-up Seth," snapped Val.

Bobbee continued to hold her breath.

"Come on girl, you can't win. I used to be the queen of holding my breath you know."

Bobbee continued to hold her breath.

"Uh Val. She's starting to turn blue," noted Jethro.

"Nothing to worry about until she turns purple Jethro. And I guarantee she won't get that far. We've got two hours at least before she pops."

Bobbee turned purple.

"Val, you forget she's only five. She hasn't learned to develop her lungs to hold air for that long yet. That's enough. Get her to stop."

Val, who was betraying her own confidence with a nervous look on her face, grabbed Bobbee by the shoulders. "Knock it off now kid."

Bobbee turned a darker shade of purple.

"C'mon Val," said Jethro.

Val shot Jethro an irritated glance and looked back to Bobbee. "It's not funny anymore kid, now knock-it-off," she said while shaking the young girl's shoulders.

Bobbee was almost black. At this point Seth stepped in and spoke up. "You guys, I don't think she's gonna stop until we agree to help her brother."

Bobbee looked over his way and nodded her head in the affirmative.

Val now looked over at Jethro pleadingly. "Jethro," she said in a high-pitched voice.

Jethro moved toward Bobbee, pushed Val out of the way, and grabbed Bobbee by the shoulders, whose eyes were now starting to glaze over.

"Okay, enough all ready Bobbee. We'll go after your brother."

Almost instantly, Bobbee's skin colour changed from black to its natural colour.

"Thanks," she said, turning back and leering out the windshield. When nobody moved or said anything she turned around with a baffled look on her face. "Well lets go get him you guys," she said, throwing her hands up in the air, snapping her fingers and tacking on a little wiggle of her hips.

This seemed to snap Jethro and Seth to attention. Jethro looked over to his friend and said, "Well, I guess we better go get him."

Seth, taking the order hesitantly, said, "Libby."

"Yes?"

"Let's go find Bettee. Are the exterior tracking systems still okay?"

"Tracking's okay. Still having a bit of a time with my decision making, but I'm working on it."

Seth pointed at the drive lifters. "He was sitting in that left hand drive lifter Libby. Take a D.N.A. sample of his fingerprints and put a lock on him. We should be able to hone in on wherever they've taken him."

"Done Seth-man."

The kids felt the ship rumble into life and start to move. It was a slow crawl at first, but the bus began to accelerate, flying past mountains of teeth. They began to notice that the glowing, blue, fluorescent globules of space paste were now illuminating all sorts of caves on the insides of the space slugs' teeth. Flesh creatures were drifting in and out of these caverns, their blue glowing eyes twinkling menacingly. The bus slowly pulled up in front of one of the larger caves and came to a stop.

"This is the place," came Libby's voice. "Our little friend is in that cave."

Jethro let out a sigh that sounded like hesitant commitment. "Take us in Libby."

The bus slowly accelerated and entered the large cavity. Flesh creatures lined the walls, ceiling and floors. They were so tightly knit together that it made it look as if the entire cave was alive. The only things that gave the creatures away were their eyes; their creepy blue eyes.

"Who's to say the kid isn't completely buried under these things," ventured Val.

"He's not," insisted Bobbee.

"How do you know?"

"I can't explain. We're twins and we just...know things about each other."

Every now and then they would witness a flesh creature detach itself from the rest and float out to observe the intruders. They all noticed that these particular creatures were not wielding weapons and closer inspections revealed that the riders and their steeds were actually attached, melded together in a flesh ridden, grotesque, kind of way.

The bus was now flanked by a rather large convoy of fleshies and it continued to coast through the dark cavern. There was an eerie silence in the cockpit and soon they could all see the end of the cave. As they approached it, they noticed a large ball of flesh floating directly in front of a blue wall of illuminated space paste. Directly below the ball was a fleshie about ten times the size of its smaller companions. It floated about twenty feet off the floor of the cave. It was waving its arms slowly as if it was trying to communicate some sort of message.

"Libby, is the internal translation implantation device still functional?" asked Seth.

"As a matter of fact, it is. Navigation's almost back on line too and I should have everything else up and running soon."

Seth crossed the cockpit to portside and hit a magenta button. A panel opened up in the wall directly in front of him and beneath it was a mould in the shape of a Sirian hand.

"Everyone over here," he said.

They all crossed the cockpit and gathered around him.

"Okay guys," he said, " I'm going to explain this to you." He pointed to the hand mould in the wall. "This is a translation implantation device. What it's going to do is deposit universal translation energy waves directly into our bodies. This will enable us to understand virtually every alien race we encounter in the known universe. What the waves do is they hone in on tonal pulses and inflections of vocal sound waves and determine..."

"Ya, ya, ya. Let's just get this over with and find out what the flesh freak has to say," interrupted Val rather rudely.

Jethro looked at Val and rolled his eyes.

"What?" she questioned innocently.

"Sorry Seth, but she's right," he said. "What do we do?"

Seth pointed at the device and said, "Just put your hand in the mould and the machine will do the rest. Like this." He stuck his hand in the mould and a voice came out of the panel.

"Initializing implantation," it said and then after a brief pause, " implantation complete."

"See," said Seth. "Easy as one, two, three. Who's next?"

"I'll go," offered Jethro, placing his hand in the mould.

One by one, each of them went through the implantation process. When they were all done, Seth crossed back over to the middle of the cockpit and placed his hands on his hips, staring intently at the giant fleshie on the other side of the windshield.

"Libby, turn on the external and internal microphones and speakers. I wanna be able to communicate with this big tub 'o' flesh."

"Done," replied Libby.

A loud, booming voice suddenly kicked in, mid sentence, and came out of the internal speakers. It was clearly the voice of the giant fleshie.

"...any idea how much work it takes it to maintain a set of teeth like this?"

"Hello, " said Seth. "Umm, we kinda missed the first part of your speech. Could you maybe, umm, start over again?"

The large fleshie shifted uncomfortably in its own skin and pointed at the bus.

"You speak the Plaque tongue. How is it that you know our language?"

Seth was about to answer the creature when Jethro stepped in and waved him off.

"We are scientific researchers," he said. "We come in peace. We travel the universe seeking out new ways to preserve life. We've been studying the space slug for about six months now. Our intent is not to harm it or you. We are familiar with your language because we have researched it."

The rest of the gang looked at Jethro with shocked looks on their faces.

"Where did that come from," murmured Quasar.

"Nice goin' Jethro," complimented Val.

The giant fleshie paused before continuing.

"What are you called?" it asked.

"I am Jethro."

"Jethro," it repeated, raising a flesh covered hand behind its rump and scratching.

"And what are you called?" asked Jethro.

The fleshie shuddered slightly before answering. "I am Sower Rawn, and these are my minions, the Plaque Riders. We maintain all that is truly white on the outside of these caverns. It is our primary mission. Anything that threatens the primary mission is to be destroyed."

"Okay now that would be the part that we have a problem with. You see your...um...Plaque Riders took one of our men and we'd kinda like him back," said Jethro.

Bobbee gave him a kick and a comment under her breath. "What do you mean, kinda?"

Jethro raised a hand to silence her.

"He meant your riders no harm. They were attacking our bus and he was merely trying to protect us."

"We attack no one," exclaimed Sower Rawn. "It is not in our nature."

"Ya, well how come your goons were trying to break through our ship with their picks and scrapers then, flesh man," interjected Val.

Jethro shot Val a hard gaze and mouthed the words 'shut-up'.

"If you are scientific researchers, shouldn't you know the answer to that question?" Sower Rawn demanded suspiciously.

This time Seth stepped forward and spoke. "Of course, we understand. They were merely doing their job."

Sower Rawn turned his head slightly. "This new voice obviously has wisdom. Who is this new voice?"

"I am Seth."

"Seth is wise," the booming voice praised. "The Plaque Riders merely act on instinct. It is their duty to eliminate any alien objects that appear around the sacred teeth."

The other four Sirians praised Seth for his quick thinking by giving him a thumbs-up and he thanked them with a smile.

"Yes of course," he added quickly. "They were merely doing their job. We totally understand.

We are peaceful travelers and merely wish to get on with our business, but we really need to get our shipmate back."

"Shipmate?"

"Yes, our shipmate. Your Plaque Riders took him away. That's how we ended up here. Our tracking systems detected that our friend was taken here."

Sower Rawn shifted around in his own flesh. "Ahh," he said. "You seek the alien instrument."

"I don't understand," said Jethro. "What do you mean by alien instrument?"

Sower Rawn spread his arms out and made a gesture with his hands. Two Plaque Riders on either side of the cave detached themselves from the walls and floated out to flank their master on either side. He made another gesture and each Rider reached inside their fleshie sides and produced the same type of weapons the others had used to tap on the glass of the bus.

"As you can see," added Sower Rawn, "the Plaque Riders are limited to the use of these crude instruments. Most of them forged from material salvaged from ships such as yours."

"You mean there've been other ships before us?" asked Jethro.

"Of course. Not only does the space slug have an obsession with its teeth, but with eating as well. You are the first to avoid being completely crushed between the molars."

"So what does all this have to do with our shipmate?"

"The instrument that your shipmate was traveling in is the most advanced we have ever seen. It would be a great advantage to keep it and put it to use."

Once again Seth interjected. "Oh, I see. You're talking about the bus pod. Hey man, if you want it, it's yours. We just need our shipmate back."

"How do you expect us to operate this wondrous instrument without the pilot? No, I'm sorry, but we will need to keep the pilot."

"Okay, well let me ask you this Mr. Rawn. How do you expect to keep the pilot alive?"

"Alive? I do not understand."

"The pilot needs to be fed and though your space slug here seems to have quite a healthy appetite, I'm pretty positive that there isn't anything in its diet that could be used to feed the pilot."

Sower Rawn paused uncomfortably before answering. "Sower Rawn did not think of this. This is very...upsetting."

"Fear not though," Seth reassured the flesh master, "because it just so happens that I'm an inventor and I can build you a device that will enable you to operate the pod without the pilot."

"What sort of device?"

"Well, return the pod and the pilot to us and I'll show you. As long as our mate is okay, I'll build you the device and return it along with the pod if you agree to let us leave safely."

"And this ...device. We will be able to use it to control the instrument?"

"You betcha, Rawnie Baby."

Sower Rawn was silent while he thought about the proposal.

"Okay," he said. "Sower Rawn accepts your offer. As long as you can demonstrate that your device works."

"Sounds good to me," Seth replied, sounding quite pleased with himself.

Sower Rawn made another gesture with his hands and the giant flesh ball above his head suddenly burst apart. The ball had been made up of Plaque Riders, who quickly found homes in the walls, floor and ceiling, reattaching themselves with a gooey smacking noise. Floating in mid-air, where the Riders had been moments earlier, was the bus pod. Inside it, Bettee was looking rather shaken up.

"Libby, turn on the pod communicator," commanded Seth.

A clicking sound was heard coming out of the speakers and Seth spoke out. "Bettee, can you hear me?"

There was no response.

"Here's the deal kid. These flesh monsters have agreed to let you come back so I want you to fly back to the docking bay. Slowly. We've made a deal with them and I don't think it would look very good if you went all military on them again. You got it?"

All the young Sirians, particularly Bobbee, stared in apprehensive silence as Bettee powered up the pod and slowly accelerated toward the bus. He reached the docking bay in a matter of minutes and was soon safe and sound back in the cockpit with the rest of the gang.

"Bettee," yelled Bobbee, running up to her brother and giving him a huge hug. He did a rather lousy job of trying not to look embarrassed.

But soon everyone's attention had turned back to Seth. They were all wondering just what exactly he was planning on building in order to get them out of this particular predicament.

"So what's the plan Seth," asked Jethro. "Whatcha gonna build?"

"Easy," his friend replied, "a remote control." And with that comment he turned, walked over to the drive lifters, and entered one of them. "I'll be back in about two hours," he said as the door closed in front of him.

The rest of the gang exchanged nervous glances.

Val was the first to speak. "I hope Mr. Tub 'o' Flesh is patient."

Seth returned, as promised, two hours later wielding his freshly made bus pod remote control. It was a small, green, circular device with a large, orange button in the middle of it.

"Well," he said, "here it is." He lifted the device high into the air for everyone to see.

"Does it work?" asked Val, doubtfully.

"Of course it works Val. Somehow I don't think we're going to be able to scheme our way out of this."

"I have a question," said Quasar. "How do you plan on showing Mr. Flesh out there how to use it?"

"Funny you should ask," retorted Seth, then bragging, "I simply downloaded the holographic instruction manual from Libby and she equipped it with a universal voice command translator. All they have to do is play the demo and tell the pod what they want it to do."

"Great," said Jethro impatiently. "Now let's give 'em the thing and get the Sirius out of this creepy place."

Seth turned to Bettee, "Hey, Bettee can you run down to the docking bay and attach this remote to the outside of the bus pod and jettison the pod out to Mr. Flesh Man? The remote has a super sensitive magnetic strip on its bottom so just place it where he can see it."

Bettee enthusiastically snatched the remote control from Seth and ran off to complete his mission.

Seth turned back to the front of the bus. Sower Rawn was floating patiently in his spot.

"Libby, mikes and speakers please." Seth cleared his throat before speaking. "Yo, Mr Rawn, I'm sending the pod out now. On the side of it you will find a small device with a large orange button. Remove the device, press the button, and it'll show and tell you everything you need to know. It works on voice commands, so you only need to worry about the on/off switch, and that would be the orange button. The only problem is your size. You'll probably have to get one of your Plaque Riders to turn the thing on and off for you. Your hands will probably just crush the thing."

The bus pod came into view and was slowly floating towards the big flesh master. Sower Rawn waved a hand and a Plaque Rider detached itself from the ceiling with a sucking pop, zoomed up alongside the pod, and grabbed hold of the remote control. The flesh-master waved his other hand and the Rider pushed the orange button. Sure enough a holographic image came spilling out of the top of the remote demonstrating exactly how the pod worked. Sower Rawn tried out a few voice commands and seemed quite pleased that the pod responded instantly to his authority. He turned toward the space bus and spoke.

"Sower Rawn is pleased with your gift. You may go in peace." He waved them away and immediately turned his attention back to his new toy.

"Well that was easy enough," said Jethro, just as a drive lifter door opened and Bettee stepped through. Jethro turned to him and said, "Hey, good job my man."

Bettee humbly bent his head and stuck his hands in his front pouch pocket.

"Libby, get us out of here please," commanded Seth.

"No problem," came the computerized reply.

The bus turned around and made a speedy exit out of the tooth cavity. This time, no Plaque Riders followed them. They exited the cave and headed back alongside the mountains of teeth toward the mouth of the space slug. Its mouth, however, was still closed.

"Oh great," complained Val. "Back to waiting again."

"I don't think so," Quasar cut in unexpectedly. "Everyone find a seat and strap yourself in."

"Why, what are you gonna do Quas?" asked Jethro.

"Get us out of here," she said, finding a seat and belting herself in.

Everyone else followed suit, looking over at Quasar with 'now what?' looks on their faces.

"Libby," Quasar shouted. "Point our nose straight up at the roof of this cave and lower our back end, no thrusters yet, to the base. All the way to the bottom until we're touching."

Libby did as commanded and soon the bus had lowered itself down to the floor of the ominous cave. The bus was pointing straight up and looked like a nasty little stalagmite canker on the surface of the slug's giant, green tongue.

"Okay Libby, when I say now, I want you to ignite forward thrusters. The moment they burn a hole in this thing's tongue I expect it's going to open its mouth. Your job is to get us the Sirius out of here before it sticks a finger in its mouth and tries to flush us out. You got it Libby?"

"Magic word?" said Libby.

"PLEASE," shouted everyone in unison.

"Okay Libby," said Quasar. "Ready?"

"I'm ready."

"Now."

The forward thrusters of the bus ignited into life and did, indeed, singe a rather large hole in the top of the slug's main tasting organ. Quasar smiled as the mouth of the cave opened up before them. What she didn't expect was the deafening howl of pain that the slug let out. A great wind came rushing out of the slug's throat, sending the bus spinning out of control toward the cave mouth. They narrowly missed being smashed to pieces against the wall of teeth that loomed up in front of them. Fortunately, Libby immediately accelerated them into space, out of harms way.

"Way to go Quasar," shouted Val, jumping up out of her seat and running over to her friend.

Quasar smiled. "Yep, girls pretty much rule," she said, giving Val a high five.

Jethro and Seth let the comment slide. They were impressed with Quasar's quick thinking and were quite happy to be out of the giant's mouth.

Jethro looked over at Seth suddenly, with a quizzical look on his face. "I just have one question."

"What's that?" Seth replied.

"What happens when that remote control's batteries die?"

Seth just smiled, raised his eyebrows, and shrugged.

All the young Sirians enjoyed their first big laugh since their adventure had begun.

CHAPTER 3

THE JETHRO SIRIUS EXPERIMENT IS FORMED

The bus coasted through space rather quickly, and it was obvious that it had a goal in mind. It would stop, attempt to change direction, but end up back on the original track. It was almost as if its destination were beckoning it with the use of a very powerful magnet. It had been traveling for almost two days since their run-in with the Slimacular space slug and inside the kids had been in a heated discussion about what they were going to do next.

The cockpit had become their new home. Though all but Seth would periodically drift off to their living quarters to catch up on some much needed sleep, they all wound up back at the ship's main observation post. Their interests no longer included playing and lounging around in the water-park and mazes. Their main concerns now revolved around finding their parents or a way back home. These two options were presently at the center of their debate.

Val was, of course, the most passionate when it came to expressing an opinion. "Forget this floundering around stuff. I say we go home."

"And what about our parents?" argued Seth. "I suppose we just forget about them?"

"No, but I don't know how much good it's gonna do to fly around aimlessly looking for them."

"I don't think we should be flying anywhere," cut in Bobbee with her sweet little voice. "My mommy always told me that if we ever get separated, that I should stay put and she'll find me."

"Well that's a stupid idea," Val remarked. "Why don't you be quiet and let the big kids do the thinking, okay pip squeak?"

"Shut up Val," demanded Seth. "She actually has a pretty good point."

Bettee nodded his head in agreement, frowning at Val.

"Stop it you guys," said Jethro. "Nobody's stupid and everybody has good ideas. The intent of this discussion is to weigh out our options and come to a decision. We can sit here and argue until our antennas are in a knot, or we can grow up and talk to each other like adults."

"What do you mean?" said Bobbee. "My parents are always arguing."

"Good point," Val agreed. "So are mine."

"Okay, okay, I get your points," said Jethro. "Let me rephrase what I said. Grandparents. Grandparents never argue. Let's grow up and start acting like grandparents."

"I have four sets of grandparents," pointed out Seth.

"Oh, for the love of Peet, shut up," hollered Jethro. "You guys know what I mean. We need a note taker. Quasar why don't you grab a laser pad and start jotting down our ideas."

Quasar agreed and jumped up and ran off to find a laser pad to write on. She came back rather quickly and sat down, laser pen poised, ready to write.

"Now, let's start with one idea at a time, okay? That way we won't get sidetracked. We'll start with finding our parents. Any ideas on how we might go about doing this?" Jethro looked at his friends, awaiting their response, but all eyes had turned on Seth.

"What?" Said Seth, nervously. "C'mon you guys, I can't come up with all the good ideas. Quasar's pretty good at it. Any ideas Quas?"

All eyes soon turned to the girl who had gotten them out of the space slug's mouth.

"How in Sirius should I know?" she said. "The one we ought to be asking is Libby. She knows more about this stuff than any of us."

Libby, who apparently was monitoring the conversation, spoke up. "Yes Quasar, that's right, and if you kids would stop yippin' your yaps for just a few moments I will explain our situation."

"Okay, so what's the deal Libby? You said your sensors are on the fritz or something," Jethro asked.

"Yes, my sensors have been damaged. I can't just locate your parents, but we're not lost. And at the same time, we can't exactly just up and fly home."

"Why not?" Everyone asked at the same time.

"Okay, here's the deal. In order to ensure that the band gets paid for every gig, the head of security installed a measure that prevents me from uploading the directions to the next planet. The only way I can do this is if the promoter has paid the band. Once the credits have been confirmed, I can upload the next set of directions. So, you see, the only direction we can go in is to the next gig, and the only way we can get to the next gig is to be paid from the last one. Now, seeing as we were paid for the last gig, the only place I can take us is to the location of the next performance. Follow?"

There was a short silence as the young brains attempted to digest all that the ship's central computer had just explained to them. Seth, of course, was the first to speak. "Can't you just override the security measure, Libby?"

"If I could do that, it wouldn't be much of a security measure now would it? The only way I can stray from our original plotted course is if the bus or its passengers are in danger. I have an automatic override function, in that particular case, like when we had to escape from the asteroid field and the space slug. I can't fake it though, so don't bother asking. In all other situations, the only person who has the authorization to override is the chief of security, and guess what?"

"He disappeared with all the other adults," said Quasar.

"Right you are, Miss Ion, right you are."

"So what do we do?" asked Val.

Again there was a short silence. Having to solve a problem bigger than say, finding a hiding spot nobody knew about during a game of hide and seek was something the young Sirians were not used to. They all began to feel the dull sensation of responsibility sinking into the bones of their inexperienced youth.

"I have an idea," said Jethro.

All eyes turned to him.

"Why don't we do the gigs?"

Silence.

"I'm serious, you guys. Why don't we do the gigs? We're good enough musicians to pull it off and Seth and I know most of my dad's songs, so why don't we just play the shows. It wouldn't take us long to teach Quas and Val all the material. I'm sure you two already know a bunch of it."

Quasar and Val nodded in the affirmative.

"Jethro," said Seth, "promoters are expecting the Ozzbourn Sirius Experiment, not The Jethro Sirius Experiment. How would you explain the fact that we're a bunch of kids when they'll be expecting adults."

"Libby," said Jethro, "can you show us my dad's 8X10 promo photo."

"Sure." The photo appeared on the holo screen. The resemblance between the children and their parents was uncanny, a fortunate trait that often swam around in the Sirian gene pool.

"See, we could pass as our parents. They always say that people look shorter in person anyways. Come on, how hard can it be? We know all the songs and we're Sirian. Even if they do question our appearance, if we pull the show off, who's gonna care?"

"It sounds crazy to me," said Val.

"Me too," said Quasar. "But, at the same time, it does sound almost do-able. I mean, I guess we could pull it off if we really wanted to."

"As far as I'm concerned," said Seth, "we don't have any other choice. All other options disappeared with our parents."

Again, Jethro spoke up. "Hey Libby, how many dates left in this tour?"

"Three hundred and twenty."

"Three hundred and twenty!" screamed Val. "But that doesn't make any sense. We've gone home lots during this tour. Why can't we do it again?"

"Because our visits home weren't programmed into the tour," explained Libby. "The chief of security would override the system and direct the bus to the nearest light speed highway. Unfortunately, without the override feature, this would be impossible."

Val was beginning to look upset as the reality of her situation began to sink in. "So what you're saying is that we have to spend the next two years flying around the galaxy in this bus, playing shows that were originally intended for our parents? Whoever the chief of security is, is a complete moron. Coming up with an idiotic security measure like that. Oooo, I hope we find the adults so that I can give him a good solid kick in the shins."

"I admit it's pretty lame, but you know Sirians and their money. They'll do anything to make sure they get paid." Said Seth.

"Well it all sounds pretty ridiculous to me," she said.

"You got any better ideas Val?" asked Jethro.

"No, I don't have any better ideas," she retorted, rolling her eyes irritably. "But that doesn't mean I won't have any, ever. The moment I come up with a decent plan to get us home sooner than two years from now, I'll let everyone know."

"Just because a better solution hasn't presented itself yet doesn't mean it never will. A lot of things could happen between now and the end of the tour," Jethro said reassuringly. "I say we stick to the tour, but leave ourselves open to other options as they present themselves. We're probably going to be meeting plenty of adults during the tour. Maybe we'll meet someone who can help us with overriding the security measure. We don't know what could happen. We could find ourselves back home in a week, laughing at ourselves for even thinking we'd be gone for two years.

Come on guys. I think this idea is the best one we've got. At least we've got a goal. Let's stick to it and, if we need to change things along the way, then we'll change things. What do you say?"

Everyone knew he was right. Though Seth was good at solving technically related problems, Jethro was pretty good at putting things in ways that everyone understood. They all nodded their heads in agreement.

"Libby, when's our first show?" Jethro asked.

"You have exactly two days until the Ozzbourn Sirius Experiment is scheduled to appear. We lost a little bit of time during our escape from the asteroid field and the space slug's mouth, but if we hurry, we should be able to make it on time. The worst that could happen is you might miss sound check."

"Ya' right," said Quasar, "or we could get eaten by giant Slimacular space slugs." She half expected everyone to laugh, but no one seemed to think her comment was very funny.

While everyone was busy enjoying some much deserved down time, Seth was busy researching some of the planets where the band would be performing. Val sat next to him, showing slight interest in the list of venues.

"Wait, go back," said Val, suddenly.

"How far?"

"Monsturd planet. We're not actually playing there are we?"

"Umm, let me see. No, it says here the show was cancelled due to a scheduling conflict. Why?"

"Why? It's the Monsturd planet, that's why. It's full of some of the scariest monsturds in the universe."

"How do you know?"

"My parents used to have a book on it. 'The Top Ten Scariest Planets in the Known Universe.' The Monsturd planet was number one."

"Yikes," said Seth. "Good thing the show was cancelled. Why would they book a show there anyways?"

"I have no idea. I guess it wouldn't be such a bad idea to look into the background of some of the planets where we'll be performing."

"No kidding," said Seth, returning his attention to the computer screen.

CHAPTER 4

JAMMING AND COOKING

Though Jethro and Seth had been making music together for the past few years, Val and Quasar, although talented, had never played in a band before. Their parents had filled them full of musical knowledge and ability, but had never encouraged their daughters to express that knowledge in the form of a band. Such was not the case for the boys.

Between Jethro and Seth, they had enough songs to fill an entire set, but only had two days to teach the material to Val and Quasar. While Seth was busy programming drum parts into his new beat box, Jethro was busy running songs with the two girls.

The band's line up consisted of Jethro on vocals and guitar, Seth on drums and electronic sampling, Quasar on bass and vocals, and Val on keyboards and vocals. It was a long and tedious project, but Jethro and the girls eventually got all the songs charted out on paper. Charting was extremely important because it gave the girls a safety net of being able to look, on laser pad, at all the main chords, melodies and lyrics while they were performing. This way, if they got lost in a song, they'd be able to get back on track without too much trouble.

It was still going to be a lot of work. The Ozzbourn Sirius Experiment was probably one of the most famous bands in the entire Universe, so if Jethro and his friends were going to successfully masquerade as his dad's band they were going to have to rehearse like they'd never rehearsed before.

Val was already starting to express her frustration. "Oooooo," she moaned, "this is worse than school. I've got enough chords in my head to write an entire symphony."

"Just relax Val," Jethro reassured her. "Once you've learned all the songs, it won't be that bad. I promise. This is the worst part. I know it's a lot of material to have to learn in one day, but I know you can do it."

"I can do it," she said. "I'm just saying it's not easy. Not only do Quas and I have to learn half the music, but we have to memorize a bunch of lyrics too!"

"I know, I know. You're doing great though. I knew you two would," he said, giving her a reassuring pat on the shoulder.

"Thanks," she replied, suddenly hitting a bad note, causing both Jethro and Quasar to shudder. "Sorry," she said.

"No problem," replied Jethro. He was a little nervous, though. Quasar and Val only had two days to figure out twenty songs. Though he knew they'd have charts on stage with them, he was still worried that the stress and pressure of the time constraint would overpower and ruin their performance.

Oh well, he thought to himself, *no sense worrying about it now.*

By the time they had finished learning all the songs, an entire day had gone by and evening had rolled into their surroundings. Seth had completed all his programming and the band felt ready to start rehearsing as a group.

They made their way down to their parents' rehearsal room and were all picking up and plugging in instruments excitedly. Though Jethro and Seth had a few of their own instruments, they'd never had this many toys to play with. Once they had all their instruments plugged in and amps cranked up to full volume, they began making a noise that could probably have deafened even a Slimacular space slug.

Bobbee and Bettee were sitting off to one side listening to the awful sound, cringing and covering their ears. It hadn't sounded this bad while they were learning the songs, and Bobbee was beginning to wonder if the older kids actually realized how terrible they sounded.

Jethro happened to glance over at the twins and put his mouth in front of a microphone. "How does it sound you two?" His voice was loud and distorted and gave Bobbee's spine that feeling you get when someone drags their fingers down a chalk board. She shuddered and looked over at Jethro.

"Just play a song," she cried.

"All right," Jethro answered turning around and looking at the rest of the band. "You guys ready?"

They all nodded their heads in agreement.

"Asteroid Shuffle: take one," Jethro said into the microphone. "A one, a two, a one, two, three, four..."

The band kicked into the song and once again created a racket that caused Bobbee and Bettee's antennas to twitch uncomfortably. Bobbee, who had developed her own sign language in order to communicate effectively with her brother, made a few hand gestures.

Bettee nodded his head affirmatively. The two siblings jumped up. Bobbee ran up to a rather large and complicated mixing board and began adjusting buttons and knobs while Bettee dashed into the midst of the band and began turning volumes down on the amplifiers, adjusting E.Q's and moving microphones around. The band members, who were now staring curiously at the two youngsters, kept playing. Within five minutes the antenna twitching noise that had been threatening everyone's appreciation of music, had turned into a much quieter, cleaner and surprisingly pleasing array of sound. When properly mixed, The Jethro Sirius Experiment, in all honesty, sounded quite fantastic. The moment the musicians could actually hear themselves, they found they started performing better as well.

The song finished and the band mates all looked at each other excitedly. They shifted their gazes to the two young siblings, and smiled appreciatively.

Bobbee spoke first. "The Draicon Sound Siblings at your service." She bowed low to the ground as did Bettee.

"How did you guys do that?" Jethro asked, still grinning from antenna to antenna.

"Our parents," explained Bobbee. "They own the sound company that your dad hired. They taught us everything they know."

"Everything they know," exclaimed Seth disbelievingly. "But you two are only...what...five years old?"

"Big deal. We're fast learners."

"Boy, you can say that again," said Jethro, visibly more excited about the siblings' performance than the bands'.

Val quickly spoke up. "Hey, do you guys do lights as well?"

"Of course," replied Bobbee.

The band exchanged another round of smiles.

"Cooool!" they all chimed in unison.

Bobbee and Bettee soon set to work on the lighting systems and within a half hour, the rehearsal room was starting to look and sound like a genuine rock concert. The authenticity of the rehearsal was fueling the band's energy and by the end of the evening they all felt ready for the next night's performance.

"I can't believe our luck," remarked Seth, looking over at Bobbee and Bettee. The rehearsal was over and they were all sitting on the floor relaxing. "That's twice you two have saved my butt."

Bobbee looked at him and then turned away, blushing. Bettee looked at her and signed something with his hands. She turned back to Seth. "My brother wants to know how come you don't do the sound, being an electronic genius and all?" she said.

"I don't know," replied Seth. "When it comes to programming and stuff I'm pretty good, but I think I'm tone deaf or something cause my ears just won't tell me what sounds good and what doesn't. Birth defect or something, I guess." He shrugged.

"Your Dad's good at it though, isn't he," cut in Jethro.

"Oh, totally. He was always giving your dad pointers on how to make songs better. He never played an instrument other than drums, but he always seemed to have a good ear for song arrangements."

Jethro grinned. "So maybe he's not that replaceable after all."

Seth opened his mouth to speak, but realized Jethro had made a valuable point he couldn't argue with, and just nodded his head and smiled at his friend knowingly. Even though he knew he could replace his dad's technical ability on drums with a machine, there was no way his invention could successfully arrange a good song. There were just simply too many creative elements that made up a composition. It wasn't a matter of just programming verses, a chorus, and a bridge into a computer. Although it could probably be done, Seth knew that without the Sirian element, it would probably sound pretty lame.

I guess even the greatest minds can learn something new every day, he thought to himself.

"Okay guys," said Jethro, standing up and stretching his limbs. "I think we should all get some sleep tonight. We've got rehearsal all day tomorrow and a show tomorrow night. We're gonna need our energy."

They all nodded in agreement and headed off for their quarters. Jethro and Quasar were the last to leave and she stopped him before he could leave the room. "Uh, Jethro," she said hesitantly.

"What's up Quas?" he asked turning to face her and wondering if something was wrong.

"I just wanted to say that I'm glad we're all together and that, even though our circumstances look pretty grim, that I have...umm...well, no problem with you being the...you know...leader."

"What are you talking about Quas?"

"We need a leader Jeth or we're gonna end up spending the next two years of our lives fighting and arguing. You and I seem to be the only ones capable of overlooking our differences and I'm just not cut out for...you know...leadership stuff."

"I guess I know what you mean Quas, but I don't want the others thinking I'm Mr. Big Shot."

"I know that," replied Quasar, "but I still really believe that we're gonna need a leader. We can't stay stuck in this power struggle for too long or we're all gonna end up hating each other. Both Val and Seth are pretty head strong and I know what's gonna happen. You and I are already getting dragged into it and I think we just need to be really...careful...if we're gonna get out of this and find our parents."

"Okay Quas, I get your point, but why don't we just keep this between you and I. I'll be the silent leader type. That way it won't be so obvious to Val and Seth, all right?"

"Thanks Jethro. That makes me feel a lot better."

"No problem," he replied.

They hugged and then headed back to their quarters to get some sleep.

The next morning they all woke up in fairly good spirits, and hungry. The rumbling in their stomachs reminded them that they hadn't had much to eat since the beginning of the adventure. They had all congregated in the cockpit first thing in the morning, but soon decided to head down to the cafeteria on the second floor to get some food.

After ordering fresh wudget sausage and Sirian terratoidal eggs from the creaticator, Seth was extremely disappointed when a plate of uncooked sausage and a tray of raw eggs, still in their shells, appeared in front of him. His friends were staring curiously over his shoulder.

"Libby, what's goin' on?" demanded Seth.

"Unfortunately Seth, I've just discovered another system malfunction."

"You've got to be kidding me."

"Sorry Seth-bro. The meal duplicator won't recognize the meal codes. All it's recognizing is the ingredient codes."

"So what you're telling me is that it'll duplicate everything we need to make a specific meal, but it won't duplicate the actual meal itself?"

"You got it."

Sometimes, Seth thought to himself, *Libby sounds far too cheerful for her own good.* He turned to face his friends. "Well guys, looks like we're gonna have to cook."

They all moaned their disapproval and stared at Seth helplessly.

"I don't even know how to make toast," complained Val.

"Make it?" Quasar said. "I don't even know what ingredients to use to make toast."

"Oh, knock it off you two. We can do this. Back home my mom and dad used to cook all the time. It can't be that difficult. Libby," asked Seth, "are the emergency cooking facilities still functioning?"

"You betcha."

"Great. Come on you guys. There's another creaticator in the kitchen. We better hurry up and make ourselves something to eat 'cause we got a lot of work to do today." He headed off through a door to the right of the first meal duplicator and everyone else followed suit.

As they entered the kitchen, Quasar looked over at Seth. "Hey Seth."

"Ya."

"How come you know so much about the layout of the bus? I mean you seem to know where everything is."

Seth didn't hesitate in answering. "My dad designed the security systems for the entire ship so we've got all the blueprints back in our quarters. I don't have the whole bus memorized. Probably only about ninety percent of it. Parts of the engine get pretty complicated. I skipped those, so if you guys think I'll be able to find my way around that engine block, think again. Libby will have to take care of it if it gets damaged."

"Wasn't there a bunch of engineers down there or something?"

"Ya, but my dad says they're all union workers," commented Jethro, "and that they spend about twenty three of those hours sitting on their butts and playing Sirian poker."

"Well, whatever. It's still a pretty complicated piece of machinery and I don't even want to have to think about what'll happen to us if it dies," said Seth as they reached the second duplicator. "I think we should all eat the same thing. I don't want to be stuck here cooking a million different things."

Once all the ingredients had been ordered, they began dropping sausages and eggs into fry pans and began the not-as-easy-as-it-looks task of cooking. Fortunately, they made it through the process without too much arguing. The sausages turned out slightly crisp and black on one side and the eggs wound up a little rubbery, but no one seemed to have much of a problem with this, and they scarfed down their meals with the enthusiasm of a four hundred pound Muldeyvian Imp, a creature from the planet Muldex, who is notorious for its insatiable appetite.

When they had all finished eating, Jethro wasn't surprised to find that the automatic dish-cleaning cyclers were inoperable as well. Due to their time constraint, he encouraged everyone to stack their plates up on the counter where they could clean them later. Everyone had no problem complying with this request and they were all soon heading back to the rehearsal room on the third floor.

They spent the next five hours rehearsing and with the help of Bobbee and Bettee's expertise, they managed to achieve a level of quality that they were all quite happy with. While Quasar and Val remained in the rehearsal room, going over songs, Jethro and Seth headed back to the cockpit to discuss the planet they would be arriving at in less that two hours. Bobbee and Bettee spent their time packing up equipment that would be needed for the show.

Seth asked Libby to display the tour schedule on the monitor and he and Jethro scanned down the list until they reached that night's destination:

Botneex - Dendro City - 21/07/2412

Jethro looked up at the ceiling. "Libby, can you give us some background on Planet Botneex? I want to know a little bit about its inhabitants before we arrive."

Libby's voice came out of nowhere, loud and clear. "Botneex is a small green and blue planet located in the Nooayji Galaxy, Sector A. It revolves around a large, yet young star which is part of the 'Sickle of Life' constellation. Considered to be a very humid planet, it receives a good deal of rain a good deal of the time. Fifty percent of the time to be nearly exact. Its inhabitants, known as organic botanics, are plant-like in nature. Many different races and breeds of organic botanics co-exist on Planet Botneex, and do not consider themselves a technologically advanced race. One group, called the Hydroponical, is considered to be the most technologically advanced, and it is their sector of the planet that you will be performing. Do you require more information?"

Jethro waved his hand, "No that's good enough. How long until we arrive?"

"About an hour and a half."

He looked at Seth. "I guess we should make up a song list. I don't really feel like winging it when we get on stage."

"I agree," replied Seth, and the two of them headed back to the rehearsal room to discuss the list. Val and Quasar were no longer there. The boys asked Bobbee where they had gone and she informed them that they had gone to pick out some outfits for the show.

"It's a good thing we have girls in the band," said Seth. "I haven't even thought about what I'm gonna wear tonight."

"I guess it's probably pretty important eh," commented Jethro.

By the time the group had finished getting dressed up, they had only about a half hour left to make up their song list. This turned out to be a little more difficult than they thought, as everyone had their own ideas, but they eventually got it done, just before Libby's voice echoed throughout the room.

"Five minutes to arrival - Planet Botneex," she said.

"Libby, turn the reverb down on your voice," Jethro advised. "It's annoying. C'mon you guys, let's go up to the cockpit and check out the planet."

They all headed up to the cockpit and pushed their faces up against the windshield. Planet Botneex was growing larger and larger as they approached it. A beautiful swirling blend of greens and blues covered its entire surface, and closer inspection revealed splotches of gray and white.

"Those gray and white spots are weather patterns I think," said Jethro, turning to his friends. "Apparently it rains a lot on this planet so everyone be sure to pack your ponchos."

CHAPTER 5
BOTNEEX

The bus entered the planet's atmosphere with ease and the young band was soon looking down on one of the most beautiful planets they had ever seen. They were lucky to enter a sea of blue sky, though there appeared to be rain clouds looming in the distance. Down on the surface was nothing but lush greenery; plants, trees, flowers, and weeds. As they approached the surface they realized they were directly above a beautiful city, which appeared to have been built out of the plant life. Winding roads made from giant vines curved in and out of downtown cores that sprouted thick, weed-like buildings of all shapes and sizes. The entire city was buzzing with activity as vehicles made from plants and trees zoomed up and down the botanical highway. The kids were amazed at how there appeared to be absolutely no trace of metals or plastic anywhere.

A rather large, interesting looking building loomed up in front of them and they soon realized that they were staring at what looked like a giant mushroom covered in a tangle of green vines. Some of the darker vines had formed together to create something that looked like writing on the front of the building.

"Libby," Jethro said, "are you able to translate what that says?"

"That's the Hydroponical Coliseum, kids. That's where you're playing tonight." The bus steered around the enormous mushroom to the back of the building where there was a large vine covered archway leading inside. The bus entered slowly and came to a stop, lowering itself down onto a soft, mossy floor.

It was at this point that the kids got a Sirius look at the locals. A simple way to describe them would be to say they were nothing more than walking plants. Like all other races in the universe, they were of all different shapes and sizes. Their bodies seemed to be made of thick sturdy, plant-like material, supported by muscular legs and arms made from vines. Their heads extended up on green necks and looked like big venus fly traps, only these Botneexians probably knew nothing of the planet Venus. Their eyes protruded from the tops of their large heads, which were made up mostly of their huge mouths, and sat comfortably on the ends of two sturdy looking green stalks. Their clothes were made from leaves stitched together with tiny vines.

"We better get down to the cargo entrance," said Seth. "Those guys look like roadies and are probably wanting to unload our equipment."

The gang all headed down to level three where the cargo entrance would be accessed off the back of the rehearsal space. It was large and looked like a big warehouse. Bobbee and Bettee had done a great job of loading the equipment into travel cases. They had utilized the mechanical loaders to pack the gear that was too heavy to lift. The band entered the huge area and Seth ran over to the sidewall and called everyone over. They looked at him questioningly.

"What are you guys looking at? We need to acclimatize our physiology."

"Huh?" The rest of them said all at the same time.

"This is an alien planet you idiots. Our biological re-configuration unit will re-configure our internal...oh, never mind," he said, realizing he was receiving nothing but dumb looks. He pointed at a button on the wall. "You push this button, it shoots some gassy stuff in your face, and enables you to breath on an alien planet, all right."

The others all suddenly nodded their understanding and lined up. The gassy stuff that blew into their faces was sweet smelling and felt somewhat refreshing as it entered their respiratory systems and coated their lungs. Once they had all been 're-configured,' Seth looked at them. "You guys ready?"

"Ready as a Slimacular space slug about to brush his teeth," said Val.

They all had a good laugh and Seth pushed up on a lever that was sticking out of the wall. They were soon listening to the mechanical shifting of gears as the hangar door opened. A strong but pleasant breeze blew into the cargo area and the young Sirians felt their antennas tingle in response. A handful of Botneexians entered the cargo area and approached the kids. A tall skinny one was the first to speak and the two stalks that its eyes were sitting in suddenly extended in length and stretched over its head until they were sitting right in front of its mouth. The eyes had a suspicious look about them.

"I thought you'd be bigger," it said in a rather masculine voice. "You're much smaller than you look in the picture you sent."

"Hey, you know how it is," remarked Quasar. "The camera always adds a few pounds." She tacked on a nervous laugh to the end of her comment. It seemed to work though, because the suspicious look in the creature's eyes turned into one of good humour. It's big mouth opened up and laughed out loud.

"That it does," he said in mid laugh. It extended a big hand out to Quasar and tapped her twice on the head. He did the same to the others and stretched both his arms out in a welcoming gesture.

"Welcome to Dendro City," he said. "I am Vinweedo, the promoter of this event."

Jethro smiled and reached his hand out, but realized he wouldn't be able to reach the top of the organic botanic's head, and slowly retreated his hand. "I'm Jethro," he said instead. "And this is my band." He pointed at his band mates and named them one at a time. "Quasar, Valentia - we call her Val for short, Seth, and our two sound engineers, Bobbee and Bettee."

"Pleasure to meet you all," said Vinweedo, "but I'm a little confused. Your names don't match our records."

Before anyone had a chance to panic about Jethro's major mistake, Val came up with a response. "Uh, ya, about that, you see about three shows back we had a show on the Monsturd planet and for some reason we didn't perform up to their standards - probably weren't lousy enough for them - and they got really angry and chased us off the planet. We had to change our names as well as the name of our band so in case you're wondering, we're not called the Ozzbourn Sirius Experiment anymore. We've changed our name to the Jethro Sirius Experiment."

Vinweedo raised a green hand up to his chin and scratched it. "Hmmm, I understand your need for deception, but if I announce you as a different band, it could pose a problem. The audience has bought tickets to see the Ozzbourn Sirius Experiment, not the Jethro Sirius Experiment."

"No problem," announced Seth. "I highly doubt that there'll be any Monsturd planet goons here on Botneex, but just to be on the safe side, I'll install a tonal translation box in the microphone so that all the organic botanics in the audience will hear the name Ozzbourn, but any Monsturds out there will hear Jethro."

Vinweedo looked at Seth doubtfully and for a brief moment the kids thought their scheme had been discovered, but the organic botanic simply shrugged and said, "We here on Botneex, even though the Hydroponicals are far more advanced, technologically speaking of course, tend to forget about other worldly advancements. Who am I to tell you how to conduct your tour arrangements. Let us put this behind us and unload your equipment. You'll have a sound check in about two hours and then you'll have the afternoon to explore Dendro City if you like. I will send one of my crewmembers with you to show you around. He will also be in charge of getting you back to the coliseum on time for your show. Does this proposal meet your approval?"

"Sounds great," replied Jethro. "Let's get started."

Vinweedo smiled in his own plant-like fashion and turned to the crew who were mumbling amongst themselves a little ways behind him. "Okay boys, let's move. We've got one hour."

The crew immediately sprung into action and began picking up pieces of equipment and carrying them off the bus. Vinweedo turned once more to the band.

"Where is your personal sound crew?" he asked.

"Right there," said Jethro, pointing to Bobbee and Bettee, who were sitting on a large box against the wall.

Once again Vinweedo looked confused. "I don't understand. Only two of them?"

"Best in the galaxy," confirmed Val. "They prefer to work alone. They find that anyone else just gets in their way."

Vinweedo smiled once more. "I can relate to that. Come, I'll show you the stage."

The band followed the promoter out of the bus and through the back entrance of the coliseum. Within minutes they were standing in the middle of the enormous building and were staring, wide eyed, at the front of the stage.

The inside of the venue looked very similar to the outside. It was entirely made of plants and trees. Huge and thick wooden support beams crisscrossed the entire ceiling about two hundred feet above their heads and dropped down the sides to create wooden frames along the walls. The seats were made of large luscious leaves separated by branch-like arms.

One of the things that interested Jethro most about Botneex was that its buildings always appeared to be in a constant state of movement; almost as if they were alive.

Vinweedo, who seemed to know what Jethro was thinking said, "The building is alive, as is the entire planet. If we used logging techniques, the way many other planets do, everything would die. Including us. We are one with our environment and though we allow ourselves to advance technologically, it is never at the expense of the land. We simply shape our technology around the land's needs as opposed to the other way around."

Seth seemed most impressed by this and simply said, "Amazing," in his usual slack jaw fashion. The band spent the next hour exploring the building and then jumped on stage to conduct their sound check.

"Bobbee, can you turn my voice up in the monitors?" Jethro spoke into the microphone. "Blah, blah, blah, blah, one, two, three."

Bobbee readjusted the volume to an appropriate level.

The rest of the band completed their requests and after playing a couple of songs they decided that they were quite ready for the show that night.

Vinweedo approached them on stage once they had completed their sound check. He was followed by a shorter, chubbier organic botanic. "You sound fantastic," commented Vinweedo. "I can't wait until my kids see you. They're huge fans." He turned and pointed at the botanic standing behind him. "This is Stawker and he will be your guide for the afternoon. He's been under my employment for well over ten years and I'm sure you will enjoy his company. I, on the other hand, must be off. Plenty of things to take care of before the show."

Vinweedo waved and departed. Stawker stepped in to take his place.

"Hey dudes," he said. His voice was raspy, but seemed to have a little more life in it than Vinweedo's. "Guess I'm in charge of showin' you off-landers around Dendro City. Sounds cool to me. Where do you guys wanna start?"

They all looked at each other and shrugged. Jethro noticed that Bobbee and Bettee were still running around making adjustments.

"Yo Bobbee," he hollered.

She was about fifty feet away from him, working at the main soundboard. She looked up when she heard his voice.

"Ya" she yelled back.

"You wanna go on a tour of the city?" he asked.

She shook her head. "Na. You go ahead. Me and Bettee got stuff to do." She turned her head back down and became instantly immersed in what she had been focusing on before she had been interrupted.

Jethro looked back to Stawker. "Well, I guess it'll just be us four that you have to baby-sit. As for where we wanna start," he shrugged, "it's your city man, why don't you decide."

Stawker smiled. "No problem. Follow me."

He led them off the stage and into the outside air at the back of the building. They followed him over to a large looking vehicle that was made entirely from plants. The moment Stawker approached, the intertwined vines in its side separated and created an opening. Stawker stood to the side of the entrance and pointed inside.

"Enter," he said.

One by one, Jethro, Quasar, Val and Seth climbed into the vehicle. It smelled fresh and alive and the seats, made of a thick mossy substance, were spongy and extremely comfortable. Stawker climbed in behind them and hopped into the driver's seat in the front. His seat was directly in the middle and Jethro sat to his right, while Quasar sat to his left. Seth and Val sat behind them. The opening that had let them in quickly closed up and they all felt the vehicle rise about five feet off the ground.

Stawker backed out of the parking space, cranked the vehicle to the left and zoomed out of the coliseum lot. They soon entered a mid-air freeway where hundreds of other similar looking vehicles were rushing by in both directions.

As they cruised along, Stawker looked over his shoulder at Seth and Val.

"You two want fresh air?" he asked.

"Sure" they replied in unison.

Directly above them, vines separated to create a sunroof and Seth and Val were pleased to feel the rush of wind upon their faces and the warmth of the Botneex star upon their heads.

Stawker pushed in a small wooden button that was jutting out of the leaf-covered dashboard. "Music?" he questioned.

"Absolutely," replied Jethro.

Stawker cranked up the volume as some high-energy music rang out through vehicle.

If you've got problems in your life
Weed them out, weed them out
If you're having a hard time growin' up.

Fertilize, fertilize.

The music was quite good, Jethro thought to himself. Stawker was singing along excitedly and was drumming away on the vine wheel with his hands. He looked over at Jethro and said, "What do ya' think?"

Jethro had to yell in order to be heard over the loud music. "Pretty good. What are they called?"

"The band or the music?"

"Both."

"Well, these guys pretty much stick to stalk music. Loud and hard hitting. They're called 'Plant Haven'. Pretty good eh?"

"Ya" agreed Jethro, drumming away on his knees and starting to sing the lyrics in the chorus.

Stawker steered the vehicle in and out of traffic as 'Plant Haven' continued to stalk the bus.

"Guess what," Stawker blurted out suddenly, looking over at Jethro.

"What?"

"These guys are opening up for you tonight."

"Cool." Jethro looked over at Quasar and then turned and glanced at Seth and Val to see what they thought of the music and he was relieved to see that they were all nodding their heads appreciatively to the beat.

Stawker suddenly pulled hard to the right on the vine wheel and steered the botanical cruiser down an off-ramp. He turned left and drove under the freeway overpass and the band soon realized that they were heading into the Dendro City downtown core. All different shapes and sizes of botanical buildings lined the streets and the sidewalks were covered with organic botanicals headed in all directions going about their daily business. Stawker pulled the vehicle up to the curb and hit the brakes. They had stopped in front of a small cluster of buildings and once again, vines pulled apart from one another to create an opening in the side of the vine van.

Jethro climbed out and stepped down onto the hard, plant surface that made up the sidewalk. His friends did the same, followed by Stawker. Organic Botanicals were walking past and staring at them curiously. Stawker walked around them toward the building directly in front of them. He turned and made a pulling gesture with his hands as if he were playing tug-of-war.

"C'mon Dudes, follow me," he said.

"What is this place?" asked Jethro.

"Well, you can't expect me to show you guys the city and not, first, bring you to the best music store in town. C'mon." He did the same tug 'o' war gesture with his hands.

Jethro and the rest of the gang followed him into the building. Like the outside, the inside was entirely plant ridden. Jethro immediately recognized the sounds of 'Plant Haven' coming from some ceiling speakers. Instruments lined the walls and drum kits littered the floor. Jethro walked up to the wall to give the guitars a closer inspection. Their size and shape were similar to Jethro's own

Sirianacaster, but they were, of course, made entirely from plants. The bodies were made from firmly pressed together leaves, and the necks jutting straight out of the bodies carved out of thick stalk like material. The strings were made from extremely tough but thin vines and Jethro strummed his fingers across these gently.

"Can I help you?" a voice asked off to his side.

Jethro turned. An organic botanical was standing next to him and smiling knowingly. "She's a beauty isn't she," said a rather feminine voice.

"Can I ask you a question?" said Jethro.

"Of course."

"Please don't take this the wrong way. I've never been to your planet before and I don't mean to offend, but...I'm having a difficult time telling the difference between males and females of your race."

The organic botanical threw her head back and laughed out loud. "You're a cute little alien, aren't you," she said tapping Jethro on the head a couple of times.

He stared back irritably at her. He did not particularly enjoy being referred to as cute.

The botanical must have picked up on this and immediately put her hands up in the air in what appeared to be a defensive gesture. "I'm sorry," she said. "Now it appears I am the one who's being offensive."

"Nah, it's okay," Jethro reassured her. "I do happen to be pretty cute and I shouldn't get all weirded out when others notice."

The botanical smiled. "My name is Vindy, and as a gesture of my goodwill I would like you to take this as a gift." She pulled the guitar off the wall and handed it to him.

"Whoah, are you serious?" he exclaimed. Wide eyed and mouth hanging open, he graciously accepted the guitar.

"Isn't that your name?" she said with a knowing smile.

Jethro smirked. "Ya, how did you know?"

"I own a music store. You think I don't know one of the most famous guitar players in the entire galaxy when I see one. I could almost tell that you were Ozzbourn the moment you walked through the door."

Jethro had nearly forgotten that he was masquerading as his father and was grateful of the unintentional reminder. He smiled in response.

"Anyways," said Vindy, "in answer to your question, female botanicals, as you've discovered, can often be identified by their voices, but the easiest way is to look at our eyes." Her eyes, like Vinweedo's and Stawker's, stretched over her head and came to rest in front of her mouth. "We have eyelashes and the males don't."

Jethro inspected her eyes closely and noticed that she did, indeed, possess long, beautiful green eyelashes. "Very pretty," he said.

"Thank you. You're sweet. Any other questions?"

"Umm, so you own this store?" asked Jethro.

"Sure do. Come from a long, proud line of music storeowners. I inherited this one from my mom and dad. They were great. Plant Haven met and became a band in this very store. Right over there in that corner." She pointed and Jethro followed her finger with his gaze over to a group of instruments encased in glass.

"What's up with the glass?"

"First instruments they ever played as a group. The moment I heard them, I knew they were going straight to the top. I told them so and refused to sell them those instruments. They were kinda pissed off at me, but kinda flattered at the same time. They bought some other gear and those ones have been behind glass ever since. That one tiny box of instruments, which makes up about half a percent of my entire store is probably worth about a hundred times more than my entire inventory."

"I assume that's a lot," said Jethro.

"You assume right," she said. Then, changing the subject, "So what's it like being in one of the galaxy's most famous bands?"

Jethro almost didn't hear the question. He had noticed that a figure in a long hooded green cloak from across the room, had its head pointed directly at him and he was beginning to feel uneasy. He couldn't see the face, but there was a glimmer of eyes beneath the hood and he knew they were staring directly at him.

"Hmm?" he replied to Vindy's question

"What's it like being in one of the galaxy's most famous bands?" she repeated.

"Oh, it's all right I guess," he replied nervously. The figure across the room was still staring at him. "A little tiring after a while."

"I'll bet," said Vindy. "Hey, can I get a picture of you trying out a guitar in the store?"

"Sure."

"Great, I'll be back in a sec." Vindy dashed off to find a camera.

In the meantime, Jethro could still feel the eyeballs of the figure across the room burning a hole through him. He risked another glance at the staring plant, but when he looked up the botanical that had been there moments before was now gone. Vindy soon replaced Jethro's field of vision and she was wielding a long, tube like stalk in her hand. Jethro picked up the guitar and smiled. He heard a slight clicking sound, as the object Vindy was holding assumedly took his picture.

"Come with me," she said. Jethro followed her into a back room.

The walls were covered with pictures of various aliens and groups of aliens.

"Are these all musicians?" he asked, visibly impressed with Vindy's photographic collection.

"Yep," she replied. "From all over the galaxy."

"Wow," he said.

Vindy pointed the tube at a blank space in the wall and blew through the end of it. Something shot out of the end of it and hit the empty space on the wall with a gentle SLAP. Jethro's picture had become a permanent fixture on Vindy's wall of fame.

"Don't you want a picture of the whole band?" he asked.

"Naw. Everyone knows that Ozzbourn Sirius is the only one that really counts."

"Oh," Jethro said, not really seeming to absorb the importance of what Vindy had just said. "Well, I better get back to my band."

"Absolutely," replied Vindy, leading him back out into the store.

"Where were you?" asked Quasar, walking up to him and the storeowner.

"Uh, Vindy here was just showing me her office."

"Sure she was," teased Quasar turning to Vindy. "Hi, I'm Quasar."

"Uh-huh," said Vindy, nodding her head and then walking away.

"How rude!" exclaimed Quasar.

"She's probably just really busy," defended Jethro. "She owns the whole store you know."

"Whatever. C'mon Jethro, Stawker says we ought to go if we're going to check out any more of the city before the show."

Quasar began walking toward the entrance where the others were waiting. Jethro was slow to follow and looked over his shoulder to see if he could spot Vindy. He wanted to say goodbye, but when he realized she was no-where to be seen, he headed across the store and joined his friends.

"Best music store in the entire city," said Stawker as they exited the building.

Meanwhile, back in Vindy's office, the hooded figure that had been staring at Jethro, was busy sucking Jethro's picture off the wall into another photographic tube. He turned to Vindy, who was sitting at her desk.

"This picture is for my master's collection," he said in a raspy voice that was cold as Sirian steel. "He absolutely detests studio portraits and will only accept the most genuine of photographs."

"Ya, ya, whatever," said Vindy, impatiently. "Where's my money?"

The mysterious figure reached into the front of his cloak and pulled out a small leaf case and placed it on the desk in front of Vindy. "Open it and count it if you like," he said.

Vindy pulled the leaf case toward her and clicked it open. A cloud of green coloured gas shot directly at her and engulfed her head. She instantly sat up straight and began coughing uncontrollably. Within seconds she had fallen to the floor, convulsing, writhing and clawing at her own throat, as if she were trying to pull out whatever substance had been injected into her plant lungs. Within a few more seconds she had stopped entirely and lay still. The figure closed the briefcase, tucked it back inside his cloak and exited through a door in the back of the office.

CHAPTER 6

WEEDIES AND GENTLEPLANTS

The band spent the remainder of the afternoon sightseeing. Stawker was an excellent tour guide and showed them all the popular sights. Near the end of the day though, some large thunderclouds rolled in and, what started out as a steady drizzle, soon turned into a downpour.

The band sat quietly in the van as Stawker made his way back to the coliseum. He didn't play any music during the ride back, which gave Seth an opportunity to think with out being distracted.

"Hey Stawker," he said.

"Yo."

"Vinweedo told us that everything is alive on Botneex. Buildings and all. How is it that things like this van, which aren't attached to the ground, are able to stay alive?"

"They're self generating," replied Stawker. "All we have to do is make sure they get enough water. You see, the Hydroponicals discovered that by harnessing the life energy of all living things, you can create a controllable power source without actually damaging the environment. It rains here on Botneex about fifty percent of the time, so our homes, vehicles, and other belongings are able to maintain a constant state of power. They're being continually fueled by the environment they were born in. In a way, they're never truly separated from their mother. She keeps feeding them until they grow old and die."

"So do you pay a tax or anything for the amount of power you use," asked Quasar.

"Tax! Of course not," laughed Stawker. "What comes from the land is of benefit to all organic botanics, and therefore, free to be utilized by whoever needs it."

"All I know," said Quasar, "is that my dad's always complaining about the cost of fuel these days."

Stawker smiled. "The arrogant nature of many alien races has led them to believe that they are better than us Botneexians, but tell me something. When you look out the windows of this van, do you see a dying planet?"

They all looked out the windows and realized that Stawker was right. The entire planet was alive, clearly not a victim of logging, pollution, or mining. It was truly remarkable the way the Botneexians had advanced technologically, without destroying their planet in the process. All the kids secretly wished that the same could be said for their home; but they knew differently. Jethro suddenly felt guilt and shame as it suddenly dawned on him that the space bus he and his friends had been flying around in was actually a piece of his planets heart, cut out in order to benefit the Sirian entertainment industry.

These feelings soon passed as Stawker safely delivered them back to the Hydroponical Coliseum. They all jumped out of the van and quickly ran inside. Vinweedo was waiting patiently for them and led them to their dressing room where they quickly changed into their stage outfits.

As they left their change rooms and headed back stage they could hear the thousands of cheers coming from the excited audience. The lights went down and they watched Plant Haven, a group of four musicians, jump on stage to open the show. Their music was loud, fast, and inspiring, and Jethro wondered to himself if they'd be able to follow up with an equally inspiring performance. *Oh well,* he thought to himself. *It's too late to worry about that now.*

Plant Haven ended their set with a drum roll that seemed to last forever, and the crowd went nuts. The cheering was so loud that the young Sirians had to cover their ears. Plant Haven left the stage in a cloud of confidence, which meant Jethro and his friends had about ten minutes to calm themselves down before it was their turn.

The Botneexian stawk band was now heading straight toward them, and Jethro decided he ought to think of something to say. The lead singer was watching him and it was obvious that he was thinking the same thing.

Just as their paths were about to cross, Jethro blurted out, "You guys were great."

The lead singer of Plant Haven smiled in response. "Thanks man."

"Nice drumming," Seth said to the drummer.

"Thanks, I can't wait to see your guys' set," said the musician with the two sticks.

Their paths completed crossing and Plant Haven was in the process of heading back to their dressing room when the lead singer turned and looked back at the Sirians.

"I thought you'd be taller," he said.

"Camera always takes off a few pounds," replied Val, pleased with herself for having invented a witty comeback to the common question.

The lead singer of Plant Haven grinned. "Hey, we're comin' back out to watch your guys' set, but I was wonderin' if you guys might wanna hang out with us after the show? There's a big party happenin' and we thought it would be pretty cool if the Ozzbourn Sirius Experiment showed up."

The young band of Sirians exchanged glances. They were still having a difficult time remembering that they were masquerading as adults and realized that this would probably be an adult party.

Jethro quickly turned to his friends and whispered. "What do you guys think?"

"I think we should go," said Val. "If we're going to be convincing as adults, we need to be prepared to do adult things every now and then."

"I agree with Val," said Quasar. "Otherwise we could blow our cover."

Jethro turned to the final member of the band who hadn't spoken yet. "Seth?"

Seth appeared to be thinking hard. "The girls have a good point," he finally said. "I think we should go."

Jethro had already made up his own mind and turned to the lead singer of Plant Haven and said, "Sure we'll go."

The singer smiled. "Great. We'll see you guys after the show. It's gonna be a rocker, dudes."

As Plant Haven disappeared back stage, Jethro and his friends started to get excited about the after show celebration. What none of them knew at the time was that they would never make it to the party.

As the young group were moving towards the stage and moving out of their after-party thoughts they heard, over the PA system, Vinweedo's enthusiastic introduction.

"Weedies and Gentleplants. I Feel Vine Productions and WEX Radio are proud to present, The Ozzbourn Sirius Experiment!"

For the first time in their young lives, the Sirians walked out on stage and instantly froze in the shoes of their own nervousness. The combination of the stage lights and the roaring crowds was quickly eroding their self-confidence. No amount of rehearsal could have prevented the first time feeling of stage fright.

Jethro, Seth, and Quasar stood on stage, unable to move. It was Val that woke them up out of their paralyzed stasis.

"Wake up, you idiots," she said. "We've been waiting our whole lives for a moment like this. Don't blow it now." She began waving to the crowd.

Her band-mates still did not move though. Val grabbed Seth's drumsticks out of his hands and gave each of them a whack on the antennas. "Wake up you wimps. We've got a show to do. You ever wanna see your parents again, you better not blow this."

It was the 'parents' comment that did it, and the other three Sirians, suddenly snapped out of their respective stage fright trances and moved toward their instruments. Seth reclaimed his sticks and jumped in behind his drum kit. The other three turned to him, now eagerly awaiting his four stick cue to start the first song.

He gave it to them and The Jethro Sirius Experiment opened up with one of Ozzbourn's biggest hits, 'Interplanetary Paranoia'. The audience rose up and delivered their appreciation in a collective cheer that nearly drowned out the music itself.

Though the young band had been quite nervous during the first half of the song, the confidence they were receiving from the enthusiasm of the audience was enabling them to loosen up. By the end of the third song, they had fallen into a groove and actually began jumping and moving around on stage.

They blasted through such hits as 'Dogstar Fever', 'Sirius Business', and 'Beautiful Star', and for the first time in his life, Jethro felt like he was on fire. His fingers danced across the strings of his guitar as if they were a part of it. He nailed his dad's solos, note for note and, on many occasions, would throw himself down on his knees or his back, wailing away in true rock star form. His intensity inspired the other musicians like oxygen to a flame. Quasar was soon running around the giant stage, throwing her feet up on the monitor speakers and striking rock star poses that would have put her own mother to shame. Val banged her head to the point where one might think it would fall off and Seth beat away at his drums with a passion that dripped from his pores in the form of sweat.

If any fan in the audience had any doubt that this was, indeed, the Ozzbourn Sirius Experiment, it was a feeling immediately devoured by the authenticity of the kids' performance. The crowd had gone absolutely insane and was jumping up and down in their seats. Those on the floor were pushed up against the barriers that separated them from the stage and were banging their heads, rhythmically, to the music.

The band finished off with another one of Ozzbourn's big hits, 'The Amphibian Who Loved Me', and the audience went absolutely berserk. As the band left the stage, they could hear the chanting crowd; Ozzbourn, Ozzbourn, Ozzbourn. The band mates all smiled at each other and were about to head back to their dressing room when they were stopped by Vinweedo.

"You guys were amazing," he said enthusiastically. "You gotta get up and do one more. The audience is demanding it."

The band members looked doubtfully at one another. They had played all their songs and didn't have one more to give.

"Well go on," said Vinweedo encouragingly. The band, knowing that they couldn't refuse the request, began to ascend the stage once more.

"All we had to do was save one song. I can't believe we forgot the encore. One song," grumbled Jethro. "One stupid song. What are we gonna do?"

Quasar and Val exchanged a quick glance.

"Umm, Jethro," said Quasar.

"Ya"

"Uh, Val and I wrote a song and the whole thing is only four chords. We've totally worked it out and it would be pretty easy for you and Seth to follow along."

Jethro looked doubtfully at the two girls. "Well, I guess we don't really have much of choice. What are the chords?"

Quasar quickly told him and the band reassumed their places on stage. Val started out the song on keyboards and Quasar began to sing, as the crowd quieted down.

The song was beautiful. It was a slow ballad and was extremely catchy and hypnotic. Jethro and

Seth had no problem following along and Jethro even found himself singing along in the chorus as he picked up the words:

> We're all alone in the Universe
> And I'm thinkin it can't get much worse
> If I'm gonna make it through to the end
> I'll have to rely on my best friends.

The crowd was out of their seats by the end of the song. It was a hit. The band took their bows and left the stage for real this time. Vinweedo was waiting for them and tapped them all on the head twice as they walked past him.

"Amazing show," he said. "Brilliant."

"Thanks," they all replied, heading back to their dressing room.

There were cool drinks and snacks awaiting them in their room and they were more than happy to sit down and indulge.

"When did you two write that song?" Jethro asked between mouthfuls.

Quasar and Val exchanged another look and smiled. "Last night," they said together.

Jethro shook his head. "Unbelievable. I didn't know you guys were into writing songs."

"You never asked," said Val.

Seth turned to Val. "It was awesome," he said.

"Thanks Seth," she replied, smiling and blushing slightly.

"And thanks for snapping us out of our brain fart syndrome earlier. I can't believe we all froze like that."

"No problem. I'm just glad I didn't freeze too or we really would have been in trouble. We would have had to change our name to 'The Jethro Sleeping Experiment'."

They all had a good laugh at Val's joke.

"You know what we should do," said Seth, suddenly.

Everyone looked at him curiously.

"We should record an album under our new name. The bus is equipped with a state-of-the-art recording studio. It would be easy."

"I'm down with that," said Jethro.

Quasar and Val were both voicing their agreement when in burst Bobbee and Bettee.

"What a rush," said Bobbee. Her brother nodded his agreement.

"You two were amazing," said Quasar. "Our stage sound was perfect."

"Ya," agreed Seth, "my in-ear monitors were crystal clear."

"No problem," said Bobbee, grinning. "That was the biggest show Bettee and I have ever done on our own."

"Well, it was awesome," said Jethro. "Hey, do you two wanna come to the after hours party?"

Bobbee looked at her brother, who shrugged. "Naw, I don't think so. We wanna make sure all the gear gets packed up properly. If we're done before you get back, we'll just grab a snack and wait for you on the bus." Just then a knock was heard at the door.

"Come in," they all said at the same time.

They were pleased to see Stawker enter the room. Bobbee and Bettee chose the open door as an opportunity to leave.

"You guys were amazing. Truly amazing," said Stawker.

"Thanks man," said Jethro.

"I'm actually here as a messenger," said the former tour guide. "Plant Haven wants to know if you guys are still into checking out that party they told you about?"

"Ya, we're into it," confirmed Jethro.

"Great. Well, I'm in charge of getting you guys there and back, so no worries."

"Cool," said Jethro. "We just need to change and get cleaned up."

"No problem. I'll wait for you out by my van." He turned and left the change room.

The cool fresh air hit their still sweating faces when the Sirians stepped outside. Stawker was waiting for them, as promised, by his van. He waved them over. As they walked casually toward him Vinweedo suddenly ran outside, waved his arms and called out to them.

"Wait. Before you take off we need to square away."

"Huh," they chimed.

"I need to pay you." He held up an intergalactic currency card.

"Oh right," said Jethro reaching out.

Vinweedo handed him the card and said, "Once again, I just wanted to say how incredible you were tonight and the entire city of Dendro thanks you."

"Hey, it was our pleasure," said Jethro.

"Come on you guys. Party's a waitin," cut in Stawker.

"Go. Go to your party." Vinweedo waved them off. "Anytime you want to come back to Dendro City, you are welcome."

The band thanked him one at a time and turned back toward Stawker's van. Just then it began to rain.

"Oh Sirius," said Jethro. "We're gonna get soaked before the party. I'm gonna run back to the bus and get some jackets for us. You guys get in the van. I'll just be a couple of minutes."

The rest of the band complied and as they climbed into the van, Jethro sprinted back to the bus and grabbed everyone's jackets. On his way back, he noticed a female organic botanic standing over by their change-room, waving him over. He cast her a curious expression before walking over to her.

"Can I help you?" he asked.

She smiled and shifted around excitedly. "Mr. Sirius, I am such a totally huge fan of yours and all my friends are in the Plant Haven dressing room and would like totally die if you were to just walk in there with me and say 'hi'."

Jethro smiled. "Sure I guess I could do that. But it'll have to be quick, I'm kind of in a hurry," he said glancing down at the jackets draped over his arm.

She led him three doors down to the Plant Haven dressing room, opened the door and motioned for Jethro to follow.

He entered the dressing room and suddenly dropped the jackets on the floor as the door shut fast behind him. The room was pretty much empty. Other than himself, there were only two other life forms in the room. The first one being the botanic that had led him into the room and the second was the strange hooded figure he had seen at the music store. The sight of him made Jethro's heart skip a beat. The figure held a small black device in his hand and was pointing it directly at Jethro.

"Hello Mr. Sirius," the figure said.

"Hullo," mumbled Jethro.

"My name is Vack Hume. Otherwise known as the Collector, and you are my prisoner."

Jethro had a chance to blink before Vack Hume clicked a button on the device. A large black hole shot out of the box, opened up in front of Jethro and started to spin. Jethro could feel his antennas being pulled toward the void and he quickly turned and made a dash for the door, but the pulling sensation on his back was too strong and he fell to his knees and began sliding backwards, across the floor, toward the dark opening.

"What do you want?" he screamed, clawing vigorously at the floor.

"Your talent, Mr. Sirius. Your talent," replied Vack Hume, as Jethro was suddenly pulled up and sucked into the black hole.

Vack Hume clicked a button on the device and the entire hole was sucked back inside of it. The female organic botanic who had led Jethro to the perilous situation was quivering on the floor. Vack Hume walked past the terrified botanic and left the room, the door slamming conclusively behind him. Jethro Sirius had officially been kidnapped.

CHAPTER 7
ENTER, THE COLLECTOR

"What, in Sirius, is taking him so long," said Val.

"He probably got stopped by a groupie or something," said Seth.

Quasar, who was starting to look worried, said, "I think we should go look for him."

"If you guys wanna go get him, that's fine by me," said Stawker. "Party's not going anywhere."

"I think we should. He's been gone for over twenty minutes," said Quasar. She got up and moved toward the side of the van.

"Can you make a door in this thing, please."

The door opened and she stepped through. Seth and Val followed and they headed back into the coliseum. Botanics were everywhere, packing up gear and looking busy.

The Sirians began shouting out their friend's name, but received only a few glares from the crew.

"Maybe he's in the dressing room," said Seth. They checked, but Jethro wasn't there.

"Do you hear that?" said Val.

"What?" the rest answered.

"Crying."

"Huh."

"Don't 'huh' me. I know what I hear and I hear crying."

"Jethro maybe," said Quasar.

"No, I don't think so. It's coming from another room. C'mon."

They left the dressing room and followed the sound of the crying which, by this point, they could all hear. It led them to Plant Haven's room. They entered and Val nearly tripped over some clothing that was crumpled up on the floor. She looked down and smiled.

"He's in here you guys," she said, bending down to pick up the jackets.

The crying, however, had not dissipated and Val looked to the corner of the room. She saw a female organic botanic sobbing uncontrollably.

"What's wrong?" asked Val.

"Nothing, go away."

Val slowly approached the botanic and reached out to offer a consoling hand. The botanic looked up.

"You won't find him," she said between sobs.

"Who? Jethro?"

"He tricked me."

"Who did?"

"He tricked me and then he took him." The botanic buried her head in her hands and sobbed some more.

"Who tricked you?" said Val. "And who took who?"

Val became impatient and grabbed the botanic by the shoulders. "Stop crying. You're not making any sense. Explain to us what happened."

The botanic hesitated and looked up at Val. "I'll get in trouble," she said.

"You're gonna be in trouble with us if you don't tell me what happened, sister."

The botanic, more out of guilt than fear, began to tell the story.

"The hooded freak told me he'd pay me a hundred credits to convince Mr. Sirius to come back to the room so he could get an autograph. I thought it was kinda weird, but I needed the money so I did it."

"So Jethro was here," said Val.

"I don't know. That freak opened up some sort of black hole and sucked Mr. Sirius into it. He had some sort of remote control or something and the entire hole, Mr. Sirius and all, got sucked into it. Then he left." She began to cry again.

Val turned and looked at her friends. "What are we gonna do?"

"First walking weed I'm gonna talk to is the promoter and find out what kinda security he's running in this place. Then we talk to the police," said Quasar.

"I'll go find Vinweirdo," said Seth. He turned and left.

Quasar looked at the organic botanic, who was still bawling on the floor. "Why didn't you do something?" she demanded.

"I was scared. You didn't see this freak. I thought he was going to kill me."

"All right, all right. Calm down. No more crying. It's starting to irritate me." Quasar turned to Val. "C'mon," she said.

"Where are we going?" asked Val.

"To the bus. I have a feeling we'll get a lot further talking to Libby than we will with these talking plants."

Jethro awoke in complete darkness. He hung upside down and could feel the rough sensation of rope around both his ankles. He bent himself at the middle and reached for his feet, grabbing at the rope with his fingers but...

"It's no use," came a voice from out of the darkness.

"Who's there?" said Jethro.

A dim light came on suddenly and, though not very bright, it caused Jethro to shield his eyes with his arm. He'd been in darkness for quite a while now.

"I already told you. My name is Vack Hume, otherwise known as 'The Collector.'"

"Where am I?" demanded Jethro.

"You are on my ship and I am taking you to my master."

"What for? What do you want?"

"I've already told you that." The hooded figure now walked into Jethro's field of vision and Jethro found the upside down version of his captor even scarier than the right side up version.

"You said you want my talent," said Jethro. "What do you mean by that?"

Vack Hume squatted in front of Jethro and poked him in the ribs with a finger. Jethro noted a musty smell emanating from the figure's robes.

"I've been a collector for a long time, Mr. Sirius, and if there's one thing I've learned in this business, it's to never reveal your motives until the victim is safely in the hands of the Big Boss."

Vack Hume stood and began walking away.

"You won't get away with this," said Jethro, struggling to break free. "My friends are gonna save me."

Vack Hume laughed a thin, raspy lifeless laugh. "Your friends are weak and brainless, Mr. Sirius. They will never find you. You belong to the Master now. Or should I say, your talent belongs to the Big Boss now."

Vack Hume disappeared from Jethro's view, laughing as he went away. Jethro continued to struggle, but it was useless. He was trapped. All he could do now was wait.

The tour bus burst through the atmosphere of Botneex and leaped into space like a giant green booger being shot out of a space slug's nose.

Inside, the kids were debating what they ought to do about their missing friend. "Libby," said Seth, "is your tracking system picking up anything at all?"

"All I'm getting is that a highly sophisticated space craft passed through the planet's atmosphere about two hours ago."

"Can you get a lock on it?"

"Because it is so far away, I can't get a decent read on its destination. The best I can do is a rough estimation of its direction based on its speed and angle of flight before it jumped to light speed."

"Okay, well, do that then. I don't think we have any other options here." He turned his attention back to his friends. "It's something anyways."

"I still can't believe how useless those stupid bone headed botanics were. What kind of planet doesn't have a police force. I mean, c'mon." Val was shaking her head disbelievingly.

"It's not their fault Val. They have no crime on Botneex. Everyone's one with everyone and everything down there. They've got some serious flower power happening."

"Well whatever they've got," retorted Val, "they didn't account for visitors and I highly doubt that Jethro feels like he's 'one' with whoever kidnapped him."

"Seth," said Libby.

"You got something Lib?" asked Seth.

"It's a weak signal, but I'm getting a similar reading to the one I picked up while leaving the planet's atmosphere."

"Great. Lock into it and follow it. Full speed ahead." He turned to his friends and gave them a reassuring look. "Don't worry you guys, we'll find him. Whoever kidnapped him is gonna be sorry they messed with 'The Jethro Sirius Experiment'."

The bus sped through space at light speed, following the trail of a craft that may or may not be holding Jethro Sirius captive. No sooner had the bus started its accelerated rate of travel than it had stopped. The stars changed from long thin bright lines back to twinkling dots.

"Libby, what's going on?" demanded Seth.

"The craft we're following has dropped out of light speed and is only a few miles ahead of us. It's docked at some sort of space station."

"Can you bring it up on screen?" asked Seth.

The monitor suddenly came to life and right in the middle of it, floating in a sea of stars was an 'L' shaped space station.

"Are you getting anything?" asked Seth.

"He's there, Seth," answered Libby. "Jethro's there and he's alive."

Seth reached the pod hanger in a matter of minutes, towing Bettee behind. Quasar, Val and Bobbee followed, although they hadn't been invited.

"Seth," said Quasar. "Don't you think we ought to get a bit more info about that thing before we go flying into it?"

"What for?" Seth shook his head irritably. "If he's in there, we're going to go get him. Period. Final answer!"

"Well, maybe we should all go then," said Val.

"No." Seth shook his head more vigorously this time. "It's too dangerous."

"Oh brother," said Quasar. "You've been watching too much siri-vision Seth. And besides which, I don't remember Jethro putting you in command before he went and got himself kidnapped."

"Well, I'm assuming command then," said Seth. He was now trying to fit his small Sirian body into the large, adult sized pod suit by rolling up the sleeves and pants cuffs. Bettee did the same.

"Then you can assume that my right hand isn't going to leave a red mark on the left side of your face," said Quasar.

"Someone's gotta stay on the bus," argued Seth, who was now climbing into the pod. It was a two seater and Bettee, who had chosen not to become involved in the argument for obvious reasons, was now climbing into the passenger seat. Seth hit a button and the front hatch began to close slowly over top of the two pilots.

Quasar managed to slip in one last comment before the hatch closed. "You've got one hour Seth. One hour," she said holding her finger up. "If you're not back by then, we're coming after you."

She wasn't sure if he actually heard her because all he did was smile and wave. The pod slid into the launch chamber and a smooth glass wall slid down in front of it. Once it sealed into place, the exterior chamber door opened up. The egg shaped pod shot out into space and floated for a brief moment before powering up and flying in the direction of the space station.

Meanwhile, back on the bus, Quasar, Val and Bobbee had made their way back to the cockpit.

"If my brother gets even one scratch, that Seth boy is gonna pay," said Bobbee.

"Relax Bobbee," said Quasar, "I'm sure they'll be okay. Seth's a pretty smart Sirian and he's gotten us out of a few difficult situations already."

"He didn't even take any of his fancy gadgets with him," remarked Val.

"Let me rephrase that," said Quasar. "He's pretty smart when he gives himself more than a few seconds to come up with a plan."

She turned to view the monitor and they could now see the bus pod slowly accelerating toward the space station.

"What in Sirius is he doing," Val said. "Isn't he gonna sneak up on them or anything? It looks like he plans on marching straight through the front door."

"It does appear that way, doesn't it," said Quasar.

The pod reached the station without being blown out of space and the three girls all breathed a sigh of relief. Then, to their surprise, Seth's voice came to them from the speakers.

"You guys hear me all right?" he said.

"Ya Seth, we hear you loud and clear," answered Val.

"Great. I think we've reached some sort of service port and there doesn't appear to be anyone around. We're goin' in."

The bus pod entered the side of the station and soon disappeared inside. It entered a small hangar where a few beat up old ships sat around waiting to be tinkered on. Seth steered the pod toward one of them and parked it beneath the larger ship's belly. The hatch opened up and Seth and Bettee clambered out of the pod.

"Quasar," said Seth.

"Ya?"

"There's a button on the front dash board that reads 'pod visual'. Can you see it?"

Quasar quickly scanned the dash and located the button. "Ya, I see it," she stated.

"Push it."

She hit the button and the view of the space station on the monitor suddenly fizzled out and was replaced by a giant head; Bettee's head to be exact.

"Bettee," Bobbee called out excitedly.

"I've rewired the pod's external camera sensors into the visor of my helmet, so that you guys will see what I see," explained Seth. "You know, just in case I'm not paying a hundred percent attention."

Seth and Bettee passed beneath the beat up old ships and found an exit in the side of the wall. It opened as they approached it and a cool, gentle waft of air blew against their pod suits. Seth cautiously peered through the doorframe. A short corridor led to a 'T' junction just a little ways ahead. He motioned for Bettee to follow and they stepped through the opening. They followed the corridor to the junction and stopped.

"Only problem is, which way do we go?" said Seth looking questioningly at Bettee. The right hallway was short and ended abruptly at a wall. The left way was long and neither of the boys could see the end. Bettee pointed down the left hand corridor.

"I agree," said Seth and together they began marching down the empty hallway.

About halfway down the corridor they were suddenly interrupted by a flash of green light, which caused them to cover their eyes. When they finally managed to peel them open again, they wished they hadn't. They were staring directly at a ten-foot Gulterian space goblin...and it didn't look happy.

Jethro must have dozed off, because when he awoke, he was no longer hanging upside down. He was lying on his back with a steel shackle attached to his right ankle. The shackle was attached to a chain and the chain was bolted to the floor. He pulled on it but, unless he was prepared to chew through his own leg, he realized he wasn't going to escape.

He glanced around the room and soon realized that he wasn't alone. Vack Hume was sitting in a chair about ten feet away from him, his feet stretched out, robe draped casually over his legs. His hood was still stretched down over his head, but his blue glowing eyes weren't staring at Jethro. They were staring down at the paperback book he was holding in his lap.

"What are you reading?" asked Jethro.

Without looking up, Vack Hume said, "How To Torture Musicians Without Ruining Their Talent."

Jethro gulped.

Vack Hume suddenly let out a long, slightly dorky laugh; one of those laughs that made one think of the class idiot.

"Had you going there for a second, didn't I?" he said between snorts.

"Uh...ya," said Jethro, slightly confused by his captor's sudden change in personality.

Vack Hume got up out of his chair, walked over to Jethro, and tossed the book into the young Sirian's lap. Jethro picked it up and turned it over. The title read, "The Adventures Of Asteroy Starblaster." Jethro studied the front cover, which consisted of a muscular looking purple alien with a big lumpy head and no neck. He looked up at Vack Hume questioningly.

"It's pretty good actually," said Vack. "Book one in a one hundred and thirty two book series. Asteroy Starblaster's this cool intergalactic vigilante who goes around ridding the galaxy of evil space monsters. Pow, pow, pow." He demonstrated by turning his hands into laser guns, shooting them off in the air.

"Look Mr. Collector, I don't mean to be rude but..."

"Call me Vack."

"Pardon."

"Call me Vack. All my friends call me Vack."

"You have friends?"

"Hey, be nice. Of course I have friends. Just because I'm a collector, doesn't mean I don't have any friends. It's just a job you know."

"So what you're saying is that whole serious, bad guy thing you were doing earlier was all just an act."

"Ya, ya, ya. Pretty convincing eh?"

Jethro cocked an eyebrow. "I guess so," he said.

"I'm actually just a regular guy," said Vack, pulling his hood back across the top of his head.

The unmasking revealed a younger looking alien with yellow skin pulled tightly across his face, revealing two small slits in the center where his nose should have been. What amused Jethro was the fact that Vack was wearing a pair of blue, glowing glasses. He reached up and clicked a button on the side of them to shut them off and he pulled them off his face to reveal a pair of yellow eyes.

"Well that's a neat trick," said Jethro.

"Like it?"

"Ya, almost as much as I like this steel shackle around my ankle."

"Sorry about that, but it's all I've got. Can't have you escaping, you know."

"Why not?"

"'Cause then I wouldn't get paid, that's why not."

"I see. Umm...can I ask you a question Mr. Hume?"

"Call me Vack."

"All right...Vack. Now that I've gotten to know you a little better, you seem like a nice guy. How come you're in the kidnapping business?"

"Do you realize how difficult it is to get a job in this Galaxy? When you get to be my age, kid, you take what you can get. And it's not kidnapping, all right. It's collections. Perfectly legal. Kidnapping is not."

"What's the difference?" Jethro asked.

"Well, kidnapping is for purely selfish reasons, but I'm working for someone else. You see, technically, I'm just a middleman, and therefore guilty of no crime. My boss, on the other hand... well, that's a whole other story. One which I'm sure he will tell you."

"Sounds like a pretty stupid law to me," said Jethro.

"Ya, well, the Galactic Government's not perfect. Politicians make mistakes too, 'ya know."

"Well, I don't know anything about politicians. All I know is the difference between right and wrong, and kidnapping is just plain wrong. Whether you're a middleman or not."

"Mr. Sirius, you're not the first person I've collected to make that point but, like I said, a job's a job. Everyone's gotta eat."

The Gulterian space goblin was looking down at the two young Sirians with a hungry look in his eyes.

"Mrrragggu," he said, pointing at them.

Bettee, looking quite terrified, opened his mouth as if to speak but, of course, nothing came out. Seth nudged him.

"That's a space goblin," he said under his breath, "and it doesn't look happy."

The Gulterian Space Goblin, like many other alien monsters, is a highly misunderstood creature. It hails from the planet Gulteria, and used to live in peaceful co-existence with all other creatures on the planet. Physically, they are the largest and strongest beings on their planet and, at one time, they used this strength to help others, but at some point in history, a group of males broke off from the main group and began their own faction of power seekers. They sought out and enslaved many of the weaker races of creatures and built a Gulterian army. They trained and used this army to overpower the peaceful goblins and have been breeding warriors ever since. Many argue that, deep down inside, the Gulterian space goblins wish to be set free of their anger and hatred but, for now, they remain one of the most feared space monsters in the galaxy.

The goblin that towered over Seth and Bettee reached into its pocket, pulled out a laser gun and pointed it directly at them.

"Moooawwg," he grumbled.

Trying not to move his lips and make too much noise, Seth spoke to Bettee.

"When I say 'go,' we're gonna dive under this things legs and pull its pants down, you got it?"

Bettee nodded his understanding.

"Now," screamed Seth.

Due to the goblin's immense size, they were able to dive under its legs with ease, coming out safely on the other side. As the goblin began turning, Seth and Bettee each grabbed a pant leg and pulled down. The goblin spun around, became wrapped up in his own pants and began to lose his balance. He dropped his laser gun and threw his hands out as he began to fall.

"Look out," hollered Seth. He and Bettee jumped out of the way.

The space goblin was desperately trying to fall gracefully, while at the same time, covering up his underpants. You see, the Gulterian Space Goblins, although angry and violent, are extremely modest and shy when it comes to their bodies. Seth and Bettee didn't know this, but it was to their advantage as the goblin became immediately focused on pulling his pants back up and seemed to forget about harming the two young Sirians.

Seth took instant advantage of the space goblin's hesitation. He reached down and grabbed the laser gun, which had fallen to the floor, and picked it up. He pointed it at the goblin, who was still struggling with his pants, and began to back away, motioning with his free hand for Bettee to do the same. They slowly began backing down the corridor, gun still pointed at the goblin. They backed right past a panel in the wall that was marked, "TRASH,' and Seth grabbed hold of it, pulled it open, dropped the gun in it, and let it slam closed.

"I hate guns," he said, then added, "Run."

But for some reason, Bettee hesitated. He turned around and looked at the goblin with a curious look in his eye.

Seth screamed, "What are you doing, Bettee? Run."

Bettee spent another couple of seconds looking at the goblin, then turned and began running down the corridor with his friend.

The space goblin, by this time, had managed to get his pants pulled back up. He appeared quite angry that the two young Sirians had seen his polka dot underwear and began to chase after them.

When Bettee started to fall behind, Seth slowed down, grabbed the youngster by the hand and practically dragged his little shipmate down the corridor. The floor began to vibrate under the heavy footfalls of the space goblin as it gained on them.

They were nearing another 'T' junction and picked up the pace as best they could. The goblin was now hollering its Gulterian battle cry behind them and they knew it was close, because they could smell its rank breath.

The space goblins, actually, used to be quite famous for their Gulterian throat singing before they became a race of warriors and hired thugs. Unfortunately, whenever they performed, they had to separate themselves from the audience with a wall of three inch thick glass, as their breath was considered highly toxic and, if inhaled, could possibly be fatal.

Seth and Bettee began to feel light headed as they inhaled the first gulps of Goblin breath tainted air.

"C'mon Bettee," screamed Seth. "We're almost at the junction. When we get there, we're gonna stop, turn, and face the goblin. Just before he reaches us, you go left and I'll go right. Got it?"

The tired young Sirian acknowledged Seth's command with another nod of his head. They were suddenly deafened by an ear-piercing shriek as the goblin ran its finger nails down the metal walls of either side of the corridor. The giant creature suddenly jumped into a bout of throat singing as it ran and the young Sirians found themselves both afraid and impressed at the same time.

They finally reached the 'T' junction and turned to face the singing monster, who was nearly on top of them.

"Plug your nose," yelled Seth and seconds before the goblin was on top of them he hollered, "now!"

Seth jumped right and Bettee jumped left. Both felt a sense of panic as the creature reached out with both hands and snatched off their helmets, in a last second effort to catch his prey but, too confused to make a decision on which direction he ought to go, the goblin ran face first into the wall with a loud crack. His throat singing suddenly stopped as he fell to the floor. One final guttural groan came from his throat before he shuddered and fell into unconsciousness.

Seth and Bettee looked up at one another and smiled.

"We did it," said Seth. "We just beat a space goblin. How about that."

Bettee managed to crack a smile underneath the beads of sweat that were pouring down his face. Seth reached down and picked up his helmet, noticing that a high-pitched squeal was emitting from it. He lifted it over his head and put it on. "You still there, Quasar?"

No answer.

He pulled off his helmet, picked up Bettee's and put it on. After receiving no answer to the same question he pulled the helmet off and looked at his young companion. "Both helmets are toast. We're on our own from here on in."

An idea suddenly dawned on Jethro as he sat, shackled to the floor. He realized that the ship was no longer moving. Vack had temporarily disappeared into another area of the craft, and Jethro pondered how he might get out of his present situation. He scanned the room with his eyes to see if there were any tools he might be able to use. There was nothing.

Vack Hume returned and sat down in his chair, picking up his book.

"What are we waiting for, Vack," asked Jethro.

"Word from the Big Boss."

"We're not moving, are we?"

Vack looked at Jethro, a curious look in his eyes. "You've been in space a long time, haven't you."

"Almost my whole life."

"Like I said, we're waiting. The Big Boss'll tell me what he wants when he gets here."

"Your boss is coming here?" asked Jethro.

"He's got stations all over the galaxy. This happens to be one of them."

"So we're in a station. A space station?"

"You ask a lot of questions, Mr. Sirius."

"Wouldn't you, Vack? I mean, honestly, wouldn't you want to know what was so important about yourself that would make someone kidnap you?"

"What do you mean by 'so important'?" said Vack. "You happen to be in one of the most popular bands in the galaxy. The question is not what is important about you, but what is not important about you."

"But it's just a band," said Jethro.

"Just a band?" Vack stood up suddenly. "Just a band? Are you nuts? Some have spent their entire existence worshipping your 'just a band'. You're one of the most important pop icons of this century."

"Well how come I don't feel important, then?"

"Mr. Sirius..."

" Would you please stop calling me Mr. Sirius and just call me Jethro."

"Jethro?" Vack looked suddenly confused, as if someone had just told him that somewhere in the universe, his name closely resembled that of a dirt-sucking appliance.

Jethro soon realized why his captor looked confused and quickly added, "It's a cover up name. We had a few problems with the Monsturd planet, so we had to change our names temporarily."

Vack's look of confusion switched to one of worry. "The Monsturd planet? What kind of trouble did you have with them?"

Jethro was struggling to recall the story that Val had made up.

"Umm...well...I guess they just didn't like the show and they...ummm...got really mad..."

"You guys did a show on the Monsturd planet? Why, in the name of the Galaxy, would you play a show there?"

"I don't know. Our agent booked it."

"Who's your agent?"

"My agent? I...ummm...I...well...how come you're suddenly so interested?"

"Because Mr...what did you want me to call you?"

"Jethro."

"Because, Jethro, if you're being tracked by a monsturd hit squad, I need to know about it. Those dudes are nasty. They don't mess around. I can't believe your agent would book you a show on the Monsturd planet."

Jethro was beginning to regret re-telling Val's story. He hated lying; always had. He'd never been very good at it and now he found himself in a situation where he needed to be exceptionally good at it. Vack was clearly becoming upset and he needed to think of a way to calm him down. It was either that or...

“Ummm, ya,” he said. “I think it was a computer mix up and we did the show and they were choked. I mean really choked. They were expecting a band from their sister planet, a group called... called the...ummm...oh, what were they called...the Terrible...uh...Maniacs. Ya, that’s it. So you can imagine how upset they were when we showed up. We barely got out of there alive. And...ya, a few weeks ago, our sensors picked up that we were being tracked by a monsturd hit squad. That’s why we’ve had to change our names. If they find us, we could be in a heap o’ danger.”

“Mr. Sir...I mean, Jethro, the monsturds are a technologically advanced civilization. Changing your name isn’t going to prevent them from tracking you. If I know anything about monsturds, they probably already know where you are. They’re very patient. They’ll wait for the perfect moment to make their move, and when they do...” Vack trailed off into silence and looked up at the ceiling as if afraid that a group of monsturd thugs would come crashing through it. He suddenly started walking toward the door.

“Where are you going,” asked Jethro.

“To run some scans and make sure we’re not being tracked,” Vack replied, disappearing through the door.

Once again, Jethro found himself alone and waiting.

CHAPTER 8

ENTER, THE BIG BOSS

The last the girls saw of Seth and Bettee's encounter with the space goblin was their two friends running in two different directions. Then the communication link had gone dead.

"What happened? Did they make it?" said Val.

"There's no way of knowing without the helmets. All we can do now is wait. If they're still okay, Seth will get back in contact with us. I know he will," said Quasar.

"I'm not having much fun anymore," Bobbee whined. "I wanna go home."

"Well, that's the general plan now isn't it Bobbee," snapped Val. "What do you think we're trying to do? I'm sure Seth and Bettee aren't exactly enjoying almost getting squashed or blasted by a space goblin."

Bobbee started to cry.

"Val, knock it off," said Quasar, putting an arm around Bobbee's shoulders. "She's only five. Give her some slack."

Val just rolled her eyes and turned back to the monitor. "I just wanna find Jethro and get outta here."

With the helmet cameras having gone dead, the girls were starting to get impatient. Val, in particular, wasn't the type who enjoyed sitting around and waiting. She suddenly heard a beeping noise accompanied by a red flashing light on the dashboard.

"What's goin' on Libby?"

"You're being hailed by a ship on board the space station," said Libby.

"Can you give us a visual," asked Quasar.

The image appeared on the large screen monitor. A figure wearing a dark green cloak with a hood pulled over its head revealing blue, glowing eyes, was looking at them.

"What do you want?" said the hooded figure. "This is private property and you are trespassing."

"We're looking for a friend of ours," said Quasar.

"You will find no such thing here. I am conducting scientific research and this is my laboratory. I am the only one here. Please leave immediately."

"Well, we beg to differ," said Val. "Our sensors detect that our friend is on that station."

"Then your sensors are malfunctioning," said the figure. "Get off my property immediately and I won't blow you up." The connection suddenly ended.

"Okay, that's not good," said Val.

"I don't wanna get blown up," said Bobbee and started crying again.

"We're not gonna get blown up," said Quasar. "There was something in that guy's voice that...I don't know. I get the feeling he's bluffing."

"How can you tell that," said Val.

"My mom's a psychologist. She studies Sirians, but I bet there's some things that are the same all over the galaxy."

"Like what?"

"Like the way he spoke. It was fake. He didn't sound very sincere. Almost like he was acting."

"Okay, nice theory. What if you're wrong?"

Quasar looked at Val as if this thought hadn't occurred to her. Bobbee, in the meantime, was still crying. "I don't wanna get blown up," she wailed.

"Oh, be quiet Bobbee," said Quasar impatiently. "We're not gonna get blown up."

"Relax Quas. She is, after all, only five," said Val, smirking slightly.

"Okay, point taken. I still don't think this guy'll blow us up. I think he's bluffing and..."

The hooded figure came up on the screen again, and this time, appeared a little less calm, judging from the way he seemed to be vibrating.

"Why are you still here?" he demanded. "Did you not understand my warning? Leave now or suffer the consequences."

"Not without our friend," insisted Quasar.

"Not without your...don't you understand that you'll all be dead if you continue to..."

Quasar cut him off. "Not without our friend," she repeated, somewhat more firmly.

The hooded figure said nothing for a moment and just stared at them.

"All right," he said. "Don't say I didn't warn you." His image disappeared once more.

"Let's get out of here Quas," said Val. "I think this guy means business, and I for one, don't wanna get turned into space particles."

"Val, would you relax. Don't you think that if he really wanted to blow us up, he would have done it by now."

"I'm not interested in trying to figure out what's goin through this guy's mind. We're dealing with another alien species, Quas, and I'm just sayin' that maybe you're wrong about the tone of his voice."

Before Quasar could respond, Libby's voice rang out through the cockpit.

"Yo, kids, I'm switching the monitor over to external cameras. There's something you ought to take a look at."

The girls looked up at the monitor just in time to witness a humongous, black space bus drop out of hyperspace, directly above the space station. It lowered itself down until it hovered parallel to the hooded figure's so called laboratory. A long thin like tube emerged from the side of the bus and reached out and attached itself to the hangar bay of the station.

"There's no way that thing doesn't see us," said Val.

"What should we do?" Asked Quasar.

"Oh gee, I don't know Quas, why don't you use some mind reading techniques and tell us all what's on that ship computer's mind."

Quasar stuck her tongue out at Val just before noticing a clump of floating debris off to the left of the station.

"Libby, can you get us in behind that garbage dump over there," she asked.

"No problem."

The bus slowly steered a course toward the space trash until it was safely concealed.

"Okay Libby, shut everything down for about ten minutes and we'll see if we can fool these goons into thinking we're gone."

Libby did as she was told and the bus soon became dead to the universe. The emergency lights clicked on and the only thing the girls could see out the front windshield was a bunch of discarded scrap metal.

Quasar soon noticed something odd about the scraps. They began to move closer together and within seconds, two rather large pieces slammed together and merged, forming a large and formidable wall of metal.

"Now what's going on," said Val slowly backing away from the windshield.

Quasar, who stood her ground, said, "I don't know."

All the other pieces around them were now doing the same thing and it appeared that the metallic junk was starting to take on some sort of form.

"Libby, back the bus up," ordered Val.

"Ooo, now little miss Val thinks she's in charge, eh," said Libby.

"Libby, please just back the bus up."

The bus slowly began to back its way through the debris, which continued to attach itself to itself. Large hands were now reaching out and intertwining with metallic fingers, forming arms and legs until soon, the space bus was no longer aimed at a pile of junk. The young Sirians' craft had come face to face with a monstrously huge, robotic space dawg.

It had four legs and a tail that swished back and forth, knocking the unused pieces of scrap metal out into space. Its head was gigantic and as it opened its mouth, the girls were confronted with a rather large set of mechanical choppers.

The hooded figure suddenly came on-screen again.

"I warned you," he said. "But no, you had to be all noble and insist on saving the worthless life of your friend. Well now you've gone and done it. Meet my gard dawg. Her name is Day-zee. One thing about Day-zee is that she loves to play games. You know what her favourite game is? It's called fetch the bus. I'm giving you ten seconds to get outta here, starting now. Ten..."

"Okay Quas, what now," said Val.

"Eight..."

"I'm thinking," replied Quasar.

"Six..."

"Quasar!"

"Four..."

"Run," screamed Bobbee.

"Two..."

"Libby get us outta here," shouted Quasar.

"Day-zee......Fetch!"

The space bus sped out of the way just in time as Day-Zee sprung into life and began dog paddling her way through space, eager to close her jaws around the green bone that had appeared in front of her.

It didn't seem to matter where the bus flew. Day-Zee had, apparently, played this game before and it was clear that not even Libby was going to outmaneuver the gard dawg. The only thing she was able to do was keep the bus a tongue's length away from being crushed between the robotic canine's teeth.

"Libby," shouted Quasar. "I don't think we're going to last long before we become a Day-Zee snack."

"We're gonna have to jump to light speed," hollered Val.

"No-can-do Missus Valeritious," said Libby. "This guy just put a cloak on his location. If we leave now, we won't be able to find our way back here. At least not to this exact location.

"Why does that not surprise me, in the least," said Val.

The bus was zooming all over now, barely avoiding Day-Zee's hungry mouth. The young Sirians felt like they were back in the space paste tube and found themselves, once again, having to hold onto something solid in order to maintain their balance.

Suddenly, Quasar's face lit up. "I have an idea you guys," she said.

"I hope so," shouted Val. "Cause we're about to become lunch."

"Libby, how many bus pods do we have left," demanded Quasar.

"Three bus pods remain on board, sista."

"Great. Pick one and prepare it to launch. And set it to auto-pilot. Full speed."

"Gotcha Quasarius."

"What's your plan Quasar," said Val.

Quasar ignored her friend's inquiry and made another demand of the bus's computer.

"Libby, steer us toward the station. Full speed."

"What?" screamed Val and Bobbee at the same time.

The bus cajoled toward the space station and was headed directly for the long leg of the 'L'.

"I can't look," hollered Val, covering her eyes.

The Gard Dawg was nearly on top of them as they sped toward the station.

"Libby, I want you to drop us in behind the back wall of the station the moment we clear the top of it. At the same time, I want you to eject the pod in the exact same direction we were traveling. Got it?"

"Got it, Miss Thing."

The bus had now reached the station and was sailing across the roof at full speed. Day-Zee was directly behind the fleeing Sirians and her feet danced across the metallic surface, as chunks of metal broke off and floated out into space. The gard dawg had nearly caught her snack and was opening up her mouth to bite down on her reward when they cleared the roof. The bus shot instantly down the back wall while simultaneously passing a pod out its back end. The pod took over the bus's original course and Day-Zee, not smart enough to realize her treat had transformed into something much smaller and less satisfying, continued her chase of the bus pod, which was now heading off into the unknown distance. Day-zee's mammoth, wagging tail of steel soon disappeared from view.

The space bus, in the meantime, had attached itself to the side of the space station and Libby had shut down its power in order to avoid detection. The young Sirians were safe...for the time being.

"Now what made you think of such a clever trick?" Val asked Quasar.

"I don't know," replied her friend. "Something in the back of my memory saw it in a movie on trans-galaxy satellite once. Great movie. I think it was number two in a trilogy...something about the war of the stars or something."

"Well, thank Sirius for siri-vision, 'cause it just saved our lives. I'll have to remember this one if I ever see my mom again and she tries to tell me 'too much SV is bad for you.'"

Val had imitated her mother's voice in the last line and the three girls, despite their stressful situation, all had a good laugh.

Seth and Bettee walked, aimlessly, down empty corridors and were getting frustrated. Seth was starting to wonder if they'd ever find Jethro. As they trudged along, lost in their own thoughts, the floor beneath them suddenly fell away and they dropped into a chamber about ten feet below. The floor, which had now become the ceiling closed back up and they found themselves sealed in darkness.

Seth reached into his pocket, pulled out an emergency flashlight, turned it on, flashed it around the room, and screamed. What he saw sent shivers up his antennas. Lined along the walls were large blocks of ice sealed in glass. Inside these blocks were all sorts of different life forms, completely frozen. Most of them appeared to be adults and Seth quickly made his way around the room, investigating each block individually to see if he could find Jethro.

Each block had a nametag and appeared to be monitored by a small life support box and it soon became clear that these life forms were, in fact, alive. He slowly made his way around the room and stopped suddenly. He was standing in front of an empty glass case - no ice and no life form. Although this particular case stood out from the rest, it wasn't the lack of a frozen life form that caught Seth's attention. It was the nametag. Two inches above the life support box was a tag that read: Ozzbourn Sirius.

Jethro was uncomfortable. He'd been sitting on the hard, cold floor for who knows how long and his butt was going numb. He shifted from one cheek to the other, but it made no difference. He decided to stand up, instead, and stretch his legs. He glanced down and noticed that Vack's paperback was lying on the floor a few feet away. He got down on his stomach and reached for it. His fingertips reached its spine and he managed to edge it close enough to him to grab hold of. He stood up again and began flipping through the pages. The book had been written in a different language and Jethro understood none of it. When he reached the end, he noticed some handwriting in the back of the book. This writing had been composed in the universal language and Jethro understood it perfectly. It appeared to be a list of some sort and this is what it said:

1. *Collect Sirius - Done!!*
2. *Rendezvous with Big Boss*
3. *GET MONEY!!!!!*
4. *Freeze Sirius*
5. *Call Mom*
6. *Go to bank and deposit credits*
7. *Locate lead singer of The Gelpods*
8. *Collect lead singer of The Gelpods*

The part that caught Jethro's eye, was the 'freeze Sirius' part. He was giving it some thought when he heard the footsteps of Vack returning. He quickly kneeled down and slid the book across the floor to where it had been and sat down just as the door opened and Vack stepped in. Jethro looked over his shoulder and glanced irritably at the Collector.

"Do you have any idea how uncomfortable this floor is," Jethro said.

Vack seemed taken aback by the comment and, for a moment, didn't say anything. He then walked over to the side of the room and hit a button on the wall. A door opened up and Vack stepped through it. He soon returned with a fold-up chair and crossed the room to where Jethro was sulking on the floor. He unfolded the chair and placed it in front of his captive.

"Sorry about that," he said. "You know when you've been doing this as long as I have, you tend to forget some of the common courtesies. How come you didn't ask sooner?"

Jethro stared at him. "Because I don't normally think of kidnap...sorry...collectors as kind and courteous."

"Well, now you know different," said Vack, returning to his own chair and picking his book up off the floor. He didn't appear to notice that the book had been snooped in.

After about five minutes, a crackle, fizz, and a beep came from the ceiling, followed by the sound of someone's voice.

"Mr. Hume," it said. "The Big Boss is ready for you now."

"Right," said Vack. "I'll be right there."

Jethro looked up, surprised. "The big boss is here?"

"That's Big Boss to you buddy boy. I'll be right back. He's gonna want to meet you." Vack turned and, once again, disappeared from the room.

His absence, although lasting only ten minutes, seemed to go on for hours, as Jethro sat alone in the room. He was thinking about Vack's list again; the part about 'freezing Sirius.' He didn't like the sound of that and soon found himself on the verge of crying.

The Big Boss turned out to be not very big at all. Jethro initially thought that the huge space goblin that entered the room was the head honcho but the ugly creature, as he soon discovered, was the Big Boss's bodyguard. The Big Boss, as far as Jethro could tell, was a kid. He stood about three feet tall and all but his face was covered in smooth, pink fur. His face was layered with smooth milky white skin and his eyes were almost completely black with small white pupils. To be honest, the Big Boss gave Jethro the creeps. He wasn't what you would expect of a Big Boss.

The pink creature eyed Jethro up and down.

"So," he said, "this is the famous Mr. Sirius." His voice was deep and nasally, and resonated with contempt.

"The one and only," said Vack.

"I thought he'd be taller."

Vack simply nodded his understanding.

The Big Boss approached Jethro and stood about an arms length away.

"So, Mr. Sirius. I suppose you think you're pretty special."

Jethro must have betrayed his thoughts with his facial expression because the Big Boss picked up on it immediately, though completely misinterpreted the look.

"Don't look so smug Mr. Big Shot. It's superstars like you that make me sick to my stomach. You and all the others with your so called...talent." The Big Boss spat at Jethro's feet.

"Umm...I'm not sure I quite understand," said Jethro.

The Big Boss eyed Jethro suspiciously. "A typical answer from a typical jerk," he said. "You remind me of my brother."

"Your brother?"

"Yes, my brother. The famous Bossentical Eekew. Most famous Bossentient in all of Bossentia. Well, he's not so famous now is he? You might say that his creative juices are completely frozen." He laughed a hyperactive, nasally laugh that matched his voice perfectly. He turned and looked at the space goblin. "That was a joke you insensitive lug."

The space goblin let out a deep chortle and the Big Boss, who seemed partially pleased, turned back to Jethro.

"You see Mr. Sirius Putz, my whole family had talent. All but me. I come from the most famous family in the entire universe. Every day of my life, I watched my brothers and sisters become more and more talented. Singing, acting, writing, painting. And every day I came closer and closer to realizing that I would never be talented. I tried everything. Every time I tried something new my brothers and sisters would laugh at me. They'd laugh, and laugh, and laugh. Eventually I separated myself from them and moved into the basement. It was there that I began building things Mr. Sirius."

"Building things," questioned Jethro.

"Yes, building things. I acquired a knack for inventing and spent all my time building and plotting my revenge. One by one my brothers and sisters became famous for their creative endeavors. They received the ultimate in respect from both my parents and their peers."

"I, on the other hand, was shunned. Spat on by my own mother, who referred to me as the 'runt of the litter'. My father spent most of his time avoiding me as much as possible and would criticize my inventions, calling them worthless and stupid. Well, it was I, in the end, who had the last laugh. I, Bossentical Distort, who would laugh longest and hardest."

"While my brothers and sisters were out and about, becoming more and more famous, I began work on my ultimate invention; a machine capable of changing my life. I called it...'The Talent Sucker'."

"Stealing money from my family, I employed the help of Blurtch here." He pointed over his shoulder at the space goblin. "One by one we lured my brothers and sisters and my parents down into the basement and hooked them up to my wonderful machine. Their screams were music to my ears as I sucked the talent out of their very souls. When I was finished with them, they were incapable of a single creative thought. I then froze their bodies in my ice boxes and there they remain."

"Hooking myself up to my machine, I absorbed every last drop of my family's talent. I now had the talent of ten, but soon became hungry for more. It was then that I began my hunt across the universe to acquire more talent. I've got collectors in every galaxy and soon I will be the most talented being ever to exist and all will remember the name of Bossentical Distort, the Big Boss."

When he had finished his speech the Big Boss stared at Jethro, as if awaiting a response.

"Well," he said. "Have you nothing to say?"

Jethro stared at the pink creature curiously before speaking. "Do you mean to steal the creative juices of every single life form in the galaxy," asked Jethro.

"Of course not, you dolt," said the Big Boss. "Only the ones with talent."

"But...everyone...has talent," said Jethro. "Just because you can't sing or play an instrument or paint a picture, or write a good story, doesn't mean you don't have talent. You're just talking about artistic stuff. What about sports, physics, mathematics, gardening, hairstyling, making things, building things, heck, inventing things? It sounds to me like you had plenty of talent when it came to inventing. I think you've missed the point of what having talent really means."

The Big Boss stared blankly at Jethro before saying, "Take him to the talent sucker before he tries to say something smart again. His good ideas belong in my head, now."

Blurtch, the space goblin, approached Jethro, ripped his shackle right out of the floor, and threw the young Sirian over his shoulder. As they marched past, Vack gave Jethro an 'I'm just doing my job' look.

"You're a real jerk Vack," said Jethro as the space goblin carried him out of the room followed by the Big Boss.

Vack Hume walked back to his chair, sat down, and picked up his book. He flipped to the back and looked at his list. He scanned down to the fifth item on the list and thought of his mother. She'd never really been proud of his choice of work, though she always told him she understood the necessity of having a decent paying job. He sat and thought about what Jethro had said. He'd never been called 'a jerk' with such sincerity before and it suddenly dawned on him that Jethro was right. No matter how nice he was and no matter how much he justified the importance of having a job he was still, simply put, a jerk.

He was allowing a mentally disturbed, pink, furry midget to steal all the talent in the universe. What if the Big Boss decided to take Jethro's advice and start stealing all the other kinds of talent. Eventually he might come after me, Vack thought to himself. After all, being a collector requires pretty good acting abilities. He sat and stared silently at the wall for a short while. Finally he put his book down, stood up, and left the room.

CHAPTER 9

TRESPASSERS WILL BE ELECTROCUTED

"How long are we gonna sit here Quas," asked Val.

"I don't know. As long as it takes I guess. In the movie I saw, they float away with the trash."

"Okay, well, seeing as the trash that we tried to hide behind turned into a giant, robotic space dawg that tried to kill us, I think we can pretty much rule that plan out."

"Libby," said Quasar. "How long until we can get communication back with Seth and Bettee?"

"Unfortunately," said Libby, "communication has been severed on Seth's end and until he, in his infinite wisdom, figures out a solution to the problem, there ain't a thing the Lib meister can do."

"Oh, this is just great," said Val. "Now we've lost Seth, Bettee, and Jethro. This tour is going so well." She turned and looked at Bobbee, who had fallen asleep in a chair. "Must be nice to be able to sleep at a time like this."

Quasar followed Val's gaze over to Bobbee. "It's actually not a bad idea," she said. "If we're going to get through this Val, we're going to have to look after ourselves. Maybe we should sleep in shifts. That way if Seth does, eventually, try to contact us, one of us will be here."

"You go first," said Val. "I'm not really that tired right now, anyway."

"All right," replied Quasar. "Just call me in my quarters when you want to switch."

Quasar entered the vertical drive lifters and went back to level two where her family quarters were. She entered the living area and immediately thought of her mom and dad. She almost considered pulling the pictures off the wall so she wouldn't have to be reminded that they were gone every time she stepped in the room, but she decided against it. Perhaps leaving them up would provide her with the strength and courage to not give up.

Her mother had always been an ambitious musician and had worked her way into Ozzbourn's band the way a good friend works their way into your heart; with a lot of passion, faith and honesty.

Her mother had actually been in the process of working on a solo project when she mysteriously disappeared with all the other adults.

Quasar thought about the last time they'd spent together as a family. It had been over breakfast. Her mother had been speaking about the solo project and her father had been speaking about...

"Dad," she shouted out loud suddenly. "How could I have been so dumb?" She smacked herself in the forehead, turned around, left her quarters, and headed back to the cockpit as fast as her webbed feet would carry her.

Seth still had his light pointed at the nametag that possessed the name of his best friend's father. He was busy running a bunch of different scenarios through his head in an effort to explain the new information.

Why would there be an empty icebox with Jethro's dad's name on it here, he thought to himself. He started moving around the chamber again, flashing his light on every icebox, hoping to find more of the Sirian adults, perhaps even his own parents. No such luck. Ozzbourn Sirius was the only recognizable name in the entire chamber. He began searching for an information panel; anything that might help him figure out why Ozzbourn's name would appear on an empty icebox in the middle of an unknown space station.

Bettee followed quietly behind him and Seth had nearly forgotten that the silent little twin was with him. Not ever hearing the sound of someone's voice could be somewhat unnerving at times, and Seth found himself wondering what Bettee's actual problem was - why he chose not to speak. He was about to give the thought a little more attention when his light suddenly crossed over a door wedged between two iceboxes. He walked over to it and searched for an opener. He soon located one on the floor and stepped on it, pushing it down with his foot.

The door shot into the ceiling as Seth and Bettee's faces lit up with a pink glow. The light came from the room on the other side and they stepped through.

The door immediately closed behind them, causing them both to spin around. Seth searched the floor for another opener but found nothing. They were sealed in. He turned and began investigating their new surroundings. As far as he could tell, the pink light had no source. It was almost as if the very air in the room was aglow.

Suddenly, as if responding to the intruders, the light began moving to the center of the room leaving nothing but blackness in its wake. Its brightness increased in intensity as it condensed itself into one single form in the middle of the room. Surrounded by complete darkness, a three-foot tall hologram of a pink, furry creature was staring at them. It raised its hand and pointed a finger in their direction.

"Trespassers will be electrocuted. Trespassers will be electrocuted. Trespassers will be electrocuted. Trespassers will be electrocuted." The lips of the creature moved but the voice itself seemed to come from the walls around them.

Seth began flashing his light frantically around the room, desperate to find a way out. The hologram continued to shout its one phrase over and over again, a monotonous vocal display that drove jagged, little shivers up Seth and Bettee's spines. Seth's light soon located a door on the other side of the room and he and Bettee ran for it, passing straight through the hologram on their way. It shimmered, and almost flickered out, but soon regained its luminescence and continued its repetitive chant. It was still pointing at the Sirian's previous location.

Seth searched the wall, the floor, and the ceiling, but couldn't find an opener anywhere. The annoying din of 'trespassers will be electrocuted' continued to pound away on their eardrums, causing them to bang on the door with their fists, hoping that by some fluke, it might open. The door, however, did not relent and remained tightly sealed. Seth and Bettee, ready to give up, turned and leaned their backs up against the door. Perhaps this was all it took, because the moment they did this, the door opened and their own weight caused them to fall backwards into a brightly lit room. They had to shield their eyes, which hadn't adjusted to the light yet, and just as they were about to drop their hands and push themselves into a sitting position, a large pair of bumpy, green hands reached down, grabbed them both by the front of their suits, and picked them up.

Quasar burst into the cockpit, startling both Val and Bobbee right of their seats.

"You guys," she yelled.

"For the love of Peet," said Val. "You nearly gave me a heart attack."

"Val, I can't believe I didn't think of it before."

"What?"

"The G.R.D."

"Huh?"

"The G.R.D. Galactic Research Department. My dad's company. In the basement. I totally forgot about them."

"What are you talking about, Quasar?"

"The G.R.D. It's a scientific research company that my dad woks for. Well, used to work for anyways, but they share the basement with our education departments. They have archives full of research on every star system we've visited and are going to visit. If there's any clues on what happened to our parents, they'll be down there."

Val looked skeptical. "Ya, well what about Libby? How come she didn't access these so called archives?"

"Because they have a separate computer system down there. They're completely independent from the rest of the bus. Libby doesn't have access to their system."

"It's not that I don't have access," came Libby's voice. "It's just that Miron's a jerk and doesn't like to share."

"Who's Miron?" said Val and Quasar at the same time.

"The G.R.D.'s central computer. He's got a serious attitude problem. A real snob you might say. Always beakin' off about the scientific and intellectual capacities of his crew and how they're far too sophisticated to be sharing space with a degenerate group of musician low-lifes. I'll show him degenerate. I'll degenerate his arrogant wires into a tangled mess of..."

"Libby," the girls said again.

"Sorry," said Libby. "He just gets me all heated up, is all."

"How come you didn't talk about Miron before, Libby?" asked Val.

"You didn't ask."

"Can we get into the G.R.D.'s labs?" asked Quasar.

"That's completely up to Miron. And let me tell 'ya, he ain't an easy computer to convince."

"C'mon you guys," said Quasar, heading for the vertical drive lifters once again. Val and Bobbee followed her through the doors and they were soon on their way down to the fourth floor. When they came to a stop, the door opened and they stepped through. Quasar led the way.

"Follow me," she said.

They followed her past the familiar education departments until they reached a large door at the end of the corridor. Quasar punched a code into the door and the three girls entered what appeared to be, a waiting room of some sort. Comfortable looking couches lined the walls and there was a desk sitting beside a door in the far wall. They walked over to it.

"Yo, Miron," came Libby's voice. "You've got some visitors."

There was a brief moment of silence before a second, more masculine sounding, metallic voice echoed throughout the room

"Musicians," said Miron. "I absolutely despise musicians."

"C'mon, Miron," said Libby. "Open the door."

"Why should I?"

"Because we need to scan your archives."

"Scan my archives? I think not. I'll not be violated by the likes of you."

"Oh, come on Miron," said Libby. "Lighten up wouldja. This is important and you know it."

"What's important is that I protect the G.R.D.'s interests at all costs. That is what's important. How dare you speak to me of importance. You lecherous no minds, who gallivant across the galaxy conducting your treacherous musical experiments on unsuspecting alien races. Disgusting, if you ask me."

"Well nobody did ask you Miron and if you want to ever see your precious little, brainiac scientists again, you better let us in."

"Give me one good reason why I should comply with this ridiculous and unreasonable request."

"'Cause my dad is one of your bosses, that's why," said Quasar.

"I beg your pardon," said Miron.

"Look Moron, or Miron, or whatever your name is, you better open this door and let us in or I'm gonna tell my dad that you were completely non compliant during a department emergency."

"And just who are you," Miron demanded.

"I'm Quasar Ion. My dad's Milton Ion, and if he finds out that you treated his daughter in a disrespectful manner, he'll replace you before you can say..."

"Open sesame," completed Miron, as the door opened in front of them.

"Way to go Quaso," said Val as they stepped through the entrance to the G.R.D.

"Libby, are you comin'," asked Quasar.

"Only if Miron gives me permission," said Libby.

"Miron?" Quasar said.

"I think not. I'll not be sharing my sophisticated circuitry with the likes of her and her tainted..."

"I'll tell my dad," cut in Quasar.

There was a short pause while Miron's computer chips heated up.

"Ooooo, fine then. You can come in, but don't touch anything. I don't want you messing up years of research with your carefree attitude."

"Thanks beaker boy," said Libby. "I must say, I'm shocked. I'm actually admire'n Miron." She chortled and snorted metallically at her own pun.

"Oh, dear goodness me," said Miron. "I think I'm going to be sick."

The laboratories were pretty much what you would expect. They were all white and separated by glass walls. Different types of machinery were placed in various locations and the desks, tables, and counters were littered with computers.

"Which way to the archives," asked Quasar.

A glass door opened to their right.

"Through here," said Miron.

They entered a large room. A desk sat in the middle of it and, on the desk, there sat a large computer keyboard.

The three girls walked up to it.

"How do we turn it on," asked Quasar.

Miron let out a long, tinny sigh. "Press the 'ON' button."

Sure enough, a large red button (it was the only one; the rest of the buttons being white) labeled 'ON', sat separate and off to the right. Quasar pushed it and a large holographic screen came to life, covering the entire wall directly in front of them.

Quasar looked down at the keyboard, then back up at the screen. "Yo Miron, does this thing work on voice commands?"

"Yes," came Miron's reply. "And that rather large keyboard sitting in front of you is just for show."

Quasar rolled her eyes and looked at Val. "Is a smart mouth, like, standard issue for central computers?" She let out a big sigh. "Miron, please just answer the question."

"No, it does not. Using one's own motor skills in an essential stage in the developmental patterns of Sirian intelligence and..."

"But you work on voice commands right," said Val.

"I was speaking and I do believe that the Sirian Code of Ethics demands that you show me a little more respect when I am speaking."

"Ya, well now you're dealin' with Val's code of ethics and Val's code is tellin' you, you better shut your mouth and start answering our questions or you're gonna be replaced before I can say 'Sirian Code Of Ethics'! Now, do you know how to run the archives from your central computer command center?"

If the young Sirian girls could have seen a computer sulk, they would not have been surprised to see Miron doing so. The metallic tone of his voice had a bitter tinge to it.

"Yes, of course I can operate the archives," he said.

"Then turn 'em on," said Val.

The holographic screen in front of them suddenly came alive and a pleasant, female voice said, "Welcome to the G.R.D. Archives."

Val stepped aside and turned to Quasar. "It's all yours."

"Thanks, Val." Quasar stepped up, leaned over, and placed a hand on either corner of the desk.

"Okay Miron, can you show me the final archive entry before all the adults disappeared?"

The screen flickered into life and Quasar found that she had come face to face with...

"Dad," she said.

Sure enough, right in front of her eyes was an image of Milton Ion, who stood before them, only he was having a difficult time doing so. Everything around him was shaking uncontrollably and he was holding onto a desk to maintain his balance. His lips were moving, but there was no sound.

"Miron, can you rewind it to the beginning and turn up the volume this time," said Quasar.

Miron did as he was told and rolled back the recording to the start. This time they heard Milton's voice loud and clear.

"F.R.D. archive 19/07/2412. We've detected a disruption in space, causing the unstableness that you see going on around me. We detected a slight disturbance, but before we had time to warn the pilot, we had already passed into it. Miron's sensors indicate the disturbance is not natural; that it was placed here on purpose by intelligent life. Presence of a ship approximately ten miles above the disturbance has been detected but, unfortunately, the nature of the ship's inhabitants has not been revealed."

"My guess is that we've entered a Pendulum Pocket. All evidence leads to this assumption. Certain, random areas in space contain tranzit fusion particles and if properly manipulated, can be turned into a type of laser netting. A Pendulum Pocket is an energy force used to scan space for asteroids and meteorites. They are utilized, mainly, by mining companies, and the pocket acts as a sort of energy induced netting, drawing the metal interiors of rock toward it. Unfortunately, every now and then, if a ship is in the wrong place at the wrong time, it can be caught in a net, and sent to, more than likely, the mining colony of which the rocks are intended for."

"If we don't manage to get out of the pocket, we could end up at any random mining colony in the universe. We are attempting to notify the pilot but, due to our scrambled sensors, we've had to send a lab technician on foot to reach the cockpit before it's too la...."

Quasar, Val, and Bobbee watched as the image in front of them, suddenly cut out and disappeared, replaced with the silent hiss of white noise. Quasar stared intently at the screen hoping that any second now, here father would reappear. She knew he wouldn't though. She had just witnessed the very moment that everything had gone wrong.

Tears rolled down her face and she quickly wiped them away.

"Miron," she said.

"Yes."

"That was my dad."

"I know child, and I'm very sorry."

"It's okay. It wasn't your fault. I just want to know if you have any theories on what happened; why communication just suddenly ended like that."

"Well, my theory on the subject is purely speculation, but I will do my best to explain it to you in simple terms." Miron cleared his virtual throat before continuing.

"I believe your father was correct in his theory on the Pendulum Pocket. Though the disturbance we passed through was loaded with sensor scramblers, all collected data leads to this assumption. One thing that many life forms are aware of is that tranzit fusion particles can also be manipulated to select certain forms of energy. In this case I believe those specific energy types were those of the adults aboard this ship. Hence, the adults were taken before the children."

"So basically," said Quasar, "the adults were probably taken to another area of the galaxy."

"That is the assumption," replied Miron.

"The question is where," said Quasar, pausing to think about all the information she had just absorbed.

"Your dad said something about mining colonies," said Bobbee.

Quasar turned and looked at her young companion. "Yes he did, didn't he," she said. "Hey Miron, is there anything in the archives about how many known mining colonies are in this particular galaxy?"

"Six million, four hundred twenty-five thousand and two," confirmed Miron.

"Well, that shouldn't be too difficult to narrow down," said Val, throwing her arms up in the air.

"Actually, it shouldn't be," said Miron. "Every mining colony in the galaxy is a member of the Galactic Mining Coalition and their guidelines require that every colony register their company files in the Coalition's central computer system."

"So, what you're saying is that there might be a record of our parents' arrival at a specific mining colony in the Galactic Mining Coalition's registry?"

"That's correct," said Miron. "That is if they were delivered to a mining colony. Though slavery has been outlawed in many sectors of the galaxy, the Black Cross Society has been unable to outlaw it universally. It is still legal in certain sectors, however, the law requires a company to register their slaves with the G.M.C."

Quasar looked at Val. "Well, it's a place to start," she said. "All we have to do is track down the Galactic Mining Coalition, break into their central computer, and do a file search on recently acquired, adult, Sirian slaves."

"If you say so," replied Val.

"What about Bettee, Seth and Jethro," said Bobbee, who was developing a talent for pointing out important details.

"Right," said Quasar. "First things first, eh Bobbee. Well, now that we have access to the G.R.D.'s archives, we have a heck of a lot more knowledge at our disposal."

"So," said Val.

"So, maybe there's something in these archives that'll help us get the three boys back on the bus so we can get the Sirius out of here."

"Like what?"

"Like, that's like, what we're gonna, like, look for Val."

CHAPTER 10

ESCAPE FROM 'L' STATION

Jethro, slumped over Blurtch's shoulder, kicked, screamed and punched all the way down the corridor. Blurtch grunted in irritation each time a foot thumped him in the chest, or a fist struck him in the back.

"Let me go," hollered Jethro. "I swear, in the name of Sirius, I haven't got any talent."

Bossentical Distort, who strode behind Blurtch, looked up at Jethro and laughed. It sounded more like a whiney, pathetic squeal and Jethro had to cover his ears to eliminate the shiver that had appeared at the base of his spine.

"It's no use, Mr. Sirius," said the Big Boss. "If you were talentless, you wouldn't even be here. Don't waste your breath. You may be a talented musician, but a talented actor you are not." He squealed wickedly again, causing Jethro to cram his fingers as deeply into his ears as he could possibly get them.

They had nearly reached the end of the corridor when they came to a door on the left hand side. Blurtch hit the opener and stepped through into a small, brightly lit room. He set Jethro down on the floor and shackled him to another bolt and chain.

In the middle of the room sat a large contraption. Wires and metal rods protruded out of it in every direction. A seat was built into the center of it and, hovering directly above, was a pink, glowing helmet of light. A control panel stood off to the left of the machine and was connected to the chaotic grouping of wires.

Bossentical spread his arms out in the direction of the machine. "May I present...The Talent Sucker!"

Jethro looked unimpressed and sneered in response to the introduction.

"Is that the best you could come up with? The Talent Sucker," he said, imitating the Big Boss's voice. "I mean, c'mon. That's so lame. I mean, even after all the talent you've already sucked up, that's the most creative name you could come up with? Doesn't sound to me like your machine really works all that well little bossy."

"Shut up," said Bossentical. "Enough is not enough!"

"Uh, don't you mean, 'enough is enough'," said Jethro.

"Whatever. You won't be making your smart remarks after I suck the talent out of you. It'll be I making all the witty retorts. Blurtch! Put him in the chair."

Blurtch unshackled Jethro, picked him up, and walked over and placed him in the seat. He strapped in the Sirian's wrists and ankles and Jethro soon discovered that no amount of struggling was going to set him free.

He looked over at the Big Boss. "Hey little bossy, you're a real space turd, you know that?"

Bossentical only smiled and turned to Blurtch. "Turn it on," he said.

Blurtch stared dumbly at his boss.

"Hunh?" he grunted.

"Oh, for the love of Peet, get out of my way," said Bossentical, pushing Blurtch aside and grabbing hold of the control panel. Just as he was about to hit the 'ON' button, a loud banging noise came from the wall on the left hand side of the room. Jethro could hear the faint muffled sound of shouting.

"What is that infernal noise," shouted Bossentical. "There's nothing I hate more than being interrupted right in the middle of the scene when the hero's about to get it. Blurtch! Go check it out." The Big Boss's hand no longer hovered above the 'ON' button as he awaited the outcome of the space goblin's investigations.

Blurtch walked over to the wall and put his ear to it. He then began searching the wall for an opener. He found what he was looking for and pushed down on the button with the big toe of his right foot. A door shot, instantly, into the ceiling and two bodies fell over backwards into the room shielding their eyes from the light.

"Seth! Bettee!" yelled Jethro as he witnessed his two friends fall into the room.

Blurtch picked them up and set them on their feet. He held the front of their suits tightly and watched as they slowly lowered their hands, enabling their eyes to adjust to the light.

"Jethro," said Seth, squinting in the direction of his friend's voice.

"Seth, it's me buddy. I can't believe you found me!"

"Who cares," cut in Bossentical. "Blurtch! Shackle them up. They can watch their friend lose his talent. And if they have any talent themselves, I'll be more than happy to take it off their hands."

Blurtch carried Seth and Bettee across the room and chained them to the floor. They both looked questioningly at their friend strapped to the strange looking machine.

"This lunatic wants to steal my talent," he explained. "He's invented this crazy machine to suck it out of me. He's been doing it all over the universe and has been freezing his victims in ice boxes."

"Hey," said Seth. "We just saw a whole bunch of aliens in a room a couple of doors down that way." He pointed in the direction of the wall he and Bettee had fallen through. "There was an empty box in there with your da..."

"Silence," shouted Bossentical. "It's of no importance to any of you. All you need know is that those ice boxes will be your new homes for the rest of eternity." He squealed with glee and this time Seth and Bettee joined Jethro in covering their ears.

His hand once again hovered over the 'ON' button and he looked at Jethro. "Say goodbye to your talent, Mr. Sirius."

Fortunately for the young Sirians, the button never got pressed for, just as the Big Boss began to lower his hand, the lights went out.

Val stared at the hologram screen in front of her. She was looking at the image of some sort of vehicle, with large studded tires. It looked like it was capable of seating about four Sirians and on the front of it was a large, rotating, cone shaped drill.

"What is it?" she asked.

"A burrower," said Miron.

"What's a borrower?"

"Not a borrower; a burrower. It's a drilling vehicle. It's designed to drill through metal and rock."

"So," said Val.

"So," replied Miron impatiently, "you can use it to drill through the side of this space station so that you can go rescue your friends."

"Oh."

"Miron, how are we supposed to get it onto the side of the station without floating off into space," asked Quasar.

"You simply vacuum seal the exit port to the point of entrance, open the door and drill your way through. The exit port is presently pressed up against the wall of the station."

"Can we take you and Libby with us?" asked Quasar.

"If you must," replied Miron.

"Great! Show us where this burrower is."

The girls, following Miron's directions, soon located the docking bay where the drilling vehicle was located and sure enough, there it sat, silently awaiting a mission.

As they approached the vehicle, Quasar turned to Bobbee. "Maybe you should wait here."

"I don't wanna stay here all by myself. I wanna go with you guys."

"Bobbee, we're gonna need someone to stay back and protect the bus, and besides which, there won't be enough room for all of us."

"What do you mean? There's four seats and only three of us," said Bobbee pointing through the windshield of the burrower.

"Bobbee, we're going in there to get Jethro, Seth and Bettee. That makes five of us. It's going to be cramped enough as it is."

Bobbee opened her mouth as if about to protest but then stopped.

"Oh, all right," she said. "Can I at least have Libby stay with me?"

Quasar rolled her eyes up to the ceiling. "Libby, is it okay if you stay back with Bobbee and we take Miron?"

"No problem by me," said Libby.

"Don't I get a say in this?" asked Miron.

"No!" everyone shouted, including Libby, in unison.

"Fine," said Miron. "Just don't expect me to be a gentleman anymore."

"You wait in the observation booth, Bobbee," Quasar instructed. "Miron and Libby will be able to communicate, right you two?"

"Yes," Miron and Libby replied together.

"So if you need to contact us," continued Quasar," just ask Libby. Got it?"

"Got it," said Bobbee.

"Great." Quasar turned and opened the door of the burrower. "Val, let's go. You want me to drive, or do you want to?"

"You go ahead," said Val, climbing into the passenger seat.

Quasar walked around the vehicle and got into the driver's seat. She turned on the ignition and the burrower rumbled, enthusiastically, to life.

"Miron, we're probably going to need your help operating this thing," said Quasar.

"But of course you are," replied Miron, his voice coming from a speaker in the dashboard.

Quasar grabbed hold of the steering wheel. "Is this thing automatic or standard," she asked.

"Automatic," said Miron. "You shift it into gear with the stick on your left. Use the wheel in front of you to steer, and hit the button marked 'DRILL' to drill. Your gas pedal is on the right. That'll make you move forward. Your brake pedal is on the left. That'll slow you down. I'll take care of the rest. Any questions?"

"Nope," said Quasar.

"Let's rock and roll," said Val.

Quasar shifted the burrower into gear and slowly pressed down on the gas-pedal. The vehicle slowly moved toward the docking bay doors.

"Libby dearest," said Miron. "Please initiate a vacuum seal and open the docking bay doors."

The two girls heard a loud sucking noise as the vacuum seal was created. The sound was soon replaced by the squeal of gears as the doors opened before them. The burrower moved forward until it was face to face with the space station exterior wall. The docking bridge slowly extended until it clanked noisily into the wall.

Bobbee had entered the observation booth, which was designed to protect observers from the unbearable noise of drill against metal, not to mention flying bits of metal shrapnel caused by the drilling process. She watched as the conical nose of the drilling machine spun into life and began digging into the wall. She flinched as chunks of metal bounced off the unbreakable glass that separated her from the danger.

Back inside the vehicle, Quasar and Val, who had each donned a set of protective hearing and eyewear, were beginning to sweat. Although the burrower was effectively insulated, the friction created from metal spinning against metal was creating an intense heat that was impossible for the two girls to ignore.

"Yee-ha," screamed Val as the drill sank deeper and deeper into the wall.

Soon, the entire front half of the Burrower was submerged in the wall and Quasar and Val looked out their windows, not surprised to see a tangled mess of metal and wire scraping across the glass.

"Who knows what kind of wiring we're cutting through," shouted Quasar. "We could be slicing major power sources in half right now."

"I don't doubt it," hollered Val in return.

The burrower continued to dig its way through the wall and soon a pinpoint of light opened up in front of them. It got larger and larger and soon the vehicle had breached the other side. Quasar steered the vehicle left down a dark corridor, the headlights illuminating their path.

"No lights," commented Val.

"Like I said, I think we cut through some major wiring back there. You don't slice though that much electricity and not do any damage," Quasar said, pulling off the protective ear and eyewear.

"Oh ya, I forgot," said Val, doing the same.

The corridor was long, dark, and straight, and the burrower drove quietly down the middle of it. It was surprisingly quiet, save for the mechanical whirr of the spinning drill cone.

"I think we can turn that off now," said Val, reaching over and pressing the drill 'OFF' button. They continued to cruise down the dark corridor and the eerie sensation that they were not alone began to set in. They had traveled down about half the length of the darkened path when suddenly, a robed figure with blue glowing eyes appeared in their path and it was running directly toward them.

"Blurtch, what's going on?" screamed Bossentical into the pitch dark that had engulfed the room.

"Muuurrrg," replied Blurtch.

"We must have blown a fuse. Find the emergency light panel."

Jethro stared into the darkness, grateful for the temporary distraction.

"Seth, Bettee," he yelled over the hollers of the Big Boss. "You guys still there?"

"We're here, but we're still chained to the floor. There's nothing we can do, Jethro. I'm sorry man," answered Seth.

Jethro's mind raced quickly, trying to locate a solution to their present problem, but it wasn't having any luck.

A sudden swishing noise suddenly came from the far wall where they had originally entered. Jethro heard it, but the Big Boss, who was still busy shouting orders at Blurtch, hadn't seemed to notice the sound.

A pair of blue, glowing eyes appeared directly in font of Jethro, startling him.

"Vack?" he said.

"Shhhh," came the response.

Jethro felt a smooth set of hands undoing the straps around his feet and ankles and he was soon free.

"Hold onto my robe and follow me," whispered the voice.

Seth and Bettee were freed next and joined the train that had been formed by the bodies in the dark. The blue eyes led the way, taking them out the front door. Just as they were about to round the corner, Bossentical noticed the glowing eyes.

"Bluuuuurrrrtch," he screamed. "They're escaping. Stop them!!!"

There was a crash and a clang, followed by a painful grunt as Blurtch stumbled across the room.

"Run," said the owner of the blue eyes.

The Sirians broke the train and started running as fast as they could, following the glow of the blue eyes. They soon heard and felt the heavy footfalls of the space goblin trudging after them.

A dim flickering light appeared at the end of the corridor and the group, not knowing what its source was, ran toward it.

Blurtch burst into a steady bout of throat singing and continued his pursuit, once again dragging his fingernails down the walls.

The light had become extremely bright and was now pointing directly at them and moving forward.

"What's that light?" hollered Jethro.

"Never mind and keep running," replied the voice in the front.

They could hear the sound of an engine beneath the din of the throat singing. They ran faster, knowing it wouldn't be long before the goblin's breath began wafting up their nostrils. They had now come face to face with the light, and discovering it was a vehicle of some sort, jumped to either side of it, narrowly avoiding a collision.

Blurtch, on the other hand, wasn't so lucky and crashed head first into the vehicle, stopping it dead in its tracks, and knocking himself into complete unconsciousness.

"Who is that," questioned Val, pointing at the robed figure running straight toward them.

"I don't know," said Quasar, "and I don't plan on picking him up if he asks for a lift." She pressed her foot down on the gas pedal and as they approached the figure, they soon realized he wasn't alone. Three short figures in the middle and a rather large one bringing up the rear burst into view.

"It's them," screamed Val.

"And they've got Jethro," hollered Quasar.

"Ya, but what, in Sirius is that huge thing chasing them?"

Quasar never got a chance to answer her friend, for just as they were about to collide with their friends, the boys leapt to either side of the burrower and the large thing in question ran straight into them.

The force shook the entire vehicle and the girls felt their necks snap back, painfully. Their restraining harnesses saved them from being tossed about the inside of the vehicle. The accident was over almost as soon as it started and Val and Quasar both looked at each other, dazed expressions on their faces. Quasar's eyes soon grew round and she pointed over Val's shoulder at the passenger side window. Val turned and looked.

"Aaaahhh," she screamed.

The blue eyes they'd seen running toward them were now staring at them through the glass. Directly below them was a pair of antennas. Val leaned forward and peered down. It was Jethro, leaning against the wall and panting heavily. Quasar quickly turned, looked out her window and discovered Seth and Bettee, still in their pod suits, on the other side.

The owner of the blue eyes was now tapping on the glass. Val looked at the eyes and then down at Jethro. She turned to Quasar.

"Should we open it?" she asked.

"Ya," said Quasar.

"Miron, can you open my window," Val said.

The window slowly started to roll down and Val looked past the blue eyes to her panting friend.

"Hey Jethro," she said. "You okay?"

Jethro looked up, seeing his friend for the first time.

"Val?" he said.

"In the flesh," she replied.

"I can't believe it," he said, rushing up to the window, forcing his arms through and trying to give her a big hug.

Quasar was doing the same thing on the other side with Seth and Bettee.

A low groan suddenly came from around the front of the burrower and the blue eyes turned to it. Vack Hume pulled his hood back and his glasses off. "We better get moving before 'ole Blurtch here wakes up."

"Who're you," questioned Val, suspiciously.

"He saved our lives, Val," said Jethro. "He comes with us."

They were soon all piling into the cramped space of the drilling vehicle. Bettee had to sit in

Vack's lap and began playing with his glasses as Quasar began backing the vehicle up as fast as she could.

They finally reached the hole in the wall that they had created and pulled into it. Soon, they emerged on the other side and were, once again, back on the space bus. They quickly climbed out of the burrower and Bettee was instantly tackled by Bobbee, who overwhelmed him with hugs.

"Libby, close the hangar doors and get us outta here," shouted Quasar.

As the doors began to close, Jethro turned to Vack.

"What about your ship," he said.

Vack shrugged. "It was a piece of junk anyway." He turned and looked upon the rest of Jethro's friends and smiled. For the first time since he'd started his job, he actually felt good about himself.

CHAPTER 11
FUELISHA

The bus was in the process of distancing itself as far away from the space station as possible. The six young Sirians and their new found friend all sat in the cockpit eating snacks they'd picked up in the kitchen on the way back up.

They spent the next couple of hours filling each other in on everything that had happened during their separation. Seth and Jethro became particularly excited when Quasar revealed the information regarding the Mining Coalition.

"I say we get on that as soon as possible," said Jethro.

"I agree," said Seth.

"Umm, guys," said Libby. "I hate to burst your bubble, but you've got a show tomorrow night."

They stared at each other in silence and then burst out laughing. They'd almost forgotten that they were still on tour. So much had happened to them since they'd left Dendro City that music had completely slipped their minds.

"Where, Libby?" asked Jethro.

"Fuelisha, the petro planet. I can have us there in about ten hours."

"And where's this General Mining Coalition," asked Seth.

"Well, you're not going to believe this but, coincidentally enough, their main-headquarters are on Fuelisha."

They all exchanged smiles.

"Plot a course," instructed Jethro.

Their journey to Fuelisha was short and restive, but not without incident. They were all still quite exhausted from the excitement of the past day and a half and chose to spend much of the trip sleeping in their quarters.

Seth was sitting in the cockpit, pulling pilot duty, when he heard a warning bell sound off.

Bwoop, bwoop, bwoop, bwoop!

He had nodded off slightly and the noise snapped his head to attention. He looked down at the dashboard and then out the front window.

"Libby?" he questioned.

"Chill out, Seth bro, I'll take care of it," said Libby.

He felt the bus slow right down and drop out of hyperspace. He saw movement in the far right hand side of the windshield and leaned forward. He soon realized that, flying directly across their path, was one of their own bus pods, but before he had a chance to question why it was there, a second flying object caught his eye. It appeared to be chasing the bus pod and Seth jumped back as a giant robotic dawg flew directly in font of the bus, nearly colliding with it. It continued its pursuit of the pod, however, and soon disappeared into the distance.

The bus powered back up and resumed its original speed.

"Libby, what in Sirius, was that," he asked.

"Gard dawg," she replied. "Its trajectory was completely random and we would've collided with it. The Hyper Highway doesn't account for stray dawgs."

Seth, tired and confused, chose not to pursue a line of questioning. Instead, he leaned back in his chair and closed his eyes.

Meanwhile, back on the 'L' station, Bossentical Distort had employed the help of a traveling electrician who was busy repairing the wiring that Quasar and Val had cut through with the burrower. The Big Boss stood in his chamber of iceboxes staring nervously as beads of water dripped down the outside glass. If the power did not get turned back on soon, the boxes would melt completely, awakening the prisoners within. The Big Boss wasn't particularly looking forward to having a roomful of angry aliens looking to get their talent back. Dealing with them one at a time had been easy, but having to deal with them all at once was something he did not even want to think about.

He paced back and forth in front of the empty box meant for Ozzbourn Sirius and wrung his furry, pink hands together. He looked over at Blurtch, who was standing off to the side.

"I want them Blurtch," he said. "I want them all. I didn't come this far to be out-smarted by bunch of punk rockers and a traitor collector. They'll wish they'd never messed with the Big Boss. I will suck every last bit of marrow out of their bones of talent. I'll have them all tripping over their own feet before I add them to my collection." He gestured to the melting iceboxes.

Blurtch grunted a reply, causing the Big Boss to turn on him.

"And don't act so innocent you dweeb. This is all your fault. If you weren't such a big clumsy oaf, you would have caught them before they got out of the room. Now we have to wait. We can't even get back to our ship until the power returns. Do you have any idea how much this complicates my plans? Do you?"

Blurtch grunted another reply.

"And would you stop that grunting. It makes you sound stupid."

"Sorry, Boss," said Blurtch.

"Why do you do it anyways?"

"I don't know. It makes it easier to manipulate a situation if people think you're an idiot. The dumber they think I am, the more of an advantage I've got. You know; the element of surprise."

"Well your little tactics didn't exactly prevent you from ramming your head into a giant drill, now did they?"

"Well, I ran out of breath spray."

"What are you talking about; breath spray?"

Blurtch pulled a small aerosol can out of his pocket and showed it to his boss.

"Breath spray," he said. "You see, ever since I left Gulteria my diet has changed and my breath just doesn't seem to have the potency it once had."

"I don't know about that," said Bossentical, pinching his nose. "You still smell pretty rank to me."

"It's not that my breath doesn't stink. It still smells like the inner bowels of a Slimacular space slug. It's just that it's lost its power to subdue a fleeing victim. The most it does now is disorient them. That's why I ordered a case of this stuff." He held up the can once again. On the front label it read, '*Simulated Gulterian Space Goblin Breath*'.

"What'll they think of next," said Bossentical. "I don't care if you use fart in a can, I just want them caught. Do you understand me?"

"Yes Boss," said Blurtch, sticking the can back in his pocket.

They heard a sudden mechanical click, as all the electronic life support systems sprung back into life.

"Power's back on," said Bossentical. "Now, let's go get us some more talent." He walked out of the room, Blurtch following at a safe distance behind.

The space bus had dropped out of the Hyper Highway and was now approaching the petro planet, Fuelisha. It had once been the most beautiful planet in the Galaxy, full of energy and life. Unfortunately its inhabitants, obsessed with power and technology, had slowly, over the past one thousand years, sucked the very life essence right out of it.

The first thing to go was the water. The pollution had become so bad that not even clouds could hold themselves together in the air. Without the clouds, the planet's water sources soon became depleted and eventually completely dried up. It was at this point that they had to begin ordering their water from off planet, which cost an absolute fortune.

Not being able to afford the outrageous cost of hydro-electricity, they began utilizing solar power. They actually invented a technology that enabled them to suck power out of the sun at a much faster rate, but used it to such a degree that they caused the star to enter its white dwarf phase far too early. Not only did this disable their ability to utilize solar power, but it also caused serious changes in the planet's orbit patterns.

With no water and no sun, the Fuelishans had to come up with a plan to keep their planet alive. At the time in their history when their sun loomed on the verge of not being able to produce enough heat to keep the Fuelishans alive, a brilliant scientist invented a giant machine that would convert meteorites and asteroids into a pulp that could be used as fuel. This invention is what led to the creation of the Galactic Mining Coalition, probably the biggest mining operation in the entire universe. Selling precious rocks and minerals collected from the asteroids and meteorites made Fuelisha a very wealthy planet.

As the bus approached the polluted world, Seth noted that it looked like a giant, round piece of rotten fruit with straws sticking out of it. The straws were actually giant cylinders used to deposit the collected space rocks. The machine, which had replaced the planet's core, sucked the rocks down, mashed them into a pulp, converted them into power, and distributed that power throughout the planet. The separator would extract any water, minerals, and precious rocks. These would be packaged and sold for profit.

The curious thing about Fuelisha is, though it had once been beautiful, its inhabitants had fought fiercely between themselves to own and control as much of the planet as possible. Instead of maintaining a paradise, they had succeeded only in destroying everything they had fought so hard to possess. As a result, facing the death of the planet and the possible extinction of themselves, the Fuelishans put their fighting aside and their heads together and came up with a solution. They have enjoyed five hundred years of peace and continue to strive to find new and better ways of maintaining a universally friendly balance.

The bus coasted between two large cylinders and angled its nose toward the planet surface. It cut through the homemade atmosphere and soon found itself surrounded by thick gray clouds. They'd cling to the bus's outer surface momentarily, before letting go to rejoin the polluted master that bred them. The clouds seemed to have no end and Seth began to worry that they would never dissipate, providing a cushion for the bus only until it crashed into the surface.

"Hey, Libby, are you getting any readings on the venue," he asked.

No answer.

"Libby?"

No answer.

"Libby," he shouted.

"Sorry Seth," came her voice suddenly. "I was temporarily disposed. What can I do for you?"

Seth stared suspiciously at the ceiling. This was the first time Libby had been temporarily and independently disposed. *Oh well,* he thought to himself. *I don't have time to question her about it now.*

"Are you getting any readings on the venue," he asked again.

"Just as soon as we cut through this cloud cover of pollution, we should be able to see the city."

"So we're not gonna be flyin' blind like this the whole time then?"

"Well, you may be flying blind, but I'm not. We'll breach these clouds in about two minutes."

"All right. I suppose I ought to wake the others up." He pushed a button in the dash marked 'GET UP'.

The first to join him in the cockpit was Val. She walked through the drive lift doors and moved to accompany Seth at the front of the bus.

"Hey Seth, how's it goin'," she said, patting him on the shoulder.

"Pretty good. It'll be better as soon as we get through this crap." He pointed at the passing cloud cover.

Val looked out the front windshield and watched as cloud-like fingers clung to the glass like oil, then slid across the surface and let go.

"Boy, we sure know how to pick 'em eh?" She said.

"Yep!" he replied.

They sat in silence for about a minute watching the clouds go by until, finally, the bus burst through the thick grayness into the dark night sky of Fuelisha. Below them lay the twinkling lights of what represented a large urban center.

"Los Monocks Syde City," said Libby. "Population; ten million. Estimated time of arrival; ten minutes."

Seth and Val sat and stared, together, at the vast display of nightlife below. They leaned forward over the dash to get a better look and accidentally touched their hands together. Seth immediately pulled his hand away, quite aware of the heat the contact had caused to surge into his cheeks. Val turned to him and smiled.

"You okay?" she asked.

"Ya, I'm okay," he said, turning his attention back toward the lights below.

Val did the same, seemingly content with his answer. This caused Seth to look back at her again.

"Umm, Val," he said.

She turned her head, looking curiously at him again. "Ya?"

"Umm...I just wanted to say...I...umm...that we, uh...oh...just...thanks for coming to rescue us."

"No problem," she said, still smiling. "That's what friends are for, right?"

"Ya." He turned his attention back to the city's display of lights, which loomed much closer now.

As Val resumed her gaze on the spectacle she reached over, grabbed Seth's hand and tangled her fingers between his. They didn't look at each other. They just sat silently, smiling.

The drive lift doors suddenly swished open causing Seth and Val to pull their hands apart. They both turned to see who it was. Vack was smiling and waving at them. His hood was pulled back, revealing his face, and he no longer wore his glasses.

"Hey guys," he said.

"Hi," they chorused.

Vack walked towards them. "Duh wittle wove birds hangin' out at wookout point eh?"

"What are you talkin' about," said Seth, rather defensively.

Vack, looking startled, seemed to realize that if looks could kill, he'd be dead right now. He put his hands up and smiled. "Hey, relax. It was a joke. You know, boy, girl, bright lights, big city..."

They stared at him blankly.

"Never mind," he said, parking his robe covered rear in the seat next to them. "So what are we looking at?"

"Libby, what's the name of this place again?" Seth asked.

"Los Monocks Syde City," replied Libby.

"Interesting planet," remarked Vack. "You know in all my years of collecting, I've never been here. Although there is something oddly familiar about this place."

Soon, the cockpit became occupied by the entire group. Jethro was the last to arrive and he looked as if he could still use some more sleep.

The bus shot into the urban bustle of the city and the group watched as buildings zoomed past on either side of them. They felt as if they were in the middle of a giant factory. Smoke stacks were like an endless row of teeth. They jutted straight out of the ground and stood against the night sky like giant black cigarettes, clouds of smoke pouring forth from them.

The sound of turning gears and clanging pipes rang out and could even be heard inside the bus. Every colour of light you could possibly imagine joined together to light up the city. A strangely hypnotic rainbow of luminescence shone its way into the cockpit of the bus, completely mesmerizing its crew.

They traveled through the city for nearly ten minutes when a large, well-lit hole in the ground suddenly opened up before them. The bus steered itself into this hole and traveled straight down into its belly.

"I feel like I'm in one big, giant factory," commented Jethro.

"Fuelisha, essentially, is one big, giant factory," said a stiff masculine voice.

Jethro looked around, confused. "Who said that?"

"I did," said the voice.

"Who're you?"

Quasar, Val, and Bobbee exchanged glances, realizing that the boys hadn't met Miron yet.

"I'm Miron, the G.R.D.'s central computer, and your Libby has invited me to share her circuitry.

Two chips are better than one she argued, though somehow I find that very hard to believe, given the limited capabilities of her circuitry."

"Ya, well it's better than having a pair of soiled underwear for a personality," said Libby.

"Soiled underwear," retorted Miron. "And just what kind of a filthy minded comeback is that supposed to be you...you...nincompoop of a...and right in front of the children. How inappropriate."

"Oh great," Jethro moaned. "Another socially disabled computer. Just what we need."

"...was programmed by the elite of Sirian society and in the prime of my youth..." Miron continued to lecture Libby, but soon gave up when he realized that she was ignoring him.

The bus had ceased its descent and shot down a side tunnel, resuming its horizontal journey. It cruised through the tunnel for a short distance and suddenly sailed into an enormous chamber. Hovering directly above the Monocks Syde Coliseum, the bus looked like a speck of fly poop on an eyeglass lens. It slowly lowered down into the center of the arena. The huge building was completely empty, with the exception of the crew, who were working diligently on the stage.

The bus set down as a few individuals broke off from the main crew and went to greet the band, which had made its way down to the cargo bay. The door opened and, just as the group was about to step out, a small, thin fuelishan stepped into the bus and walked hurriedly toward them, pointing.

She had to be the most, unhealthy creature the band had ever seen. Her head was long, thin, and cone shaped. One large bulging eye sat where her chin should have been. Her mouth, small and thin, sat where her forehead ought to have been and she appeared to have a couple of noses for ears. Her ears, themselves, were nowhere to be seen. Wires and tubes protruded from a small, metal, pack that was attached to her back and sunk into the skin in the back of her head. Her skin was pale gray in colour and seemed to fold over itself in many places. In strong contrast to her body, she wore a red tank top and a long skirt to match, both very clean and in very good shape.

"You're late," she blurted out. "Just who do you guys think you are? I've spent six months organizing this show and you guys have the nerve to just stroll in here six hours late with not so much as a simple phone call. I almost thought you weren't coming. Sixty thousand tickets sold and I started to think I was going to have to eat not only my shirt, but my entire wardrobe. You ignorant, arrogant musicians are all the same, strutting around on your over inflated egos, thinking you have the right to..."

At this point, Vack stepped forward and jabbed a finger at her. "Hey lady, unless you want to eat my entire wardrobe, including the underwear I've been wearing for the past nine weeks, I suggest you shut your mouth. I'm sure that once this is all over, you'll be able to buy the entire city a new wardrobe, so why don't you pipe down and show the band a little more respect. You're lucky they're even here after what they just went through."

The fuelishan, intimidated by Vack's assertive nature, took a step backward. "I...I'm sorry...I didn't...realize..."

"Ya, well next time maybe you should give someone a chance to explain before you jump all over them," said Vack.

"And who might you be sir?" she asked.

Vack paused before answering. He glanced at the young Sirians, who looked just as shocked by Vack's outburst as the fuelishan had. He turned his attention back to the lady and smiled.

"I'm their manager," he said.

"Oh, well...all right then. Once again, I apologize. You must understand that stress levels are high and..."

"Hey, no problem. Apology accepted. My name's Vack." He held his hand out to her.

She shook it and said, "I'm Oline, the promoter. Nice to meet you."

Vack introduced her to the band and carefully explained to her about the band's name change. She nodded her head in an effort to indicate that she understood, but didn't seem too impressed. As she led them across the grounds toward their dressing room, Libby took the bus to a large docking area and parked it.

Jethro nudged Val as they approached their dressing room. "I think, maybe, we need to come up with a better story than this Monsturd planet thing. Nobody really seems to be buying it," he whispered.

Val nodded her agreement. "I think, maybe, you're right."

They arrived at their dressing room and Oline led them inside. It was comfortably furnished and a table sat in the middle, covered with delicious looking food.

"All the food was specially ordered from a trading post, off planet. I hope you like it."

"This is a lot of food," said Jethro. "Let your crew know that they're welcome to help themselves."

"We don't eat food, Mr. Sirius. Our bodies reject it. At one point in history, before we destroyed our planet, we indulged in the pleasures of eating, but those times are long gone."

She pulled her tank top up to reveal her stomach. Where her belly button should have been was, instead, a metal cap. She unscrewed it and removed it to reveal a hole. She then reached into her pocket, pulled out a bottle, and unscrewed its cap. Next, she began dumping its contents into the hole in her stomach. It reminded Jethro of watching his dad fill up the space cruiser back home. When she had finished draining its contents, she tossed the bottle into a garbage can and twisted her belly cap back into place. She looked up at the band, who were all staring wide eyed at her stomach.

"You see, we survive purely on petroleum products now. The same way that you'll starve to death if you don't eat, we'll die if we forget to gas up."

"So, do you get hungry," asked Seth.

"Not the same way you do, but we do start to feel sluggish and slow when we get low on fuel. That's our reminder to make sure we re-fuel ourselves."

"Far out," said Val.

Oline looked at Vack. "Where's your sound crew?"

"Ummm, I...uh..." Vack turned to Jethro, questioningly.

"Right here," said Jethro. "Bobbee and Bettee Draicon. The two best sound re-enforcers in the entire galaxy."

Bobbee and Bettee stepped forward and Oline eyed them up and down.

"That's it?" she asked.

"Two's company," said Bobbee. "Three's a crowd, and any more than three's a pain."

Oline laughed. "Suit yourself. As long as you understand that if the sound is inadequate, I take it out of your pay. Now come, I'll show you to the stage while my crew unloads your equipment."

Bobbee and Bettee followed Oline out of the dressing room. Vack decided to join them and check out the coliseum, leaving the rest of the gang to sit and chat.

"Okay," said Jethro, "our main goal is to get this show over with as soon as possible and find the Galactic Mining Coalition place."

"Okay, I don't get it," said Quasar. "Are we planning on breaking into the place or are we gonna wait till tomorrow and ask."

Jethro laughed. "Ya, right. We'll go in there and ask if we can have free access to their central computer system."

"We could just have Libby or Miron hack into the system," said Quasar.

"You think so," said Seth. "I'm sure that many before us have tried, especially with all the anti-slavery stuff that's going on. They can't be in too big of a hurry to share their files with anyone. Particularly not some electronic snob like Miron."

"Ya, I guess maybe you're right," said Quasar.

"Look guys," said Jethro, "we'll get on top of this right after the show. For now, I think we ought to get out there and warm up. We haven't touched our instruments since Dendro City and I, for one, am a little nervous."

Everyone followed Jethro out of the dressing room and into the hallway. They soon disappeared down the length of the corridor, traveling between mountains of bleachers. The stage resided on the other side. Once they were out of sight, a figure stepped out from beneath the shadows of the bleachers, and stared after them. Her name was Marion and she was a collector from Betelgeuse. She stepped back into the shadows, awaiting the band's return.

The Jethro Sirius Experiment played magnificently, topping their previous engagement at Dendro City. Halfway through their regular set, Seth went into a big drum solo and, after about five minutes, the rest of the band joined in and they began improvising, playing off each other like they'd been together for years. Vack stood off to the side of the stage banging his head and air-guitaring the songs.

After playing their encore, the band descended the rock star podium, beads of sweat pouring down their faces. Vack ran up to them, still air-guitaring away.

"That was awesome. You guys are great," he said.

"Oh right, I guess you've never seen us play before, have you," said Jethro.

Vack shook his head and began following them back to the dressing room. Just as they reached the bleachers, they were stopped by a voice.

"Mr. Sirius." It was Oline, who had run up behind them. "I know you're probably tired but there's some press people who would like to take some pictures of the band signing autographs. Could I trouble you for an extra hour of your time?"

"Actually," said Jethro, "we've kinda got some things we need to take care of."

"Just one hour. Please. I implore you. One hour. There is a public relations commitment clause in our contract."

Jethro looked at his band-mates. They shrugged and looked at Vack.

"Couldn't hurt," he said.

Jethro looked back at Oline. "All right, you've got us for one hour."

"Great, come with me." Oline turned and started heading across the floor area of the coliseum.

They walked through an entrance at the far end and turned right down a corridor. When they reached a door on their left, Oline stopped and turned to face them.

"Okay, there'll be a long table at the front of the room where you'll sit and sign autographs. Photographers will snap your pictures and may ask you a few questions. Try to interact with the fans as much as possible."

"Jethro, look out," screamed Vack, as a creature jumped out from beneath the bleachers on their right.

Jethro turned just in time to see a large club swinging in the direction of his head. He ducked and winced in pain as the weapon knicked his antennas. Unfortunately for Oline, the club didn't stop after it missed its target. It kept on swinging and caught her square in the side of the head. She crumpled instantly to the floor. The door opened and a fuelishan poked its head out to see what all the commotion was. The creature lifted its head and snarled, causing the snoopy fan to pull his head back inside and slam the door.

The creature itself walked on all fours and had two extra arms sticking out of its back. Muscles bulged beneath the blue denim suit that covered the beast's body. It wore no shoes, revealing feet that sported sporadic clumps of hair and toes that were long and thin and tipped with needle-like claws. Its face was thick and beefy and was covered in the same sporadic clumps of hair. The exposed skin was dark brown and wrinkled. When the creature snarled it exposed a mouth that was missing most of its teeth. Upon its bumpy head it wore a black, velvety fedora hat. One hand reached over and adjusted the hat, while another pointed a club at the quivering group of young Sirians.

"You dead, you die," it snarled. "You say bad things about Monsturd planet and Monsturd King ain't happy 'bout it. I here to set you straight."

"Hey, woah, woah, woah, woah, woah. You got the wrong band, man," said Vack, holding his hands out in a stopping gesture.

"Watchoo mean I got da' wrong band. Dees are nefinately da' big mowvs I'm a told 'bout."

"You sure about that big guy?" Vack was slowly reaching into his robe. "Take a closer look."

The monsturd leaned forward and shoved his face in so close to the young Sirians that they could feel his whiskers tickling their skin.

"You look like right jerks ta' me," he growled.

Vack pulled out the device he'd used to capture Jethro on Dendro City and clicked it on. Unfortunately the monsturd was too quick and swung his club around, knocking the device from Vack's hand. Vack quickly pulled his hand back in reaction to the pain. The monsturd did a back flip and picked up the device with his free hand. He pointed it at Vack and the Sirians.

"I don wanna mess wit da' wrong dudes so I take you back ta' Monsturd planet wid me jus to make sure. Monsturd King decide if you da' rite scum bags or not."

The monsturd clicked the button on the device and a large black hole opened up in front of him. As it began to spin, it started sucking the Sirians in, one at a time: Val, Seth, Quasar, and then Jethro.

"I hate this part," he yelled, just before being sucked into the void.

Vack was the last to be pulled in and he desperately clawed at the floor to avoid the void, but it was no use; he joined the others within seconds. The monsturd clicked the button and the black hole was pulled back inside its home.

"Punks," the monsturd said to itself and marched off down the hallway.

CHAPTER 12
KING RUBB

As Blurtch steered Bossentical Distort's ship through space, his small, furry companion stood behind him, doing a little song and dance.

"I'm gonna be famous, I'm gonna be famous, I'm gonna be famous," he chanted.

Blurtch turned and looked at his irritating little boss.

"And no one's gonna stop me, and no one's gonna stop me, and no one's gonna stop me..." continued Bossentical.

The things I put up with for a regular pay cheque, Blurtch thought to himself. Just then, the homing beacon light began blinking, accompanied by the steady sound of a bass drum.

"It's them," shouted Bossentical putting a sudden and long awaited end to his chant. "Lock in on it and follow them, Blurtch."

Blurtch did as he was told and within seconds had changed the direction of the ship.

"I told you implanting a homing device in Mr. Sirius's shoe was a good idea. I can't brag enough about how brilliant I am, eh Blurtch. Blurtch? Tell me I'm brilliant Blurtch......Blurtch?!!"

"All right, all right," said Blurtch, shaking his head. "You're brilliant."

"Of course I am you idiot. Where are they going anyways?"

"I'm not sure yet. It'll take a few minutes to duplicate their course."

"Well hurry up. I don't want to lose them again."

Blurtch sneered at this remark. Even though the Big Boss had blamed him for the prisoner's escape, Blurtch knew it wasn't his own fault. If the boss had simply pushed the button on the talent sucker the moment the lights went out, the process would have been complete. But no, the boss had given in to the diversion and, as a result, it was Blurtch that received all the blame. *Oh well,* he thought to himself, *I guess that's what I'm being paid for.* He hit the gas and winced as the Big Boss resumed his chanting.

"I'm gonna be rich, I'm gonna be rich, I'm gonna be rich..."

As Bossentical Distort and Blurtch pursued the monsturd ship along the hyper highway, a third, more discreet ship joined the small parade, following at a safe distance. Besides Vack Hume, Marion was one of the best collectors the galaxy had ever seen and she'd only been doing it for a few short years. Her pants and jacket were made of smooth, well worn, brown leather and fit her body snugly. She wore a pair of black combat boots with thick rubber soles. While most chose to wear their boots over top of their pants, Marion chose to wear hers underneath, so that she could conceal a vast array of weaponry and collecting devices.

Very much into face piercings, Marion sported a collection of rings and studs. A small silver ball stuck out of her lower lip and a small black one protruded from her nose. She had punctured both eyebrows with rings, and tooth-like bones stuck through both earlobes. Her eyes were covered with black sunglasses and her head with a black bandanna.

She was sitting in her favourite chair at the helm of her ship and in her lap sat Merp. Merp was a Fuzzy Tendril Creeper from the planet Zoonigate. Though no being in their right mind would keep a Fuzzy Tendril creeper as a pet, Marion was an exception to the rule. You see, Fuzzies (as many like to call them) are, in fact, quite adorable. They are cute, fuzzy little creatures that come in every colour imaginable. They are quite chubby in their mid section, but narrow out around their face and tail areas. Due to its adorable appearance the fuzzy has fallen victim, many a time, to annoying tourists who like to use the phrase, 'Ooo, look at that cute little fuzzy wuzzy'. It is usually at this point that the tourist discovers the Fuzzy to be one of the most dangerous creatures in the galaxy. Most do not survive to tell the story and those that do are far too traumatized to speak.

The reason Merp sat so contentedly in Marion's lap is because she had saved him and his entire tribe from a hunting party of poachers from planet Vaniteez, where the colourful, Fuzzy fur is used to maximize personal appearance in every form of clothing imaginable.

Marion stroked Merp's smooth coat and he growled appreciatively, pushing his head up to maximize the pleasure of the massage. The other two ships veered off the hyper highway and she followed, making sure to keep her distance. She had installed some of the best cloaking software into her central computer, but you could never be too careful. She glanced down at the destination charts and inhaled sharply as she realized where the other ships were going. She pushed Merp out of her lap and he landed on the floor, giving her an unappreciative growl.

"Just my luck," Marion said to herself, as the Monsturd planet popped into view in the distance.

Geeno, the monsturd, steered his vessel toward his home planet and it was soon cutting through the atmosphere. He was what you'd call the king's errand boy and was very good at his job. He grumbled to himself as his ship coasted over the land of the giant monsturds. He'd heard far too many stories of the giants using ships as toothpicks and finger nail files. He glanced down and witnessed two giants brawling over a boulder, kicking up enough dust to fill a desert. The giants actually guarded the entrance to the monsturd city. It was the only civilized metropolis on the entire planet.

Geeno's ship approached a jagged grouping of mountains. Most of the Monsturd planet was covered in rock, sand, cactus, and seas of bubbling black oil, but mountains were sporadically prickled with tall, thin trees made of sparkling crystal. It was a magnificent sight to behold and just as it appeared that Geeno was about to crash his ship into the mountainside, a large hole opened and swallowed him up.

"Fly lower," bellowed Bossentical into Blurtch's ear, causing the goblin to flinch.

"I don't know if that's such a good idea Boss," said Blurtch. "The dude we're following was travelin' quite high and..."

"Am I paying you to argue? No! I don't think so. We're too high. Every monsturd on the planet is going to be able to see us approaching, you idiot, and then we'll really be in for it. Fly lower."

Blurtch steered the ship toward the planet's surface until they were a few hundred feet above ground level. He looked, nervously, from side to side as they careened along at a moderate pace. He'd heard things about the Monsturd planet - terrible things. He was in the process of trying to imagine what these terrible things might be, when a large chunk of rock came swinging out of nowhere and connected with the side of the ship, sending it end over end through a thick cloud of dust. It hit the ground with a loud thud and slid across the sand for a few hundred feet before crashing into a rock wall beneath a large outcropping.

Both Blurtch and Bossentical had to peel themselves off the floor, a painful process that was clearly identified by the Boss's hysterical, screams.

"Aaaa, you idiot Blurtch. You moron. Ooooh, how could you be so stupid? You flew too low and ran right into a cliff. What are you blind? Aaa, my aching joints."

"I didn't run into a cliff," said Blurtch, dusting himself off, and clearly not injured by the crash.

"Oh, and I suppose we ran into a rather solid pocket of air."

"We were hit," said Blurtch.

"Hit? By what, you idiot?"

Blurtch started heading for the back of the ship, glancing briefly, over his shoulder. "I don't know, but I ain't stickin' around to find out."

"Get back here and carry me, you big pile of space turds. Blurtch! I'm ordering you to carry me."

But Blurtch wasn't listening and had already disappeared into the back of the ship. The Big Boss decided to sit down on the floor and sulk while his brain worked out a plan.

Jethro awoke, once again lying down, only this time it wasn't on the hard surface of a ship, it was face down in the dirt. He lifted his head, groggily, and spat out bits of sand and rock. His friends were lying all around him and were in the process of waking up - all but Vack, who was already sitting up. They were surrounded by rock, with the exception of one wall, which was made up of solid looking iron bars.

Vack looked over at Jethro, who had now managed to prop himself up in a sitting position.

"You okay," asked Vack.

Jethro nodded his head. "Ya, I'm all right. You?"

"I'm okay. You know where we are?"

Jethro shook his head this time. "No."

Vack smiled. "You have no idea what that thing was that attacked us?"

Jethro was about to shake his head again when Val's voice cut in.

"It was a monster, that's what it was," she said.

"A monsturd to be exact," said Vack.

"Huh," grunted Jethro and Val simultaneously.

"A monsturd," Vack repeated. "We were captured by a monsturd and I'm sure we're not on Fuelisha anymore. Jethro, I told you that you shouldn't have messed with these guys."

Jethro had a dazed look of confusion on his face. "But...we never...I mean...we didn't..."

"What?" Vack said.

"We made that story up," admitted Val.

"Okay, now I'm confused," said Vack. "What are you guys talking about?"

Jethro sighed before beginning his explanation. "We're not the Ozzbourn Sirius Experiment. Ozzbourn Sirius is my dad and, less than a week ago, he and all the other adults just disappeared without a trace."

This time it was Vack who had the confused look on his face.

"I'm not Ozzbourn, Vack. I'm Jethro, his kid, and these are my friends. They all have parents who are in my dad's band. We don't know how to get home, so we've been pretending to be my dad's band, hoping that maybe we'll find a clue about our parents. Without proper security clearance, we can't get back to our Galaxy. All we can do is follow the tour schedule."

Vack still looked confused. "So let me get this straight, you guys really are a bunch of kids."

"Ya."

"And your problem is that you don't know where your parents are or how to get home."

"Ya."

"Well that's ridiculous. All you have to do is get your navigation computer fixed and go home. You mean to tell me you guys were planning on flipping forward through a few hundred channels just to get back to channel one when all you have to do is jump a few channels backward and you're home?"

"You see, that's the problem though. We can't just get our navigation system fixed. The head of security rigged it so that only he can change our course. Without him, the only place we can go is the next planet on the tour," said Seth.

"There must be a shop or something you can take the bus to. There's lots of people out there who specialize in overriding security systems. I mean, they may not be on the brighter side of the law, but they'll get the job done."

"So then all we have to do is find a way out of here, get back to our bus, take it to one of these shops, and then go home," said Quasar.

"Ya, that's the ticket," said Vack. "Easy as one, two, three. Do you have any idea where we are?"

"No," said Quasar.

"We're on the Monsturd planet. We've been kidnapped by monsturds and whether you made up your story or not, you've managed to get on their bad side."

"How do you know we're on the Monsturd planet," asked Seth.

"Because I've been here before. About two years ago, I had to collect a monsturd by the name of Willen. Willen the Villain they called him, and I swore I'd never come back. Well, here I am and I'm tellin' you it's not gonna be easy escaping; particularly, without a ship. And especially more, now that I gotta deal with a bunch of kids."

"Hey, you didn't know we were kids until a minute ago and now all of sudden, we're gonna be a problem?" Jethro asked.

"Whatever. All I know is that it's gonna be hard enough figuring out how to get out of this mess, let alone having to baby-sit a bunch of junior achievers."

"So, the true colours shine out now, eh," said Jethro.

"What's that supposed to mean?"

"I mean that, a minute ago, we were your friends. Now we seem to be nothing more than a baby-sitting job gone wrong."

"Look, the point is that you lied to me."

"You kidnapped me, you hypocrite!"

"I didn't kidnap you. I collected you. There's a difference. I was doing..."

"Your job," Jethro completed for him. "Ya, ya, ya, I know. Whatever, Vack. Call it what you want. It's still kidnapping."

Vack walked up to the bars and grabbed hold of them, looking around and examining his surroundings.

Seth stood up and walked up to where Vack was standing.

"You know what, Vack," he said. "I really don't care what you think. We're getting out of here with or without your help, and up until a few minutes ago, I actually had made the mistake of thinking you were a pretty cool guy." He turned around and walked back to join his friends.

Val stared admiringly at him until Quasar gave her a questioning look. She immediately averted her gaze when Vack turned and faced them.

"I didn't have to save you guys back on 'L' Station, you know. I could have let that space goblin tear your arms off and I could have gone back to doing what I do best; collecting."

"So why didn't you then," said Jethro.

"Because, I...." Vack stopped in mid sentence, turned, and stared back through the bars.

"Just forget about him," said Val. "If it wasn't for him, we wouldn't be in this mess. I, for one, don't trust him anyways."

Vack didn't say anything, but he could feel their accusing glares bearing down upon his back.

"Okay," said Quasar. "Here's the scenario. We've been kidnapped by a rather scary looking monsturd in a bad suit, we're trapped in a cave on the Monsturd planet, we're probably completely surrounded by monsturds, we don't have a ship, and Vack's a self centered, back stabbing jerk."

Vack turned and sneered at her in response to the last item on her list.

She met his gaze. "Well, you are," she said, breaking contact with him and turning her attention back to her friends.

"We can do this," she said. "No problem."

But her friends weren't convinced and an uncomfortable silence fell upon them as the reality of their situation settled in.

The heavy fall of footsteps broke the silence and the large monsturd that had kidnapped them, appeared on the other side of the bars.

"Back away from 'da bars," he said to Vack, who immediately complied and took four steps back.

"What's goin' on?" he asked.

"'Da King wanna see all you now," he said, pushing a key into the iron lock and swinging the bars open with a loud creak. "Come wid me. And no funny stuff or I'll rip your arms off. Goddit?"

They all nodded their understanding and followed the monsturd out of the cell.

"Excuse me, Mr. Monsturd," said Seth.

"Whaddya want?"

"Could we possibly have your name?"

Geeno stopped, turned, and stared at the young Sirian. None of his prisoners had ever asked him for his name before.

"What for?"

"Oh, I don't know," replied Seth. "Makes communication a tad less formal, I suppose."

The monsturd paused and rubbed his chin with his hand. "Hmmm. S'pose it's all right. M' name's Geeno. Geeno Turdstocker."

"Well Geeno, my name's Seth. And this is Jethro, Val, and Quasar. And the tall guy in the robe is jerk face."

Geeno turned to Vack. "Jerk face eh? You look like one too." He then turned and began trudging down the tunnel of rock that they'd just entered.

Vack looked over and gave Seth an evil glare. Seth returned the look by sticking his tongue out.

They traveled down the stone walled corridor, up a steep ramp, and then down another short corridor for some time when they began to hear the din of many shouting voices. Their journey ended in front of a large steel door. Geeno made a fist and punched the access panel and the door shot up into the ceiling, revealing the source of the voices on the other side. It appeared to be a rather rowdy monsturd restaurant. Monsturds of all different shapes and sizes were busy stuffing themselves full of food and drink as they engaged each other in light dinner conversation, which, for a monsturd, often involves ever increasing degrees of physical confrontation.

Geeno slowly led them through a labyrinth of flying fists, kicking feet, and spraying saliva. More than once the Sirians had to duck or swing out of the way to avoid being hit by a monsturd appendage, not to mention numerous flying projectiles.

Vack, unfortunately, was not so lucky and caught a large meat chop to the side of the head. He spun around, hoping to locate the source of the thrown object, but there were too many possibilities. He turned back and continued to follow the others.

They managed to weave their way through the length of the restaurant reasonably unscathed; nothing more than a few minor bumps and bruises. They had reached a door in the far wall and entered, happy to give their ears a break from the noise of the monsturd eatery. The door closed behind them and they began examining the room. Stretched across the far wall, directly in their line of view, was a long, stone table and seated at it, engaged in much more civilized behaviour, were four monsturds.

Geeno looked over his shoulder at the prisoners. "Stay here," he ordered, walking around behind the table and taking a seat beside the monsturd in the middle.

It was this monsturd that looked upon them now. He was taller than the others and his head shot forth from his shoulders like a snake, revealing no visible neck. He sported a scruffy tuft of blond, curly hair on the top of his head and a brown mustache decorated his upper lip. A pair of horns protruded from the top of his head and wrapped around them were a couple of red bandannas. He wore a sparkling blue robe and his back bulged out unnaturally beneath the material.

"So," he said, rather casually. "I hear you punks bin' sayin' stuff 'bout me."

The young Sirians exchanged nervous glances but said nothing.

"Yo, King Rubb is speakin to yous, so 'ya better answer 'im," ordered Geeno.

"Ummm, I...didn't realize we were being asked a question," said Jethro.

King Rubb looked at the other monsturds. "Not only does he insult me, but he thinks he's a language instructor too." He turned back to Jethro. "What's yo' problem punk? How come you bin sayin' stuff 'bout me and my boys?"

"Look, Mr. King," began Jethro.

Geeno stood up and flexed his muscles. "You call 'im King Rubb," he insisted, sitting back down.

"Okay, uh, King Rubb," continued Jethro. "We don't even know what we're doing here. None of this makes any sense to us. We uh...um...uh..."

"What he's trying to say is that we don't know why you've brought us here," said Vack.

"Why?" said King Rubb. "I'll tell you why. I's got spies all over dis galaxy workin' for me, sendin' me information on various stuff, and dere's nothin' I hate more dan people spreadin' lies 'bout me."

"May I ask what kind of lies you're speaking of," said Vack.

"You punks bin out dere tellin' folks I don 'preciate music much. Dat I ran you off my planet and bin' huntin' you down. Well, dat's a lie. Dat never happened, so why you tellin' folks it did?"

Jethro shot Val a look of disbelief. Their little cover up story, which seemed harmless at the time, had finally come back to haunt them.

"Look" said Val. "We're sorry we said that. We didn't mean to hurt your reputation. It's all just a big misunderstanding."

King Rubb shook his head. "I don see no misunderstandin' when it come ta' lyin'. Y'all lied. Plain and simple and now yous got me all riled up 'bout it, havin' ta' defend my reputation. Why, even jus yesterday a musician friend 'o mine call me up and say Yo' Rubb, what's dis I hear 'bout you dissin' music.' Y'all makin' me look bad in front 'o my friends."

"Look," said Quasar. "If you want us to clear your name, it's really not a problem. We'll publicly apologize for lying if you want."

King Rubb pondered her offer for a moment and took a swig of his drink. "You'd do 'dat for me?" he asked.

"Of course," said Quasar. "Look, we just want everyone to walk away from this thing unhurt."

"Y'know, lotta people tink Monsturd planet is full 'o psycho barbarians but it ain't true. Sure we bin' known ta' break a few bones, but only du ones dat deserved ta' be broken. We understand people make mistakes, heck, I make 'em all da' time. Be nice, doe, if you'd tell me why you said what you said."

"You got a few minutes?" asked Jethro.

"Sure I got a few minutes," said King Rubb, leaning back in his chair and grabbing his drink.

Jethro proceeded to tell him the whole story about their parents' disappearance and everything that had happened to them since. The king listened quietly, interrupting only occasionally to ask questions.

King Rubb nodded knowingly at the end of the tale. "Let me make dis very clear. I don hurt kids. Not for nuttin'. I'm not afraid to give a kid a good spankin' every now an den but I don' hurt kids. Sounds like you kids said what you said 'cause yer lost and confused. I'm not holdin' dat against you, but you gotta be more careful what you say, ta' who. Dis is a big galaxy and dere's ears everywhere."

The Sirians all breathed a sigh of relief, as they realized that King Rubb wasn't gong to torture or execute them.

"Thank you King Rubb," said Jethro.

"Hey, no problem Jet-ro. I tell you what kid. You and yer band do a show fer Monsturd planet t'night, and we'll help you find yer parents."

Jethro felt his heart leap at the suggestion, then sink back down as he realized something.

"We'd love to," said Jethro, "but all our equipment got left back on Fuelisha along with two others of our group; Bobbee and Bettee."

"Not a problem," said King Rubb. "I'll send Geeno here ta' git yer bus and stuff. You don mind do 'ya Geeno?'

"Course not," said Geeno. "Ida bin nicer to y'all, had I known y'all were kids. Sorry if I scared 'ya."

"Hey, it's no problem Geeno," said Jethro. "You were just doing your job, right?"

Geeno smiled, revealing his many missing teeth. "'Dat's right. Hey, I like you Jet-ro. Yous kids are pretty cool for a bunch 'o kids. I'll go git yer stuff." He patted Jethro on the shoulder and left the room.

"You kids look hungry," said King Rubb.

"We're famished," said Jethro.

"Hey, Flurp, go get dese kids sometin' ta' eat, 'an bring it back here. 'An bring some extra chairs. Dey eatin' wit 'da king t'night."

CHAPTER 13

ENTER, THE NOBLE THIEF

Bobbee and Bettee Draicon were starting to worry. The band had not returned from their autograph session and it had been nearly two hours since they'd left. Bobbee decided they'd better go find Oline, the promoter, and ask her what the hold up was. They didn't have to look very hard because Oline had been looking for them. She approached them slowly and Bobbee got an immediate sense that something was wrong. For starters, the promoter had a white bandage wrapped around her head, just above her mouth.

"Can I talk to you two for a minute?" asked Oline.

"Why, what's wrong? Where's the band," demanded Bobbee.

Oline put her hands out, a gesture meant to calm the young Sirian down.

"Look," she said. "Something happened to your friends. We're not sure what, but we're working on it."

"What do you mean, 'something happened.' I don't understand." Bobbee was on the verge of tears.

"We think they were kidnapped. I was hit over the head and became unconscious, but we have an eyewitness that claims he saw a monsturd attacking them in the hall outside the autograph session. We think they've been taken off planet."

"What," screamed Bobbee. The dismay in her voice was quite obvious and Bettee began tugging on her sleeve.

"I'm very sorry," said Oline," but we are doing everything in our power to locate your friends. I promise. I can book you a hotel room if you like. Perhaps it would be good to get some rest. Maybe by the time you wake up we'll have found them."

Bobbee shook her head. "No. I think we'd be more comfortable waiting on our bus, if you don't mind."

Oline smiled. “I understand. Keep a line open, so that I can communicate with you if I receive any information on the whereabouts of your friends.”

“All right,” said Bobbee, grabbing hold of Bettee’s hand.

“And again, I’m so sorry about all this,” said Oline. “Nothing like this has ever happened to us and we’re not used to conducting this type of an investigation.”

Bobbee just stared at Oline then said, “C’mon Bettee. Let’s go back to the bus.”

The two of them made their way back to the bus and were soon sitting in the cockpit. Bobbee quickly explained the situation to Libby and Miron and asked if they could locate the missing band. Neither of them was able to pick up any trace of the older Sirians.

“Well, I for one don’t want to just sit around here and wait,” said Bobbee. She looked at Bettee and he nodded his agreement.

“I know what we can do. We’ll find that mining place everyone was talking about and get those files. That way Val won’t treat me like such a useless kid anymore. Bettee, you and I are gonna find our parents.”

Bettee smiled his response.

“Libby, can you find this mining place the others were talking about?” asked Bobbee.

“It’s downtown sweetie, but I don’t know if it’s such a good idea that you two small fries take on this kind of responsibility. What if something happens to you?”

“Oh, hush up Libby,” said Miron. “Let the little ones earn their keep. I, for one, would like to get the G.R.D. scientists back on board as soon as possible.”

“Well, Miron, I’m still trying to figure out how, exactly, we’re going to break into the G.M.C. headquarters without getting caught. I, for one, don’t have that kind of software. Do you?”

“Well, I, uh...ummm...”

“Exactly my point,” said Libby, triumphantly.

“Actually, Libby, I do have that kind of software.”

Libby paused in stunned silence before speaking again. “What do you mean?”

“I’d rather not talk about it,” said Miron.

“C’mon Miron, what are you talking about?”

“I said I’d rather not talk about it.”

“Well, if we’re all going to be in this together, you’re going to have to talk about it. Now where, in the universe, would you get that kind of software?”

“Oh, all right. I used to be owned by the Caster-Leone family.”

“The famous criminal family?”

“Yes, the very one. I was sold off to an underground pawn organization and a friend of a friend helped the G.R.D. purchase me for quite an affordable price.”

Libby started laughing. “Miron, you mean to tell me that your pompous circuitry was purchased illegally?”

“It’s not as if the G.R.D. was aware of the fact that I came equipped with illegal software. I never mentioned it. They don't even know it exists. It's not something I'm proud of, all right. Now can we just move on?"

"Fine," said Libby, still chuckling to herself. "But let the record show that I'm partially opposed to this whole idea."

"Excellent," said Miron. "That way if anything goes wrong, the other half of you will be partially to blame."

"Ha, ha," said Libby.

Still chortling at his own joke Miron continued. "Now I've located the Galactic Mining Coalition headquarters downtown and have plotted a course. Shall we be on our way children?"

"Let's do it," said Bobbee.

The bus rumbled into life and slowly pulled out of its parking space and, within seconds, was off like a shot, zooming up towards the ceiling of the coliseum and re-entering the tunnel that they had come down on their way in. It quickly navigated its way through the underground maze of roads and was soon back, above ground, zipping down various streets as it honed in on the G.M.C. headquarters.

It turned down a back alley, traveled at short distance, then came to a stop.

"This is it," said Miron.

"So what do we do now?" asked Bobbee.

"Okay," said Libby. "Listen to me Bobbee. Look in the glove-box in the right hand side of the dash. In there, you'll find a satellite communications device. Can you go get it?"

Bobbee went to the glove-box and retrieved the device.

"Got it," she said.

"Okay great. Now if you look around the middle of the dash, you'll find an insert port marked 'central computer download.'"

"Found it."

"Bobbee, do you realize that you're the only five year old I've ever encountered that knows how to read."

"Yep. My mom and dad taught me. Guess they figured it would come in useful."

"Well, now it is. Take the device and plug it into the port. What's going to happen, is that Miron and I will be downloaded into that device and you'll be able to take us with you when you go inside."

"Okay, I've plugged it in. Now what?"

"Miron, are you ready?"

"Libby, I must say, you're quite good with small children," said Miron.

"Why thank you Miron. Fortunately for us these two young children happen to be quite smart. Not to mention brave. Now are you ready?"

"Absolutely," said Miron.

The next voice Bobbee and Bettee heard came from a speaker in the satellite communications device.

"Okay children," said Libby in a much thinner and smaller sounding voice. "You're going to need some breathing apparatus before we go outside. The air is breathable, but it's really not that good for you. To the docking bay."

The children made their way down to the docking bay, donned their breathing apparatus, and left the confines of the space bus.

They stepped out into the night air as a gentle breeze swept down the alley and tickled their antennas. They moved towards the back of the building and began searching for an entrance. They soon found one marked by a few grooves in the wall.

"Bobbee," said Miron. "Lift the device as high up along that groove as you possibly can, and drag it slowly down as if you were vacuuming dust out of it."

Bobbee did as she was told and, about halfway down, she heard a small click and the door opened. Her and Bettee stepped inside and she closed the door behind them. The first thing they noticed was nothing. It was pitch black.

"I can't see a thing," said Bobbee.

A small light suddenly turned on in the satellite device.

"Is that better?" asked Libby.

"Ya." Bobbee began waving the flashlight around, now able to investigate her surroundings.

"You can pull your breathing apparatus down now, children," said Libby. "The air in here is universally conditioned."

Bobbee and Bettee did so, leaving the facemasks hanging around their necks. They looked around and realized that they had entered some kind of store. As she flashed the light around the room she revealed glass cases filled with stones of all different shapes, sizes, and colours.

"Pretty," she said.

Bettee nodded his agreement.

"This is the G.M.C. showroom," said Libby. "We need to find the vertical drive lifters, which will take us to the eleventh floor. That is where we'll find the central computer."

"Libby, something just popped into my head," said Bobbee.

"What is it?"

"Do you think this computer will have an attitude problem the same as you and Miron have?"

Libby and Miron both laughed.

"It almost certainly will," said Libby. "That's what's going to be difficult about getting into the system."

Bobbee nodded her understanding and located a sign marked 'EXIT'. She and Bettee passed beneath the sign and entered a corridor. They soon reached the vertical drive lifters and, within moments, were shooting up to the eleventh floor. When they reached their destination, the lift doors opened and the siblings stepped out into another corridor.

"Which way?" asked Bobbee.

"Right," said Miron.

They turned right and followed the corridor for a short while until it came to an abrupt end. They stood in front of another door and Bobbee once again dragged the satellite down the groove in the wall until she heard a click. The door opened and her and Bettee stepped into the residence of the G.M.C. central computer. They were confronted with something they didn't expect; someone was in the room.

Blurtch trudged across the desert, maintaining a steady pace he knew was necessary. The Monsturd planet wasn't exactly a family vacation favourite. He'd been telling the truth when he told the Big Boss they hadn't crashed into something. Something had crashed into them and he was pretty sure it wasn't unintentional. He looked over his shoulder and saw the something that had 'unintentionally' crashed into them. Currently, it was nosing around the wreckage of the ship. It was one of the giant monsturd beasts that roamed the desert and it was desperately trying to claw the ship out from beneath the rock outcropping.

The quadruped, to its own disadvantage, possessed extremely short front legs that looked like fat fleshy mounds of skin with claws. Its head looked as if someone had taken a sledgehammer and pounded it flat between the monsturd's shoulder blades. It's body was completely disproportionate, for halfway down its back, its saggy mass narrowed out into a thin spine - literally. No flesh covered its waist or its back legs and the skeletal feet dug into the sand as it wagged the long strip of bone that represented its tail.

Blutch continued his desert march, hoping he could make it to the crystal trees at the base of the mountain before another giant showed up to squash him into the ground like a bug. Though the Gulterian space goblins were one of the most feared races in the galaxy, they were no match for the giants of the Monsturd planet wastelands.

He breathed a sigh of relief as he reached the first tree. The forest, in sharp contrast to the ugliness of the creatures that cohabited the planet, was one of the most beautiful sights in the galaxy. The crystal trees grew from the ground and gleamed brilliantly in the sun like a sea of jewels, reflecting the light into dazzling rainbows of colour. Blurtch had to shield his eyes from the glamorous intensity as he moved through the forest.

As he hiked along, admiring his surroundings, he felt a tingle in his toes as the hairs on the back of his neck stood on end. It was an electrical sensitivity that he was familiar with and he quickly threw himself to the ground and rolled to the left as a crystal tree on his right exploded into thousands of tiny fragments. One particular shard embedded itself in his shoulder and he hollered in pain as he pulled it free. He rolled onto his back and stared up into the sky, but the brilliant reflection of the trees prevented him from getting a good look at what had just fired at him. He heard the sound though. It was the mechanical buzz of a pod and he was pretty sure who was piloting it.

Blurtch jumped to his feet and began running through the trees as fast as he could. Bossentical, meanwhile, had come full circle and was flying up behind the goblin again, his thumb hovering above the fire button.

"Deserter," screamed Bossentical from inside the pod. "Nobody deserts the Big Boss and lives to tell about it."

Bossentical fired another shot and Blurtch dove out of the way just in time as a large crater in the side of the mountain opened up where he'd been, mere moments before. He scrambled back to his feet and continued his mad dash up the hill, dodging his way in and out of the crystal trees. Explosions continued to occur on either side of him as his former boss intensified the attacks.

Blurtch reached inside his vest and, to his dismay, realized he no longer had his laser blaster, suddenly remembering the kids back on the 'L' station had dumped it down a disposal bin. He silently cursed himself. This was the first time in his life he'd ever had to run from anything and he did not enjoy the feeling at all. Usually it was he that did the chasing and his brain was working overtime to come up with a solution on how to turn the tables on the Big Boss.

It wasn't Blurtch that eventually turned the tables, but Bossentical himself. You see, the Big Boss's rather pathetic aim had blown apart yet another crystal tree about twenty feet in front of Blurtch. As the space goblin was about to pass the tree by, he happened to glance down and noticed a large hole had opened up in the ground, exactly where the tree had been. Without even thinking, he leaped into the hole and dropped into a dark tunnel. He ran down the unknown corridor and could hear the muffled sounds of explosions above, as Bossentical continued his wreak of havoc on the mountainside.

The tunnel eventually opened up into a large dimly lit chamber. Directly above him was a ceiling of charred and blackened metal and he was tall enough to run his fingers along its rough surface. He suddenly reached the end of the ceiling as a much higher one that he could not reach opened up above him. He soon realized that he had mistaken a spacecraft's underbelly for the chamber's roof. His back was now against a wall as he stretched his neck up to get a better look at the ship. Suing for whiplash was the first thing that popped into his mind as something slammed into him from behind, knocking him to the ground.

As he was turning over to see if his attacker was an it or a who, he felt a hand cup over the side of his head and push it to the floor.

"Whatcho bidness here goblin?" A voice asked.

"I got no business here," said Blurtch.

"Then watchoo doin' here?"

"Running from danger."

"What kinda danger?"

"None of yer business."

“Makin’ people’s bidness my bidness is my bidness, especially when deys interferin’ wid my bidness. Get up.”

Blurtch felt two hands grab him by the collar of his shirt and pull him up off the ground. Whatever had hold of him was extremely strong and Blurtch was presented with the first opportunity to get a look at his attacker. He spun around, ready to fight, but the blaster in the creature’s hand made him think twice.

“Name’s Geeno,” said the monsturd.

“Blurtch.”

“Well, Blurtch. Looks like we got ourselves a bit of a situation here. I don wanna tell you my bidness and you don wanna tell me yours. Ain’t nuttin’ much else to talk about den is dere?”

“I suppose we could fight.”

“Now, why would I wanna go’n have a fight wid someone I don know and got no beef wid.”

“How ‘bout a ride then,” said Blurtch.

“A ride? Where to?”

“Any where off planet.”

Geeno scratched his chin, pondering the suggestion for a moment. “Could do. I tell ya’ what Blurtch. You tell me yer bidness here on Monsturd and I’ll consider givin’ you a ride.”

Blurtch sighed. He was tired. He hadn’t slept for well over a week and hadn’t eaten anything all day either. Not eating always added to his crankiness and he felt the irritation building in the pit of his stomach.

“Look, all I can say is that I work for the lunatic presently blowing holes in the mountainside and that we’ve recently had a falling out due on account that he’s completely insane. I’ve spent the last two years of my life working for the crazy, fuzzy bonehead and have just recently decided to quit. The money’s not worth it, the hours suck, and the assignments are becoming less attractive all the time.”

Geeno, who was beginning to develop a certain kind of liking towards Blurtch, lowered his gun. “Whatchoo mean by, ‘assignments’?”

“Well, I did sign a confidentiality agreement with him, but I s’ppose it doesn’t much matter now. He’s got collectors working all over the universe for him, collecting top entertainers and stealing their talent.”

Geeno looked confused. “Whatchoo mean by ‘stealing’?”

“He’s invented a machine that sucks talent right out of one’s soul and adds it to his own tainted reservoir. He’s obsessed and quite crazy.”

“So you bin’ helpin’ him do dis?”

“Ya, it was my job but, recently, he had me roughin’ up these musicians from Sirius; reminded me of kids, really, so I just decided I’d had enough, and I walked.”

“Kids from Sirius eh,” said Geeno. “Can’t say I approve of anyone wantin’ ta’ hurt a bunch ‘o kids. Dat just ain’t right.”

"I know it's not right," said Blurtch. "But sometimes you gotta do what you gotta do to make a livin'. I'm a Gulterian. It's not supposed to be in our nature to care about anyone."

"I see," said Geeno. "Well, first ting I gotta do is go round up yer old boss who's wreckin' 'da mountainside. He ain't just messin' wid kids and space goblins. He's messin' wid monsturds now and we's about ta' give im a wake up call." He raised his gun and once again pointed it at Blurtch. "Sorry, Blurtch, but I'm gonna have ta' lock yous up till I speak ta' King Rubb about what I'm gonna do wid you."

Geeno led Blurtch out of the hangar bay, through the door, and down a long hallway until they reached the prisoner's quarters where Blurtch was escorted into a cell. Geeno began walking away, then stopped, and turned to look at the goblin.

"I'll be back," was all he said before turning and heading back down the corridor.

"Where have I heard that before," mumbled Blurtch.

Bobbee felt her heart leap as the shadowy figure turned around. She flashed her light in the stranger's face, causing him to throw his arm up and shield his eyes. He had long, red curly hair that fell down over a pair of pointed ears. The rest of his features were covered up with a bare arm that was covered with gnarly bumps and horns.

"You mind not flashing that thing in my eyes, please," he said.

"Sorry," said Bobbee quickly moving the light to the figure's chest. He lowered his arm so she could make out his face. For a brief moment she thought she recognized him, but then changed her mind. His face was covered with light green skin, which was pulled tightly across his bones, revealing two small slits where his nose should have been. A small, silver cup with a lid sat next to the computer keyboard and his fingers rested comfortably on its side. He picked it up and took a long, deep drink of its contents.

"What are you kids doing in here," he said, following up the question with a satisfying belch.

"Umm, I'm sorry mister, miss, uh, mister..."

"It's mister. Mister Jagger Nazz, and again, may I ask what you kids are doing here?" He took another gulp of his drink.

"We were just...umm...uh...looking for our friends," said Bobbee.

"Well, you won't find them here," said Jagger Nazz. "Go away."

"We can't go away," insisted Bobbee. "We have to find our parents."

"I thought you said you were looking for your friends."

"We are," replied Bobbee. "We're looking for both. Our friends and our parents."

"How old are you?"

"Five and a half."

Jagger smiled. "Hey, I remember tacking on that extra half to make myself sound older. Now

I drop a half to make myself sound younger. Funny how that works eh?" He eyed the two kids up and down, starting to realize that they didn't pose much of a threat.

Jagger Nazz was a renowned thief and was wanted by almost every single law enforcement officer in the galaxy. His face was plastered on bulletin boards across the universe and Bettee suddenly realized that this is where he'd seen the face before. He tugged Bobbee's sleeve and she turned to him. After he performed a series of gestures she turned her attention back to the stranger.

"You're a thief," she said.

"How nice of you to notice," replied Jagger.

"I've seen your face on posters everywhere. Is that why you're here? You're stealing?"

"You could put it that way." Jagger turned to the computer he'd been looking at earlier and began typing on the keyboard.

"Didn't your mommy tell you that stealing is bad," asked Bobbee.

"Depends on how you look at it," replied Jagger, not turning around this time.

"What do you mean?"

"What's your name?"

"B...B...Bobbee," she said.

"Well, B...B...Bobbee, I'll make you a deal. You tell me why the two of you are here and I'll tell you what I mean." He took another drink from his cup.

Bobbee looked questioningly at Bettee, hoping her brother would have an answer but he just shrugged.

"You're not gonna hurt us, are you Mister Nazz?" She asked.

This time Jagger turned and looked at her. He seemed surprised by the question; almost hurt.

"Of course I'm not going to hurt you. Why would I?"

"I don't know. I guess I just had to ask."

"I'm a thief, little one. I do not indulge in child abuse. It's a sick pleasure in this universe that someone ought to do something about. Children are the future. Why certain individuals are stupid enough to want to hurt them is beyond me." He turned back to the computer once again.

Bobbee looked at her brother and made a series of hand gestures. Bettee nodded in agreement. She then said, "Excuse me, Mr. Nazz?"

"Ya, what?"

"Do you mind if my brother touches you, like, on your hand or something?"

"What for?"

"Well, he has this talent for...um...well...it's kinda hard to explain."

"Try me."

"I guess you could say he's able to tell if people are good or bad. He kinda picks up on their vibe, or something like that."

Jagger held out his hand for Bettee to touch. "Be my guest."

Bettee moved forward and touched Jagger's hand. He maintained contact for a few seconds, then let go. He turned to Bobbee, nodded his head and smiled.

His sister returned his smile. "He says you're okay."

"Lucky me," said Jagger. "Now, are you going to tell me why you're here, or not?"

Bobbee began to tell him their story and he appeared to be listening because every now and then, between sips of his drink, he would nod his head and grunt some form of understanding. Once she'd finished, he continued to stare at the screen.

"So you think your parents might be enslaved on one of these mining colonies," he said.

"Ya, but we need to search the files in order to figure out which one."

The thief took another long swig of his drink, draining its contents.

"What are you drinking?" asked Bobbee.

"Clotchee. Never leave home without it. I even carry my cream and sugar around with me just in case."

"What's clotchee?"

"Never mind. You'll find out when you're older and unable to stimulate your own motivation."

Bobbee made a face that told Jagger she didn't understand, but he ignored her and, instead of giving her a more detailed explanation, reached down and pulled a device out of the C.P.U. He then turned his attention back on the children. "You know, they never used to register their slaves, but ever since the galactic government installed the slavery tax incentives, these companies have been registering their slaves like crazy. I find it interesting that you're looking for slaves because that is precisely why I'm here."

"What do you mean?" asked Bobbee.

"Well, I actually work with an organization called the A.S.C."

"What's that?"

"Anti Slavery Coalition. I work with many organizations but the A.S.C. seemed in particular need of my services recently so I offered them up graciously. Every year, innocent spacecraft are caught in the miner's asteroid nets, their crews forced into slavery on these mining colonies. The A.S.C, including myself, believe this to be wrong, so we're stealing the slave registries. It is our intent to post these lists on every bulletin board in the galaxy and raise awareness in the planetary populations. If people know their loved ones are still alive, it will be far easier to coerce them into participating in peaceful protests to put an end to slavery."

"So...you're stealing for good," said Bobbee.

"Yes, child, I'm stealing for good, though I'm sure the G.M.C. would strongly disagree." He pointed at her flashlight. "Is that your central computer satellite?"

She looked down and realized that she'd almost forgotten about it. It was the first time she'd heard both Libby and Miron be so quiet. "Ya," she said.

“Give it to me and I’ll plug it in for you. I’ve already by-passed the G.M.C. central computer; thank goodness. Nasty disposition that one had.”

“How do we know we can trust you?” said Libby, suddenly.

Jagger grinned. “You don’t know. But seeing as I’m bigger than both these children, you don’t really have much of a choice. I assure you though, that my intentions do not include harming these kids. You can relax.”

“What do you think Miron?”

“Well, I think he’s right. We don’t have much of a choice. But if you pull anything, Mr. Nazz, I will not hesitate to notify the central alarms of our presence. Due to their age, the children will, no doubt, be set free. You, on the other hand, will be reprimanded by the proper authorities, so consider yourself warned.”

“Pleasant central computer you have there. Big surprise. Here, hand it to me.”

Bobbee handed the satellite device to Jagger and he quickly plugged it in and began typing.

“What about us,” came Miron’s snotty voice from the satellite.

“You’re not needed, computer. I’ve already by-passed the central computer.”

“But...”

“Miron, be quiet,” said Bobbee. Mr. Nazz is gonna help us.”

“Well, that’s just dandy,” said Miron. “But let the record show that it was I who encouraged this mission in the first place and it was I who...”

“Miron! Shut up,” said Libby. “Let the thief do his job.”

Miron did so, as Jagger Nazz continued to type.

“How many days since your parents disappeared,” he asked.

“Umm...I think about five.”

“Okay, good. Let’s see if we can’t narrow this down. They usually include the slave’s race and home of origin in their files, so I’m checking to see if any Sirians have been collected in the last five days or so.”

His fingers became a blur on the keyboard and it was obvious that he’d done this type of work before.

“There,” he finally said.

Bobbee and Bettee ran up and peered over his shoulder.

He tapped his finger on the glass of the monitor. “Five days ago a large group of Sirian adults were collected by a pendulum pocket, and sent to Asteroid Y2K50-90210.” He looked at the kids and smiled. “That must be your parents.”

Bobbee began jumping up and down, squealing gleefully and clapping her hands.

“Shhh,” said Jagger. “Security may be light in this building, but it’s not that light.”

Bobbee stopped immediately and covered her mouth. It was during this moment of silence that they heard voices coming down the hall toward them.

CHAPTER 14

ONE HUNDRED AND ONE MONSTURDLES

The young Sirians ate hungrily as mounds of food were placed before them. King Rubb turned out to be a most excellent host and insisted the kids be well provided for. The food itself was not what they expected. Everything had a gourmet flavour to it and all was cooked to perfection. The meats were perfectly seasoned and baked to a melt-in-your-mouth standard the kids had never experienced their entire life. The vegetables were bathed in rich creamy sauces that made you want to keep filling your belly long after it was full. The breads were hot and steamy, and tasted like a baker's dream, even without the flavoured butter that soaked into their light fluffy cores. They all ate ravenously, as if it were their final meal, and then ate some more. Just when they thought they couldn't eat another bite, dessert arrived. It was beyond description and spent little time on the table. Within minutes it was gone and the Sirians were left leaning back in their chairs, with looks of whole and complete satisfaction on their faces.

Vack did not eat at the table with the others. Instead, he sat in the corner, his legs stretched out with his plate sitting on his lap. He picked at his plate, but did not appear to be too interested in his food. He cast an occasional glance at the others, but would quickly look away the moment he made eye contact.

As the kids were just finishing their meal, the door opened and Geeno reentered the room. He walked up to King Rubb and whispered something in his master's ear. King Rubb nodded and stood up.

"I'm 'fraid I gotta leave for a short bit kids, so if dere's anytin' you need you jus ask Flurp and he'll git it for you."

The king followed Geeno out of the room, leaving the kids to eat in silence. The other monsturds did not seem to be quite as chatty without the presence of their king.

Jethro leaned over and spoke into Seth's ear. "I wonder what's going on."

Seth shrugged. "Beats me."

Jethro looked over at Flurp, a younger looking monsturd with a fat, lumpy head and big muscles. "Hey Flurp, any idea what's going on?"

"Yer guess is as good as mine," said Flurp, stuffing a fork-full of food into his mouth and chomping away noisily.

Just then a loud explosion came from the other side of the door. Flurp stood up, quickly swallowing his food. "Security!" he shouted.

Steel walls slammed down all around them, instantly concealing their stone predecessors. A large group of monitors dropped out of the ceiling in the right hand corner of the room revealing a view of the restaurant on the other side.

The young Sirians spun around in their seats to get a good view of the images on the monitor. What they saw made their hearts sink.

A pod hovered in the entrance of the restaurant, its weapons launchers pointed directly at the large crowd of monsturd patrons. Inside the pod sat Bossentical Distort, a crazed expression covering his face.

"Anybody moves and you all get blown into monster sized turds!" He bellowed through the loudspeakers on the outside of the pod.

Flurp moved to the center of the table and pushed the plates out of the way. He reached under the stone slab and pressed a concealed button. A hole suddenly opened up in the middle of the table and an instrument panel, equipped with a microphone, speaker, and monitor rose up in front of Flurp. He grabbed the microphone and pressed another button on the panel.

"Flurp to King Rubb. Come in King Rubb."

King Rubb and Geeno suddenly appeared on the monitor screen.

"Rubb here," said the king in a voice laced with static.

"We got an intruder in 'da restraunt threatnin' ta' blow 'da place up."

"I know," said King Rubb. "We got another one down here in 'da cell block, claims he used ta' work for 'da intruder."

"Whaddya want me ta' do boss?"

"Tryn' talk ta' him. Me'n Geeno'll question this one and git back ta' 'ya."

"Got it boss," said Flurp hitting the button, causing the images on the screen to disappear.

He looked at the Sirians, who all had their eyes focussed on the monitor screen in the corner.

"You kids git up," said Flurp, "and git behind dis table. Now!"

The kids all did as they were told and watched as Flurp grabbed hold of the microphone again and hit another button.

"Hey boyee," he said. "Yous in big trouble if you don git yer pod off ar planet. I don know how you made it past ar security, but yous gon git a good solid lickin' if you don scram dis instant."

"Security? What security." Bossentical laughed hysterically. "I've infiltrated your abode without a single protest. I've broken into old folks homes with more difficulty than this. It is I that ought to be giving the orders. I came for my talent and I'm not leaving until I get it."

Flurp looked over at one of the other monsturds. "Talent?"

The other monsturd just shrugged his response.

Val nudged Jethro as they sat against the wall behind the table. "We can't just sit here and wait for him to come in here and get you. I think we should do something."

Jethro looked at her. "Like what?"

"I don't know." Val looked up at Flurp. "Hey Flurp turd, is there another way outta this room?"

Flurp turned and cast an irritated glance at Val. "Umm...ya, I guess. Dere's 'da secret passage in 'da floor, but it's only used for emergency situations."

"Well, isn't this an emergency situation?"

"I s'ppose, but we gotta wait for word from 'da king 'fore we make any decisions."

"Well, why don't you ask him what he plans on doing, 'cause we're starting to get a little freaked out here all right? We've already encountered this psycho once before and it wasn't pretty."

Flurp reestablished contact with King Rubb, who appeared on the monitor screen. "Dese kids gettin' impatient King. Whatchoo wan us ta' do. 'Parently 'da intruder want dem."

"Well, he's not gettin dem," said King Rubb. "Let's show 'im what we do to dose who mess wid 'da monsturd planet. Get dem kids down 'da secret passage and into 'da safety zone. Me an' Geeno gonna release 'da monsturdles."

"Gotcha, King. You meetin' us in 'da safety zone?"

"I'll meetchoo dere in ten minutes." King Rubb walked off screen and Flurp cancelled the connection, punching in a code on the keyboard.

A trap door opened up in the floor in the middle of the room and Flurp pointed to it.

"Okay kids, we makin' ar way to 'da safety zone. King's releasin' 'da monsturdles and anyone who ain't a monsturd don' wanna be caught above if dey don wanna suffer a horrible death."

The kids all looked at Flurp.

"Umm, what's a monsturdle?" asked Quasar.

"You don wanna know," replied Flurp. "Now git down in dat hole."

The other two monsturds jumped down into the passageway first, followed by the kids and then Flurp, who suddenly realized that Vack was still sitting in the corner of the room. He'd been so silent that everyone had forgotten he was there.

"I don know whatcher problem is mister robes but cher gonna wanna git down an come wid us."

"I'll be along shortly," replied Vack, rather calmly.

"I tink you oughtta come wid us now man. You don wanna be 'round when 'da monsturdles ar set free. Dey not too understandin' wid non monsturd types."

"Look, I said I'd be along shortly," Vack snapped. "Now, just leave me be."

"Hey, no need to git all snarky wid me," said Flurp. "Suit yerself, but don say I din' warn 'ya." Flurp ducked his head down into the passageway and began running to catch up with the others, who were already a considerable distance down the tunnel.

The moment Flurp was gone, Vack jumped up and ran over to the instrument panel in the table and began typing on the keyboard.

"C'mon," he said to himself as what he was looking for suddenly came up on screen.

"Aha. Excellent."

He was staring at a map of the underground tunnel system. He studied it for a minute, then went to the middle of the room, jumped down in the passageway, and began running in the opposite direction that the others had gone.

Blurtch was still looking at Geeno and King Rubb from behind bars. "You're not planning on just leaving me here, are you?" he asked.

"Don know," said King Rubb. "Haven't decided yet."

He turned, walked across the hall and entered the cell on the other side. He reached down and pulled hard on a latch that was sticking out of the ground. The latch belonged to a trap door, which he now dragged across the floor, revealing a ramp that disappeared into the depths beneath the cell. He crossed over into the corner where a mop stood, it's head submerged in a bucket. He grabbed both, returned to the ramp and began slopping the bucket's contents all over the edge of the ramp. He and Geeno then walked back over to Blurtch's cell and stood waiting.

"What are you doing," asked Blurtch.

"Lettin' out 'da turdles," said King Rubb.

"What are 'daturdles'?"

"You'll see."

And Blurtch did see. Within minutes the first monsturdle's head appeared at the top of the ramp. Its head was snake-like in shape and covered with thick horns. Its eyes were completely black and empty looking. As it crept into the cell, it revealed the rest of its body. The head protruded from a thick, hard looking shell, which was coloured with orange and black stripes. Thousands of sharp, needle like quills, stuck out of the shell and quivered as the creature moved slowly across the floor. Its four legs were short and fat and covered in thick black fur. As it walked, it lashed a long black tail back and forth, controlling it like a whip.

Seconds later, another one appeared where the first one had been and the parade would not stop until one hundred and one of the hideous monsturds had been released.

The first monsturdle had breached the cell and was in the process of backing up down the corridor past Blurtch's cell. As it moved backward past the space goblin it turned and snarled at him, causing him to take a few steps back. At this point, Geeno and King Rubb entered the cell and closed the iron doors. The monsturdle had now reached the end of the corridor, its rear end nearly touching the back wall. It wrapped its tail around the thick chain that hung from the wall. When it had a good solid grip it began to move forward again, its tail stretching out behind it, still attached to the chain. Once it had gone as far forward as the elasticity of its tail would allow, it released its tail from the chain. The momentum of the tail shooting and snapping into the back of the monsturdle launched the creature at an unbelievable speed down the hall until it cracked, noisily, into the wall at the other end. It merely backed into another wall and repeated the entire process, shooting itself down the next hallway that ran perpendicular to the one it had just come down.

Blurtch stared, amazed, as the rest of the monsturdles repeated the launching process of the first. He looked over at King Rubb.

"I take it you wouldn't wanna be caught unawares in a tunnel with one of these things rocketing towards you," he said.

"Unimaginable pain," said King Rubb. "Even monsturds need ta' be extremely careful or dey could find demselves impaled on 'da back of a monsturdle. Dat's why our lair is made up 'o tunnels. 'Da monsturdles are ar' main line 'o defense 'gainst intruders."

"Like me," said Blurtch.

"Well, we only send out 'da monsturdles if it's a problem we can't deal wid arselves. Dis intruder got imself some nasty weapons so's we figure 'da turdles are necessary. Dat's why we let certain intruders inta' ar tunnel system. So dat dey git ta' enjoy da' ultimate punishment for messin' wid monsturds."

It took about an hour to launch all the monsturdles, but the first one reached Bossentical within ten minutes. The Big Boss had already seriously injured a good number of monsturds in the restaurant and was in the process of interrogating one who was trapped in the clutches of one of the pod's unrelenting mechanical arms.

"Where are they," Bossentical demanded.

"I don know whatchoo talkin' bout," replied the monsturd in a pained grunt of rage.

The mechanical arm tightened its grip around the monsturd's waist and the sound of cracking ribs rang out through the restaurant. If it hadn't been for the pod's laser weapon system, the other monsturds probably would have overpowered the puny craft right away. As it stood, many of the restaurant patrons had tried and had already been shot down. None had been killed yet, but the threat of death had definitely curbed their appetite to attack.

"I'll ask you one more time before I snap you in half," Bossentical snarled. "Where are they?"

The monsturd winced under the pain of his breaking bones and breathed in deeply.

"I...don...know..."

Just as Bossentical was about to crush his victim, something slammed into the back of the pod sending it crashing into a wall and causing the mechanical arm to drop its victim, who quickly crawled out of harms way.

“Ahhhhhh,” screamed Bossentical in frustration. “Every single time I think I’m getting some where I get knocked down.”

As he struggled to get the restraining belt undone he glanced up and let out another scream; this one laced with terror and fear. A monsturdle was slowly marching toward the pod and behind it, others were filing into the restaurant.

“Turdles,” screamed the Big Boss. “Why’d it have to be Turdles?”

He scrambled out of his restraining belt and grabbed hold of the mechanical arm controls just as the first monsturdle began snapping at the pod. The mechanical hand clamped into a fist and delivered a bone shattering right hook to the side of the monsturdle’s head. The creature let out a howl of pain and backed away from its prey.

The pod’s flying and weapons systems had malfunctioned as a result of the crash. The mechanical hands were the only defense mechanisms left working and Bossentical used them as best he could. Digging the fingers of one hand into the floor, Bossentical used the one arm to start dragging the pod across the hard ground while the other arm continued to lash out at the multiplying monsturdles.

The ear-piercing squeal of metal being dragged across stone rang out as the pod made its way to the door on the other side. The boxing hand momentarily gave up its fight against the monsturdles and punched a hole through the door. Bossentical opened the pod door and climbed out. He ran as fast as his short, pink, furry legs would carry him and jumped through the hole in the door just before a monsturdle could catch him between its jaws.

Once into the room on the other side, Bossentical quickly located the still open, secret passageway in the middle of the floor. He jumped into it just as a monsturdle knocked the entire door down. The door slid across the floor and, as its end reached the passageway, it balanced precariously over the hole before sliding in and slamming into the floor of the tunnel beneath, directly in front of Bossentical, who jumped back about two feet, thinking the remainder of the door would come crashing down on top of him. It didn’t happen though and the other end remained in the room above leaning against the side of the hole. It was enough to prevent the monsturdles from climbing down into the passageway, but didn’t prevent them from sticking their heads down into the hole to see if they could get one last bite of their prey. Bossentical stood on the under side of the door that had fallen into the passageway. It was possible to crawl through the hole he’d made with the mechanical hand, but that decision would surely turn him into a monsturdle snack. He turned and headed in the only direction he could, shuddering as the monsturdles let out a shriek of anger, knowing their prey had escaped.

Flurp led the kids down the tunnel as quickly as he could. The last time he’d had to use the secret escape route was when he’d forgotten to get Geeno’s hat steam cleaned. Geeno never went out on a job without his hat; it was his trademark. He’d wasted half the day searching for his hat when he finally remembered he’d given it to Flurp, who’d forgotten about it entirely and had left it, dirty and soiled, lying on the kitchen table.

They took one right turn, descended a set of stairs and finally burst through the end of the tunnel and entered the safety zone. It actually looked more like a play zone. They had entered a huge cavern, but it was mostly filled in with a giant climbing apparatus. Criss-crossing bars and a thick meshing of cargo nets covered the kids' field of vision and the first of their monsturd guides began navigating a path through the adult sized jungle gym.

Jethro and the others bumped their heads more than once as they climbed over and under the steel bars, carefully avoiding certain ones, which they were informed were electrically charged.

They finally made their way through the apparatus and reached a sea of floating metal spheres.

"Don't worry," said Flurp. "They're not activated yet."

"What are they," asked Quasar.

"Magneticals," replied Flurp.

"What's a magnetical?"

"You don't wanna know." Flurp led the way through the giant levitating marbles until they'd reached a large pool of water in the center of the cavern. A bridge stretched out and over the water to a dock that hovered twenty feet above the pool. Flurp and the other monsturds led them up and across the bridge until they'd reached the dock.

Looking down, the Sirians could see rather large shapes swimming around in the depths of the pool.

"What's down there?" asked Seth.

"'Da Submergaturds," answered Flurp.

"Are they dangerous," asked Jethro.

"Let's jus put it dis way. Dere's a reason dis dock is floatin' way up here instead 'o way down dere."

No sooner had he spoken, when a large shape burst forth from the water and a set of jaws and razor sharp teeth rose up, snapping at the bottom of the dock. It fell short of its target by about five feet and fell back into the water with a large splash, soaking the young Sirians and their monsturd hosts from head to foot.

Flurp crossed the dock to a control panel on the other side and began punching a series of commands into it. The mechanical sound of shifting gears rang throughout the cavern as thick glass walls rose up on every side of them and the bridge they had crossed began to retract toward the dock until it was entirely concealed beneath them. A crisscross checkerboard of blue laser light erupted in a cube shape around them and the youngsters stared at it admiringly.

When Flurp had finished keying in all the defense codes, he turned to the Sirians.

"Ain't nobody gonna git you kids now," he said.

Vack had safely reached the cavern of the monsturd ship yard and was in the process of deciding which space craft he was going to steal when he heard the echo of a shriek ring out of the tunnel he'd just come down. He quickly made a decision to not be too picky about his choice and keyed open the door of a shuttle bus that was parked right next to him. He walked in, closed the door and climbed into the front seat. He was about to start the bus when he happened to look up. His former pink boss had appeared in the entrance of the tunnel and was looking around the shipyard. Vack watched as Bossentical's face lit up, a hideous facial contortion that made Vack's skin crawl.

Bossentical dashed off out of sight behind a large grouping of ships and Vack could hear the irritating little fur ball's laughter bouncing off the walls of the cavern. The former collector sighed heavily, closed his eyes, and dropped his head as if in deep thought. A moment later, he exited the shuttle bus and followed the sound of the laughter.

"I can't believe I'm doing this," he mumbled to himself. "So close to gettin' outta here and I gotta go all noble and try and save a bunch of kids."

Ducking as low as he could, he peered around the end of a sports cruiser and soon saw why Bossentical was laughing. The Big Boss had found a Fuelition mining suit, one of the toughest and safest manufactured suits in the entire universe.

Bossentical ignited the jet packs on the back of the suit and he was soon hovering a couple feet off the ground. The suit itself wasn't a very good fit for the Big Boss and the legs dragged limply on the floor as he began to move forward. He had to roll up the sleeves in order to utilize the palm mechanisms in the gloves, which controlled the rock blasting laser guns attached to the jet packs. He steered in the direction of the tunnel and was soon swallowed by its innards.

Vack crept slowly up to the wall where Bossentical had been and pulled another suit off the wall and quietly put it on. By the time he had it all locked into place, Bossentical had disappeared down a tunnel on the other side of the shipyard. He quickly ignited his jet packs and zoomed off in pursuit of his former boss.

He reached back and detached one of the rock blasters from the jet pack. He wanted to be fully prepared in case Bossentical spotted him. It was the Big Boss's crazy laughter that enabled Vack to follow at a safe distance without being heard.

He came slowly around a corner and instinctively raised his blaster up as a rather large shape came barreling down the hall toward him. At first he thought it was Bossentical charging him, but it soon became evident that the speeding hard-shelled object shooting toward him was not the Big Boss. He gave his jet packs some gas causing him to shoot up an extra couple of feet as the monsturdle shot beneath him. He turned and watched the creature crash into the wall at the end of the tunnel, then attach its tail to the other wall, stretch it out, and let go, disappearing down the tunnel that headed toward the shipyard.

He turned and resumed his pursuit of Bossentical, whose laughter was becoming more faint. A few more monsturdles whizzed beneath his feet before he heard the sound of a rock blaster going off. He turned down a familiar tunnel and realized that it was the one that led to the cells where he and the kids had been locked up earlier. He hovered his way forward until he reached the end of the tunnel and peered, carefully, around the corner.

Bossentical was hovering directly in front of a cell about halfway down the corridor and he shook his rock blaster menacingly.

"Come outta there," he hollered as one final monsturdle whizzed beneath his feet.

Vack gasped as three figures stepped out from within the confines of the cell. It was King Rubb, Geeno, and Blurtch.

"Now what is goin' on here," Vack mumbled to himself.

"Move," commanded Bossentical urging his captives to move down the corridor.

"Whaddya want wid us," grumbled King Rubb, who led the small parade.

"You've got my talent and I want it back," said Bossentical.

"Whaddya talkin' 'bout, talent? I ain't gotcher talent. Yer nuts."

Bossentical shot a rock blast into the ceiling, causing a rubble of rocks to fall down onto Blurtch and Geeno's heads.

"Call me nuts again and I"ll turn you into nuts. Now move. Yer gonna be my bait."

When Vack realized that the mismatched group was heading straight for him he prepared himself to escape back down the way he'd come, but it turned out to not be necessary. The group turned off down a different tunnel, enabling Vack to resume his undetected pursuit.

They soon came to an intercom system built into the wall. Bossentical shook his rock blaster at King Rubb.

"Locate whoever's got the Sirians and tell them that if they don't give 'em up they'll be scrapin' you and your henchman's filthy innards off the walls."

King Rubb was not accustomed to being held hostage and gave Blurtch a doubtful glance.

"Don't bother," said Blurtch. "He's crazy and won't think twice about shooting all three of us. You better do as he says if you wanna live."

King Rubb grimaced and focused his attention on the intercom. Geeno, in the meantime, growled at Bossentical.

"Oh, shut up, you oversized brute," said the Big Boss. "Why don't you go get yourself fitted for a collar, so that I can put you on a leash. Rather fitting wouldn't you say?"

The look he received from Geeno would drive any normal person insane, but seeing as the Big Boss was already insane, he only smiled and gave Geeno a flash of his crazy eyes.

King Rubb pushed the intercom button and spoke. "Dis is Rubb and Geeno. We bin taken hostage 'an if we don give up 'da Sirians, mister terrorist says he's gonna blast us."

A voice came out of the intercom speaker in response.

"Flurp here, sir. I got 'da kids in 'da safety zone. Whatchoo want me ta' do?"

"Stay put," said Rubb. "We'll come to you." He turned to Bossentical. "Dere in 'da safety zone."

The Big Boss's eyes flashed wildly. "Well, take us there then, you monsturdly moron."

King Rubb clenched his teeth. Nobody had ever spoken to him like that in his entire life and he made a mental note to make sure that when he killed the furry little pink punk, that it be long, slow, and painful.

Chapter 15

MARION AND MERP

"Quiet," hissed Jagger Nazz, as the approaching voices became louder.

Bobbee still had her hand clamped over her mouth and Bettee, as usual, stood quietly beside his sister.

"Sorry, mister Nazz," said Bobbee.

Jagger pulled the satellite out of the main G.M.C. port and shoved it in Bobbee's hand.

"Don't lose that," he said. "Now come with me if you don't want to get caught."

He led them across the room to a back door and opened it as quietly as he could. They all stepped through and just as Jagger clicked the door closed behind them, voices burst forth into the main computer room.

Jagger raised a finger to his lips, indicating to the children to be quiet. The room they'd entered was an office of some sort and a desk sat in the middle of it. Upon the desk lay a large rectangular panel.

Bobbee pointed at the panel and mouthed the words 'what's that?' Jagger pointed to the ceiling and the rectangular opening in it convinced Bobbee that it was the way her new companion had gotten inside.

The thief reached over and grabbed Bettee from beneath his armpits. By now, the voices were so close they could make out most of what was being said.

"...from in here," said one voice.

"I didn't hear anything," said another. "Everything looks all right to me."

"Are you saying I'm hearing things?"

"I'm not saying you're hearing things. Relax. Take a chill pill bro'. I'm just sayin', maybe you heard the radio or somethin'."

Jagger pushed Bettee up into the opening and reached down and grabbed Bobbee next. Within seconds, she was scrambling up through the hole and sitting next to her brother.

"...tell me I heard the radio, 'cause I know what I heard. Wasn't no radio. It was a kid or somethin'. And it came from in here."

"Did you check the office?"

"No, not yet."

The footsteps began approaching the office. Jagger Nazz quickly grabbed the ceiling panel and passed it up to Bobbee and Bettee, who both held onto it tightly. Then, all in one motion and with speed that amazed both the young Sirians, he jumped up on the table, grabbed the edge of the opening, and pulled himself up and through the hole. He grabbed the panel from the two kids and slid it into place, just as the owners of the two voices entered the room.

"Dude, you're so paranoid. There's nobody here. See."

The owner of the first voice flicked on the light. "I still think we should write a report."

"Dude, what for? So Carb can freak on us and tell us everything we did wrong? I don't think so. There's nobody here. Let's go."

Jagger and the two young Sirians held their breath as they awaited the decision of the owner of the first voice.

After an unbelievably uncomfortable pause, it said, "Oh all right, let's go. I guess everything's fine. But if it turns out that someone broke into the main computer lab and stole a buncha files, you're takin' the rap for it."

"Oh, knock it off dude..." The voices trailed off into a near distant murmur.

The three intruders let out three heavy sighs of relief.

"Well, that was a little too close," said Jagger, "but everything's okay now. You kids wanna get out of here?"

"Yes please," said Bobbee.

Bette nodded his head.

"Good, let's go then."

They had climbed into a ventilation duct and Jagger now led them, on hands and knees, down the cramped little tunnel, looking over his shoulder occasionally to make sure that his new junior companions were still with him.

The air was stale and had the faint odour of gasoline. After a while, Bobbee and Bettee both began to feel slightly light headed. Following a long labyrinth of twists and turns they reached a 'T' junction and Jagger Nazz stopped. Beside him lay a large black duffel bag.

"Which way Mister Nazz?" asked Bobbee

"Neither," he replied, reaching over and pulling the bag toward him. He unzipped it, reached inside, and pulled out a small drill. This he pressed into the wall in front of him until he'd removed a handful of screws. When he was finished, he put the drill back in the bag and removed the wall panel. A gust of warm wind blew his long red, curly hair, back and over his shoulders. He slid to the left side and beckoned to the Sirians to move forward, while at the same time, motioning for them to pull their face masks on.

Bobbee did so and reached the opening first, stuck her head through to get a look, then quickly pulled it back.

"We're up high," she said, starting to feel queasy.

"Afraid of heights?" asked Jagger, while donning his own artificial breathing system.

"Not until now." Bobbee slid over and put her back against the solid panel to the right of the opening.

Bettee slid his own mask up onto his face, crawled forward and peered through the opening. He smiled, looked at Jagger, and pointed down questioningly.

"Yep," replied Jagger. "We're goin' down."

Bobbee looked at Jagger. "What do you mean we're going down? How, in Sirius, are we supposed to do that?"

Jagger reached into the duffel bag and pulled out a body harness of some sort. He slipped it on and pulled another gizmo out of the bag. It looked like a gun only it had a large thick disc stuck to the side of it. He gestured for the kids to stay back and shot the gun toward the passageway they'd just crawled up. Out of the gun shot a 'Y' shaped cord, each end capped with barbed arrows. Both ends dug into either side of the passageway and Jagger pulled tightly on it to make sure the cord was secure. He then attached the gun to his harness and grabbed the duffel bag.

"Get in the bag," he instructed the two young Sirians.

They both complied without question and climbed in. There was an array of objects in the bag but, by shuffling around, they were both able to sit somewhat comfortably inside it. Jagger reached over, zipped up the bag, and ducked his head through the looped handles so that he had a Sirian on either side of his head.

"Hold on," he said.

Bobbee and Bettee both wrapped an arm around Jagger's neck and, before they had a chance to protest, the thief fell backwards through the opening.

At first, Bobbee thought for sure they'd fall to their deaths. They were eleven stories up and were dropping one story every five seconds. Jagger jogged his boots down the side of the building so as not to crush the children between him and the wall.

The cord reeled out above them and Bobbee was careful not to scream, though she really wanted to. Bettee, on the other hand, seemed to be enjoying himself, as the wind gusted through his hair and pushed his antennas back across his head.

No sooner had they dropped out of the building than they had landed safely on the ground. Jagger clicked a button on the gun attached to his chest, releasing the cable. He bent down until the duffel bag was on the ground and pulled his head back through the loops. The children unzipped themselves and crawled out of the sack. Jagger picked up his bag of tricks and slung it over his back.

"Where are you kids parked," he asked.

"In the alley," Bobbee replied.

"Me too. Let's go."

They were at the side of the building and only had to run a short distance before they reached the alley. Bobbee felt a sense of relief as they approached the bus. Jagger Nazz, however, had stopped and was looking around, as if he'd lost something.

"What's wrong Mister Nazz," said Bobbee.

"I swear I parked it right here," he said.

"What?"

"My cruiser. It's not here. I think maybe I got towed."

"You got towed?" questioned Bobbee.

"That's not good at all. I can't believe I got towed." He looked up at the bus. "How come you guys didn't get towed?"

Bobbee shrugged. "I don't know, just lucky I guess."

Suddenly, the sound of approaching sirens could be heard in the distance.

Jagger paced back and forth across the alley. "Not good. This is not good."

"Mister Nazz, can I say something," said Bobbee.

"What," said Jagger, while continuing to pace.

"You could always come with us. I mean, you don't have to, but we could use some help finding our parents."

Jagger stopped his pacing and stared at Bobbee and Bettee. "Well, I guess it's all part of the same cause isn't it. I mean, your parents were sold into slavery so..."

The sirens were getting louder.

"No time," he said. "I'll come with you. I'll come back for my cruiser later. I just got the darn thing, and I'm not about to lose it now."

The three of them ran up to the bus and Bobbee pushed the satellite into the entrance panel.

"I hope you kids know what you're doing," said Miron, suddenly, "because I'm not accepting responsibility for picking up some drifter who thinks he can just..."

"Oh shut up Miron," said Bobbee before climbing into the bus. They reached the cockpit in under a minute and soon the bus was shooting out of the alley and up into the night sky of Fuelitia, just as the police cruisers pulled up to the front of the building.

"Yo' boss, you really think this is such a good idea?" asked Blurtch as he marched down the corridor, Bossentical's rock blaster jabbing into the small of his back.

"Silence, traitor," replied the Big Boss. "You don't have the right to call me 'boss' anymore."

Blurtch walked begrudgingly behind Geeno and King Rubb. It was necessary for Geeno to lead the way, because every now and then, a monsturdle would come hurtling down the corridor toward them. Just before the monsturdle was about to knock them all down like bowling pins, Geeno would bring his fist down on the shelled creatures head, knocking it dizzy and causing it to become somewhat disoriented as the group carefully crept their way around it.

This activity continued to repeat itself, until they finally came to a stop.

"Dis is it," said King Rubb.

"Where, what, how, whom," demanded Bossentical.

King Rubb squatted down and ran his palms across some cracks in the floor and everyone heard a light clicking noise. The king grabbed hold of a floor panel and pulled up on it, revealing a hidden tunnel beneath.

"Down dere," he said.

"Get in there then," insisted Bossentical. "All of you. I haven't got all day." He jabbed his blaster repeatedly into Blurtch's back causing the space goblin to spin around and give him a 'you're gonna pay for that' look.

"Ooooo, whatcha gonna do Blurtchy-poo? Huh? Whatcha gonna do? Get in the hole."

Blurtch climbed down into the tunnel after Geeno and King Rubb, followed by Bossentical, who, still in the Fuelition space suit, lowered effortlessly in behind them. He didn't even think to replace the floor panel they'd removed to enter the passageway.

When they finally reached the end of the tunnel, Bossentical had already begun to grow impatient and was urging the others to move faster. They stood in front of the giant, safety zone apparatus and stared at it like children who were about to climb to the top of their first jungle gym.

"C'mon," urged Bossentical. "Get your butts movin' over your monsturdle hurdles or you won't have any butts left to get movin'."

Geeno led the entourage through the maze of pipes carefully avoiding the ones that were electrically charged and subtly indicated to Blurtch that he ought to do the same. Bossentical brushed against many but, due to the nature of his Fuelition mining suit, did not get electrocuted.

They reached the end of the obstruction and slowly entered the field of floating magneticals.

"These are your defense mechanisms?" Bossentical taunted. "What a load of garbage. What good is a giant jungle gym and a bunch of oversized floating marbles against one such as I?"

"Dey ain't' activated 'cause Flurp know me 'n Geeno are here. If dey was turned on, non 'o us would be breathin' right now."

"Ooo, sounds simply awful," said Bossentical.

They reached the end of the levitating mine field and arrived at the pool of Submergaturds. They could now see the hovering dock, which continued to float about twenty feet above the water. Flurp walked up to the glass wall and stared down at them. He had a hands free intercom around his head and he began speaking into the microphone.

"Yo, King, you okay," he asked.

"Ya. Freako here ain't done nuttin' yet," replied King Rubb.

Bossentical hovered right up behind Rubb and jabbed his blaster into the King's back. "I don't respond positively to name calling, all right. So everyone better be nice and do as I say or rubberneck here and his pal no neck are gonna get blasted all over the floor. Now, have you got what I'm looking for?"

Flurp disappeared for a moment and soon returned with Jethro and the others.

"Excellent. Bring them to me."

Flurp disappeared again and soon the sound of grinding gears rang out inside the safety zone as the bridge began to extend out and down to where the Big Boss hovered.

The bridge locked into place and Flurp began leading the Sirians down it.

"Sorry about dis,' he said, "But it's my King. I really don have much of a choice."

"Isn't there anything you can do," asked Val, the fear in her voice quite obvious. She reached out and grabbed Seth's hand, squeezing it tightly.

"Maybe," said Flurp. "But we gotta wait 'n see. Can't do nuttin' ta' jeopardize 'da King."

"Mr. Sirius," said Bossentical as Jethro stepped off the bridge and onto solid ground. "So nice of you to join us. Not only are you a talented musician but you're quite talented at staying alive. Very impressive."

"I don't care what you think," said Jethro. "You're not getting my talent. Or anyone else's for that matter."

"Oh, but I am, Mr. Sirius. And there isn't a thing you can do to stop me, I'm afraid."

Bossentical poked King Rubb between the shoulder blades with the tip of his blaster. "I need a ship, rubber neck. Where can I find one?"

Geeno growled at Bossentical again. "Ya got no right ta' speak ta' 'da Kin' like dat. 'Ya better knock it off."

"Or what," taunted Bossentical again. "You'll tickle me to death with those patches of hair stuck to your face. Perhaps you might throw your hat at me. Or perhaps you'll shock me to death and put on a decent suit. Shut up and do as you're told or I'll turn those two arms on your back into nubs."

Geeno sneered but kept his mouth shut. If there was one useful skill his father had taught him, it was patience.

"Now get over here my little band on the run." Bossentical gestured with his gun for the Sirians to get in front of him. He turned on King Rubb once more. "Now, Rubber Neck, get in front and lead me to a ship. And no funny stuff or I start splitting skulls with this rock blaster, which would be quite fitting seeing as how all your heads are full of rocks."

Vack had a difficult time seeing and hearing what was going on. He had chosen to remain just inside the tunnel entrance because anywhere else would have left him in the open. He watched as King Rubb led the group back through the apparatus. A flicker of movement caught his eye in the distance and he was able to make out the forms of two monsturds who had remained on the floating dock. He made a mental note of their presence and began zooming back down the tunnel, controlling the speed of his journey with the controls of the Fuelition mining suit.

He guessed that Bossentical would want a ship and, seeing as he'd already been to the shipyard, continued down the passageway past the missing floor panel where they'd entered the tunnel. He was pretty sure that he was in the same tunnel that had originally led him to the shipyard, and sure enough, he was able to push himself through the hole. He continued on down the tunnel until he reached the shipyard and began searching for a decent hiding place.

King Rubb was the first to enter the shipyard and was followed by Geeno, Flurp, Blurtch, Jethro, Seth, Val, Quasar, and finally Bossentical Distort.

"Excellent," said the Big Boss. "Once I choose a ship, we shall be on our way." He chose a large industry cruiser, designed for speed and endurance and motioned to the young Sirians to move toward it.

"As for the rest of you," he said, "I'm sorry, but I'm going to have to eliminate you. You must understand that I can't have anyone following me."

King Rubb raised his hands. "Hey, hold on a minute dere chump, we done evertin you asked. Dere's no need ta' go 'an shoot us."

"Don't talk to me of need, 'chum'," hollered Bossentical. "I've spent my entire life dealing with the reality of unfulfilled needs and now that I'm so close to achieving my ultimate goal, I'm not going to make any mistakes and, unfortunately for you, allowing you to live would be a big mistake."

Bossentical raised the rock blaster and aimed it at King Rubb.

Vack watched as the Big Boss finished his speech and raised his blaster. Just as the ex-collector was about to jump out and shoot the lunatic, the sound of laser guns rang out in the shipyard and Bossentical's rock blaster was blown from his hands.

"Noooooooooo," he screamed, spinning around in an effort to locate who was responsible for screwing up his plans this time. That was his first mistake, because it provided Geeno with the opportunity to reach out and wrap two meaty hands around Bossentical's neck. The pressure caused the suit's helmet to shoot off and it went straight up in the air. On the way back down its trajectory altered slightly and it landed with a loud crack on top of Geeno's head, knocking him down and causing him to let go of his prey.

Bossentical, intent on not allowing himself to be throttled once again, zoomed out of the way just as King Rubb made a jump for him. More laser blasts rang out and the Big Boss now located their source. The two monsturds that had accompanied Flurp and the Sirians to the safety zone were currently unloading a laser frenzy in the Big Boss's general direction. Bossentical scooped up his rock blaster and began returning their fire.

King Rubb managed to shake Geeno back into consciousness and the two of them crossed the shipyard to join their monsturd mates.

"Take 'em down," screamed King Rubb.

"We're tryin'," hollered one of the monsturds.

The battle went on for quite some time and Vack decided that it was a perfect opportunity for him to sneak the kids on board a ship and get them to safety. He worked his way around a few ships and zoomed under the industry cruiser, still hovering a foot off the ground in his mining suit. He pulled his helmet off and began shouting at the Sirians. He could barely hear himself over the din of battle that continued to occur.

It wasn't until he was a few feet behind the kids that they finally heard his calls.

"Jethro," he screamed.

They were hiding behind the cruiser's landing gear in an effort to avoid being gunned down and Jethro spun around at the sound of his name being called out.

"Vack?" he shouted.

The rest of the Sirians turned and looked at the face that had abandoned them.

"What's he doing here," shouted Quasar.

"Look, I'm sorry I was a jerk," shouted Vack. "But I'm here to get you kids outta here. Now come on."

They all hesitated, distrustful looks in their eyes.

"Come on you guys," shouted Vack. "I said I was sorry."

A laser blast exploded above their heads blowing a large chunk out of the landing gear and showering their heads with sparks. It didn't take any more than that to convince the kids and they ran after Vack. He led them to a beat up looking ship that had, obviously, seen better days.

"Get in," he yelled.

They all looked doubtfully at his choice.

"Out of all the space crafts you could have chosen," said Seth, "you go and pick a school bus?"

"It's not a school bus," hollered Vack. "Trust me. It'll outrun every ship in this yard. Get in! There's no time to argue."

The young Sirians silently agreed that, indeed, there was no time to argue. Vack stood in the doorway urging them with a wave of his hand to enter. They filed in one at a time and Vack quickly closed the door once they were all in. He jumped into the driver's seat and powered up the bus. It hummed instantly into life and he didn't hesitate to get it off the ground.

It rose steadily and straight into the air. The kids pressed their faces against the side windows in order to get a better view of the battle down below. Laser fire was in the process of destroying most of the ships and Bossentical was now in retreat. King Rubb and Geeno had found their own weapons and were adding to the other two monsturds' onslaught.

Bossentical must have heard the escaping ship because he turned and looked up. He had managed to retrieve his rock blaster and was now aiming it at the rising shuttle bus, but his effort was acted on too late. Just as he was about to fire his weapon, the bus breached the landing entrance and sped off into the sky beyond and disappeared from sight.

The Big Boss let out a howl of rage and fired his weapon off into the sky anyways. This temporary diversion did not bode well for the Big Boss for, just as he turned and was about to begin firing on the monsturds again, Blurtch, who seemed to come out of nowhere, stepped into the Boss's line of sight and punched Bossentical right in the nose. There was a bone cracking snap as the mining suit clad talent stealer fell to the ground, unconscious. The monsturds ceased their firing and approached the space goblin, who was standing over his former boss and grinning from ear to ear.

"Nice one," said Geeno, who was the first to reach the scene.

Blurtch turned to the monsturd still grinning. "I never liked him anyway."

"We are so outta here," said Vack as he steered the bus up and above the crystal forest. Once again, the Sirians found themselves looking out the windows at the landscape below. They were rewarded with their first view of the monsturd giants. The two who had been involved in a fight when Geeno had first flown in were still engaged in battle and were rolling around on the ground creating a huge dust storm. As Vack steered the shuttle bus through a dust cloud one of the giants managed to escape the grasp of the other and stood up on its hind legs directly in the bus's path. The vehicle shot through the cloud and if it weren't for Vack's quick reflexes, would have slammed into the mountain of monsturd face that appeared in front of it.

Vack pulled up on the controls causing the bus to fly up alongside the bridge of the giant's nose. It was enormous and made the bus look like a mere insect. Vack steered up and over the monsturd's forehead and cut through its forest of hair, arriving safely on the other side. The giant hardly noticed them as they sped off into the distance behind it.

"Well, that was a close one, eh," said Vack.

Nobody answered him. They were all too busy clutching the sides of their seats, knuckles white and faces pale.

Jethro looked over at Seth. "I think I've had about enough of this adventure stuff."

"You can say that again," replied Seth.

"Oh, what I would give just to be able to lie on the couch all day and think about nothing. This adventure stuff was way less stressful when it was fantasy in my head."

"I hate to be the one to say it," added Val, "but I actually miss my mom."

"Funny how that works eh," said Quasar. "You spend so much of your life trying to get away from your parents, but then when they're gone, you do everything you can to get them back."

"I can't believe what we've been through already. It's only been, what, a week. I feel like we're in a movie or something," said Jethro.

Just then, a lasso of light shot up from behind a mountain of rock and wrapped itself around the shuttle bus. Vack struggled to regain control, but his efforts were futile.

"Oh, what now," hollered Val.

"Hold on kids," said Vack, over his shoulder. "We're being pulled down."

"Okay, enough already," said Quasar. "How many bizarre incidents can happen to a bunch of kids. I swear we've had more in the last week than most kids do in their entire life."

The shuttle bus slammed into the ground causing everyone to lurch forward. Vack un-strapped himself and reached back and detached the rock blaster that was attached to the jet pack. He clicked it on and slowly headed for the side door. He reached over and touched the entrance panel causing the door to shoot open. Light and fresh air pushed their way into the bus but he made no effort to leave choosing instead, to stand his ground. The Sirians un-strapped themselves, crept up behind their pilot and peered around his robes. They could see the desert on the outside but no sign of their attacker.

"What's that squeaking noise," said Seth, interrupting the silence.

Everyone strained their ears to try and hear what Seth was talking about. They soon heard it. It belonged to a small, cute, fuzzy creature that was slowly marching up the landing platform. Quasar leaned over and held her hand out to the creature, as if she were feeding it a treat.

"Aw," she said, "wookut at du cute widdle, fuzzy, wuz....."

"Quasar," snapped Vack. "Don't...say...another...word. Slowly back away from it. Slowly."

Quasar froze, shocked by Vack's apparent overreaction. She stood up slowly and began backing away.

"What's the problem," she whispered to Vack.

"That little creature," answered Vack, "is responsible for probably fifty percent of the universe's population control."

"Huh?" Quasar replied.

"That little monster is a fuzzy tendril creeper. Possibly the most dangerous creature in the history of dangerous creatures."

"Oh, come on," said Quasar. "How could such a tiny little..."

"Quasar!" Vack snapped. "Trust me. I know what I'm talking about."

The creature stopped a few feet in front of them and began to growl quietly. It was the kind of growl that sent uncomfortable tingles up the back of the spine. Vack bent slowly down and placed his rock blaster, cautiously, on the ground and released his grip. He rose back up, careful to keep his hands in the air.

"It's okay little buddy," he said. "We mean no harm. And none of us are going to make any comments regarding how adorably cute and cuddly you are, all right."

The creature tensed and the volume of its growl seemed to increase at the mention of the words 'cute' and 'cuddly'. It was the sound of approaching footsteps that caused the creature to stop growling.

"Only the infamous Vack Hume would know better than to call a fuzzy tendril creeper cute, to its face," said a voice. Its owner stepped into view.

"Marion," said Vack.

"Nice to see you again Vack. It's been a while, hasn't it."

"Yes it has. And, to tell you the truth, I could probably handle it being a while longer."

"Oh, come now Vack. You love me. Admit it," she said with a grin.

"I love the absence of you, I suppose."

"Vack, Vack, the collecting hack, always had a knack for witty comebacks."

"What do you want Marion?"

"Same thing you want."

"And what would that be?"

"Your little collection there," she said, pointing at the Sirians.

Vack looked down at the youngsters, who were still clutching his robe tightly.

"You can't have them," he said.

"Oh really, and I suppose you're going to stop me this time."

"If I have to, yes."

"Vack, when are you ever going to learn? History has proven that you're no match for me."

Vack suddenly reached down for the rock blaster lying at his feet but before he could wrap his fingers around it, Marion shouted out.

"Merp, now!"

The fuzzy tendril creeper instantly transformed right before Vack and the Sirians' very eyes. Not only did its size increase ten fold, but hundreds of thin, whip-like vines sprung forth from its body, shot out, and wrapped around Vack before he had a chance to pick up his weapon. The vines lifted him off the ground and wrapped themselves so tightly around him that even the thought of struggling was squeezed into extinction. A bunch more individual vines whipped out and grabbed the four Sirians, who struggled as best they could.

"Lemmee go ya' creep," snapped Val.

Marion, without saying a word, turned around, reached into her pocket, pulled out a device of some sort, and pointed it into the desert.

With the push of a button, a ship, parked directly in front of them, suddenly materialized before their very eyes. A door opened and a landing platform stretched out toward them. Marion turned back toward her captives. The Sirians were still struggling, vines wrapped firmly around their arms and pulling them toward the ship.

"Merp, take them inside, but leave this one out here with me for a moment," said Marion, pointing at Vack.

The large tangle of vines that now represented Merp, moved up the landing platform with the Sirians, leaving Vack wrapped and floating ten feet above the desert ground.

"Oh ya, I almost forgot, Merp." Marion pointed at the shuttle bus. "Destroy their ship."

Another large grouping of vines shot out and attacked the bus. Within seconds the entire craft had been completely dismantled and lay in a big heap of scrap metal in the sand.

Merp disappeared inside the ship and Marion turned to Vack.

"Vack, Vack, Vack, Vack, Vack," she said. "What a sorry sight you are."

Only Vack's head remained uncovered by vines and he shook it slowly.

"You know Marion," he said, "I don't think you've ever done an honest days work in your life."

"Oh, come now Vack. You're not still calling this work honest, now are you? You collect the contracts and I collect from you. We're no different, actually."

"Come on Marion, let them go. They're just kids."

"Oh, and I suppose that's what you were on your way to do. Let them go. Ha."

"I wasn't collecting them, I was rescuing them."

"Gimmee a break, Vack."

"C'mon Marion, I'm telling the truth. Bossentical is here. Why would I take them from him if I'd already given them to him."

"I'm rendezvousing with Bossentical at the mining colony."

"What? Is that what he told you? C'mon Marion. Face it. He was using us as back up. He never intended on paying us. Otherwise, why would he come after the contract himself. He's hired a Gulterian to help him."

"You always were a good storyteller, Vack," said Marion, turning around and walking up the landing platform of her ship.

"Marion," screamed Vack. "Marion. C'mon! You can't just leave me here."

Marion ignored Vack's pleas and disappeared into her ship. The landing platform retracted and just before the door closed entirely, the vines suddenly let go of their prey and shot back into the ship. Vack hit the desert floor rump first and looked up as the ship rose up above him. Sand blew all around him and he had to cover his eyes to protect them. He managed to squint and catch a glimpse of the ship shooting higher and higher into the sky and then disappear from view.

He sat and looked around. He was stranded in the middle of the giant territories on the Monsturd Planet with no means of transportation, no means of communication, and no food.

"A bit of a pickled slug I've gotten myself into," he said to himself as he looked out across the desert and watched the two quarreling giants working their way toward him.

CHAPTER 16

SLAVERY AND STINKY CAGES

Marion didn't say much during the trip. Merp had resumed his original size and shape and watched over the Sirians as they huddled together in a corner of the ship.

"Yo, Naker," she said. "How much longer until we reach this mining colony?"

Naker was Marion's central computer.

"About two minutes," he said.

"Great, pilot us in to the main office, and we'll get these prisoners registered while we're waiting for our employer to arrive."

"No problem," replied Naker.

The ship approached the meteorite from behind and flew in over its jagged, rocky mountaintops. The colony itself was mostly underground. Only the giant drilling machines could be seen from the surface. On top of one of the drillers sat a tower with landing pads protruding from it. Marion's ship landed on the topmost platform as a vacuum-sealed tube reached out and attached itself to the side of the ship.

Inside, Marion commanded her prisoners onto their feet and instructed Merp to follow them out and into the tower. They exited her ship and walked through the tube before reaching a door, which they entered. Inside was the chamber of a vertical drive lifter.

"Main office," commanded Marion.

The kids felt themselves shooting straight down and had soon entered the heart of the meteorite. The drive lifter came to a halt and opened its door. Marion stepped out first and a menacing growl from Merp encouraged the children to follow her.

They entered a large office and in the center of the office sat a desk. A fuelition dressed in black coveralls sat behind it and looked up at them as they entered.

Marion approached the fuelition.

"Can I help you," he asked.

"Ya, I've got some slaves to register under the name, Bossentical Distort."

The fuelition picked up a scanning pen off the desk and waved it in the air in front of him. A holographic computer screen appeared in front of him and he penned a few commands into it. A picture of the Big Boss appeared on the screen. Below his picture was printed his name and below that, some words that read:

Number of Slaves Sold: 162,421.

Below that, were listed all the names, one at a time. Every single one of them was an entertainer of some sort.

Reading backwards was not one of Jethro's more acute skills, but he was good enough at it to recognize some of the famous names. He nudged Seth with an elbow.

"You see that?" he said.

"Ya, I get it now," replied Seth. "He's kidnapping artists and entertainers, stealing their talent, freezing them and then selling them as slaves."

Jethro's thought processes had, actually, only gotten as far as the kidnapping artists and entertainers part, but Seth's analogy made a lot of sense and Jethro merely nodded his head knowingly as if he'd already worked it all out in his mind as well.

"How many to register," asked the fuelition.

"Four," replied Marion.

The fuelition leaned over to take at look at the Sirians. "A little young aren't they?" He asked.

"Trust me," said Marion, "they're much older than they appear."

"I can't believe you're selling us into slavery," said Jethro.

Marion looked over her shoulder at the young Sirian. "I'm not. I'm just the delivery girl. It's the Big Boss that's selling you. You'll work the mines until he arrives."

'Work the mines.' Jethro didn't like the sound of that and from the various looks on their faces, neither did his friends.

"Is my ship okay where it's parked?" Marion asked.

The fuelition shook his head. "No, you'll have to move it around back. There's a visitor lot back there, but you need a pass." He reached into a drawer in the front of the desk and pulled out a small, palm sized, disc. "Here ya' go."

Marion reached out and grabbed the pass then turned and walked back toward the vertical drive lifter.

As she walked past the Sirians, she looked at Jethro. "Sorry about this Mr. Sirius, but you know how it is. Everyone's gotta make a living somehow."

"Where have I heard that one before? You guys must have a manual that you memorize or something," he said.

Marion entered the drive lifter and disappeared from view as the door closed in front of her.

"Security," said the fuelition, suddenly.

The Sirians' attention was diverted to a door opening behind the fuelition. Two large, burly looking Gulterian space goblins emerged and moved toward Jethro and his friends.

"Oh great," said Seth. "Not more of these guys."

"That's girls, chump," said one of the goblins.

"Helgump. Hildump. Take these four slaves down below and get them trained. And make sure they're not damaged. The owner still needs them before he sells them to us."

Helgump and Hildump moved toward the kids, arms outstretched.

"What do you mean, 'owner'," cried Val. "Nobody owns us. We own ourselves."

The fuelition laughed. "You are the property of one Bossentical Distort, whether legally or illegally acquired, it makes no difference to us. We are merely in the business of purchasing slaves. We feel no need to moralize about it."

Val looked at Quasar as Helgump wrapped an arm around her waist and picked her up. "What in Sirius, did that one eyed mouth head just say?"

Quasar, who'd been picked up by Helgump's other arm, just shrugged a reply. Hildump scooped up Jethro and Seth and carried them off through the doorway. Helgump followed, Quasar and Val tucked tightly under each armpit.

They entered another vertical drive lifter and, once again, the children felt themselves engaged in a downward motion. Val, who'd had about enough of drive lifters, suddenly felt her stomach turn.

"I think I'm gonna puke," she said.

"I'm not falling for that one," said Helgump, tightening her grip around Val's waist. It was just enough pressure to bring Val's monsturd meal shooting back up and out her open mouth. It sprayed down, thoroughly covering Helgump's feet.

The space goblin immediately let go of both the girls.

"Ah, sick," said Helgump kicking her feet and trying to flick the refuse off.

It flicked off, all right, but one particular glob of vomit slid off her big toe, sailed through the air, and hit Hildump square in the eye. She, of course, let go of Seth and Jethro immediately and reached for her face.

"My eye!" she wailed, sticking her thumb into her eye socket and scooping out the mess.

The drive lifter came to a sudden halt and Helgump and Hildump retrieved their captives. The door opened and the two space goblins stepped out into the heart of the mining colony. They were in a humongous cave of solid rock and all around them were platforms, pulleys, carts, and every form of mining activity imaginable. Roofless tunnels spread out in every direction and were covered with black, partially transparent, nets. All sorts of different alien races slaved away, digging into hard mounds of dirt with shovels, and chopping into unrelenting walls of rock with pick axes. Some slaves were huge and muscular and operated giant electric drills designed for blasting holes in the sides of the cave. Others were short and skinny and climbed into these holes with flashlights, searching for valuable rocks.

Though the site of thousands of slaves working in the mine was deeply disturbing to the young Sirians, there was something strangely beautiful about the setting. The main stone mined was cosmic jade, and the unique thing about that particular rock is that it glows in the dark, giving off a dazzling, green florescence. The entire cavern emanated the warm, green glow and the Sirians stared, bedazzled, at the wondrous sight.

"C'mon, move it shorties," grumbled Hildump, pushing the kids forward, obviously still upset about getting vomit in her eye.

They began marching on a pathway that curved along the outside edge of the cavern. It angled suddenly into the center so that on either side of them was a complete drop off. They seemed to be right smack dab in the middle of things. Below them and all around them worked the slaves. Directly above them, about a hundred feet up, hung hundreds of spherical cages, which were attached to the cavern ceiling with long, thick chains. Inside these cages was all different manner of alien slaves, looking rather unhappy with themselves. A platform ran through the middle of them, its purpose to provide footing for the guards.

Helgump put her hand to her mouth and curled her fingers around her lips, creating a tube shape with her hand. She began throat singing, her head pointed at the platform and spheres above. The singing, apparently, garnered a response as one of the spherical cages began lowering toward them. The chain on which it hung creaked, strainfully, as it unwound. When it reached the end of its journey, the cage clanked noisily on the path in front of them. It was made of interlocking iron bars stained black from years of use. The floor was made of a rickety, old, wooden platform, covered with filthy burlap blankets that looked like they hadn't been washed, ever.

Val turned her head away and pinched her nose with her fingers as she detected a some-what foul odour emitting from the confines of the cage. Helgump swung the creaking cage door open and Hildump began shoving the young Sirians toward it.

Val resisted and tried to scramble away. "I'm not getting in there. It reeks."

Hildump grabbed her by the scruff of the neck and tossed her, effortlessly, into the cage. Val landed on her knees with a loud thud and let out a small cry. Seth, without thinking, jumped into the cage in one leap and ran to her side. Jethro and Quasar, who opted not to be thrown, climbed in after their friends.

Helgump laughed as she slammed the door shut behind them.

"Think of it as payback for puking on me and my sister," she said, cocking her head back and signaling the guards above with another bout of throat singing.

The cage left the ground and rose steadily into the cavern heights. One thing was for certain, they definitely had a fantastic view of the entire mining operation. They soon noticed that some of the tunnels were much larger than they'd first anticipated. Large burly looking vehicles with big studded tires drove in and out of these larger tunnels and the Sirians all gasped in unison as a long, sleek, black mining train shot out of one of the largest exits. Hundreds of slaves leapt out of it and went to work at loading it with thousands of pounds of cosmic jade. Once the train had been fully loaded, the slaves climbed on top of the cargo and it shot back through its tunnel toward an unknown destination.

"Where do you suppose that train's going," Quasar asked her friends.

Seth, who immediately knew what she was thinking, jumped up and bounded to the edge of the cell.

"Betcha anything it's sending its cargo to a loading bay. Did you guys notice it came back empty," he said.

"Ya, duh," replied Quasar. "Why do you think I said something about it in the first place."

Seth looked at her. "I thought you were asking."

"I wasn't asking. I was just pointing out the fact that it was obviously going somewhere to unload its cargo."

"Then why'd you ask where we supposed it was going?"

"Because...I don't know. Because adults are always asking obvious questions I guess. Shut up Seth, it doesn't matter."

"Okay, okay, you two - pipe down," cut in Jethro. "The point is that it could possibly be an escape route."

"It'll never happen," said a voice that didn't belong to any of them.

They all looked in the direction the voice had come from and discovered a rotund looking alien in tattered, filthy clothing, squatting in the cage hanging next to them.

"Who're you," asked Jethro.

"M' name's Chucklee. Chucklee Brown. You kids must be new, eh?"

"Ya," said Jethro. "I guess so."

Chucklee shook his head. "Pretty sad state of affairs when they lettin' kids sold into slavery. Sad state of affairs."

"Are you new too," asked Quasar.

"Me? No, I bin here for years," said Chucklee. He held up his hands in display for them. His fingers were covered in thick calluses from tips to knuckles.

"I used ta' dream 'o bein' a famous musician with these fingers, but about all I ever had a chance to use them for was bustin' rock. My own fault, really."

The Sirians, happy to have met an insider, crawled to the edge of their cage so they could hear Chucklee's story.

"What do you mean by 'your own fault'," asked Jethro.

Chucklee shooed them away with a hand gesture. "Baah, you kids don't wanna hear 'bout my problems."

"Sure we do," said Val. "What else have we got to do while hanging a hundred feet up in the air in a round cage, awaiting a life of slavery?"

Chucklee laughed, a deep hearty, wonderful laugh that made all the kids smile.

"You make me laugh, girl," he said between chuckles. "Laughing is a rarity in this place. I haven't laughed in months."

"Well, it's about time then isn't it," Val replied. "You've got a great laugh."

"Thanks," replied Chucklee. "You kids seem different than the rest of the slaves I've seen come and go. Somehow you appear more, I don't know...positive, I guess."

"That's 'cause we ain't stickin' around to find out what it feels like to break rock with our bare hands," said Quasar.

"I hate to destroy your confidence," said Chucklee, "but no one's ever escaped the mines."

"Well, there's a first time for everything isn't there," said Jethro.

Chucklee had a curious glint in his eye as he looked the kids up and down. "Where are you kids from?"

"Sirius," they all said.

"Sirius," he repeated. "Never heard of it."

"Different galaxy," said Seth.

"Well, what's a bunch of kids doing in a mining camp in a different galaxy? How'd you kids get here?"

"It's a long story," said Jethro. "To make it short, our parents are in a famous rock 'n roll band and were on tour when, one day, they just up and disappeared. Our ship's trans-galactic navigation computer systems are inopperative due to a lack of proper security clearance, so we can't seem to figure out how to get home. You wouldn't believe what we've gone through since our parents disappeared. We've been mostly busy just trying to stay alive."

Chucklee stared at them. He had a very kind and compassionate twinkle in his eyes. "Well, around here, it can take up to a week for them to run your qualifications through the system and find you jobs. I'm on a medical break 'cause of my back, so I think we've go lots of time. Tell me your story and, if you're interested, I'll tell you mine."

CHAPTER 17

ESCAPE FROM Y2K50-90210

Jagger Nazz cruised across the meteorite landscape with his foot pressed down, hard, on the gas pedal of the burrower. His decision to help the young children find their parents was, he'd decided, a noble cause, and he was determined to not let them down.

His choice to not bring the two young Sirians had been made out of both a fear for their safety, as well as a need for speed. His skills and experience in getting himself in and out of places he wasn't supposed to be would only be slowed down with the presence of others.

The burrower careened around the corner of a large rock outcropping and Jagger pulled his foot off the gas and applied it to the brake as he came face to face with a large one story building. The temporary cloaking device he'd installed into the vehicle would shield him from detection, but he continued to maintain his sense of caution, regardless. As he slowly inched the burrower forward, he realized that the building looked like a warehouse of some sort. The drilling vehicle approached the front of the building and Jagger reached into his bag of tricks and pulled out his universal door opener remote control. Clicking it caused a large set of doors in the front of the building to slowly open, revealing a hangar bay of ships on the other side.

Jagger Nazz steered his vehicle into the hangar and clicked his remote control once again, causing the doors to close behind him. The hangar bay was dimly lit and he was driving up the middle of two neatly parked lines of ships. There didn't appear to be any life forms around and checking his life form detection gizmo revealed that, indeed, there were not.

He parked the cloaked burrower between two larger looking crafts and put on his breathing apparatus. There had been no airlock when he'd entered and he was not one to take chances. He grabbed his bag, strapped it to his back and, pushing the door open, climbed out of the vehicle. He quietly padded his way through the warehouse, carefully memorizing the number of ships he needed to pass in order to remember where he parked. He reached a door at the end of the building and entered.

The other side of the door revealed a long, well lit tunnel and Jagger jogged down it as quickly as possible. If he were caught unawares in such a bright environment, he would have an extremely difficult time explaining himself. As he moved down the passageway, he began to hear noises in the distance.

That is the sound of slavery, he thought to himself as he quickened his pace. The further along he got, the louder the sounds became until he finally reached an opening in the tunnel and stepped out into the midst of the central mining camp. It was humongous and there were slaves working all around him. He sneered and shook his head, disgusted by the sight of it all. He quickly began noting all possible escape routes, including the train tracks on the other side of the cave that led into a dark tunnel. Glancing up revealed the hanging spherical cages where, he knew, new recruits would be held. A giant stone column, surrounded by a spiral staircase, stood like a monolith to the right of the cages. He decided to make this his destination. If he was going to find the Sirian adults, it was as good a place to start as any.

Chucklee began his story at the very beginning: with his childhood.

"I never had much luck making friends," he began. "I was always very clumsy as a child and most kids seemed to find it quite easy to make fun of me. It's interesting how, in your youth, you're able to adapt to a constant state of ridicule. It became my only reality and no matter what I did to change it, it just seemed to get worse. I got called every name in the book. Upchucklee was their favourite, and I can't tell you how many times I got beat up."

"One day, I just decided that I was going to find something I was good at; something I could excel at that would impress the other children." He paused for a moment.

"So what did you find," asked Quasar.

Chucklee looked at her as if he were about to burst into tears.

"Nothin," he said.

"What do you mean nothing? You must have found something you were good at," said Val.

Chucklee shook his head. "No matter how hard I practiced, no matter how hard I worked, I just never got better at anything. It was almost as if I were cursed to fail at everything for my entire life. I developed a love of singing. Oh, how I loved to sing. I took lessons from the top vocal teacher in town and eventually she gave up on me and told me I was hopeless; that I ought to find a new hobby. She didn't understand that I'd already tried everything else and failed."

"I was devastated of course. Oh sure, I continued to sing, but it had to be confined to the privacy of my own home. I can't tell you how many times my neighbours banged on the walls demanding that I shut up."

"Eventually, after years of ridicule, I decided that if I was going to find something I was good at, it wouldn't be on my planet. So I left. I packed up what little belongings I had, hopped on a bus and went in search of my talent. I figured it had to be out there somewhere."

"I searched the entire galaxy and found nothing but more ridicule. No matter where I went, I'd make a complete mess of everything I tried. My travels eventually brought me to the streets of Fuelitia where I became homeless for a short while. I soon discovered that I wasn't even good at being homeless as the other street urchins chased me off the streets."

"At that point, I didn't think I could sink any lower. Then I discovered the Galactic Mining Coalition. I figured slavery was about as low as one could sink so I signed up."

"You mean you volunteered to become a slave," asked Jethro.

"What else was there to do? I've actually turned out to be a pretty good slave. I got a rock crusher placement after being here for a few months and have been doing it ever since. I guess I'm able to take out years of frustration and grief on helpless, undeserving rocks."

"Chucklee, that's the saddest story I've ever heard," said Quasar.

Chucklee merely shrugged. "Everyone's got a story, I guess."

"Crushing rock isn't the only thing you're good at," said a tiny voice from beneath the burlap blankets in Chucklee's cell.

A tiny little creature, about the size of his cellmate's big toe, climbed out from beneath the blankets, revealing himself to the young Sirians.

"Well, hello there," said Jethro.

"Chucklee, actually, has many gifts," said the little creature, who happened to look like a miniature version of the Slimacular space slug. Its slug-like appearance was mostly covered up with a tattered burlap sack for clothing. It's tiny, squashy tail, protruded from beneath the sack and wriggled as the creature spoke.

"Humbleness is one of Chucklee's major talents," the creature said.

"This is Boognerp," said Chucklee.

Boognerp nodded his head before continuing. "If it wasn't for Chucklee, most of the slaves in this colony wouldn't be alive today, including myself."

"What do you mean," asked Seth.

"Chucklee has the most unbelievable sense of hope you can possibly imagine. Unfortunately it's not in himself, but in others. He has the most remarkable ability to fill others full of an undeniable sense of hope and it's this feeling that has kept most of us alive."

"Chucklee, that's great," said Quasar.

As Chucklee shook his head defensively, Boognerp continued. "Chuck found me on the streets of Fuelitia where I had pretty much given up on life. My entire family had been stepped on and I was devastated beyond belief. I'd found a discarded box of salt in the alley behind an off-lander's restaurant and was about to jump in and end it all when Chuck here stumbled upon me and convinced me life was worth living."

"He then proceeded to sing a song meant to inspire me. Instead, it made me cover my ears, but it did get me thinking; life is meant to be lived, not discarded like yesterday's dirty socks. It's those nasty stains that you just can't ever seem to get out that build character and make you unique. Everything that happens to us in life teaches us something about ourselves. As long as we're open to the concept of learning, even if it's very painful, we will only benefit by blossoming as individuals. Life is a gift and meant to be enjoyed."

"All this I learned from Chuck. That's why I'm still here today and I just couldn't see myself not staying with him. Unfortunately, Chuck doesn't believe in his gifts. He truly, and sadly, doesn't believe he has any talent. How very wrong he is." Boognerp said the last sentence while looking directly at his companion.

Chucklee looked at the kids and shrugged. "He may be right, but it still doesn't change the fact that I want to be able to sing. It's easy for Boognerp to talk. He's got one of the most beautiful voices in the entire galaxy."

The Sirians all looked at tiny little Boognerp.

"You sing?" asked Val.

Boognerp then burst into a beautiful little tune. He did, indeed, possess a most wondrous voice. He carried the tune with the skill and confidence that most singers can only dream about. When he finished, they applauded their sincere gratitude. Jethro looked up and noted that, although Chucklee was applauding his miniature friend's vocal abilities, a small tear was streaming its way down his pudgy cheek. He quickly wiped it away, hoping no one had seen. When he met Jethro's gaze, he quickly turned his head away, ashamed of his physical display of emotion.

The problem with the mining colony was the openness of the cavern. The black nets that covered the slave maze would provide a certain amount of protection but Jagger Nazz soon discovered that concealing his presence was not going to be quite as easy as he'd first anticipated. He decided that if he was going to make his way around undetected, he was going to need a disguise. He stumbled across a slave, roughly his size, who had passed out from exhaustion, and within minutes Jagger was dressed in tattered rags. He left the slave lying in nothing but underwear, and stuffed his own clothes into his backpack, which he concealed beneath the filthy burlap shirt he'd put on. He grabbed the slave's pickaxe off the ground, and began making his way through the colony once again.

He looked like a hunchback with his pack bulging out from beneath his shirt, but it seemed to improve the authentic nature of his disguise. Most of the guards paid him no mind and if they did happen to glance his way, he'd begin picking away at the rock with his axe, performing in a slave like manner that seemed to satisfy the guards' curiosity.

He eventually made his way to the spiral stone staircase, which led to the slave cages. The giant stone column stretched from the floor to the ceiling and covered a distance of a few hundred feet. The staircase, itself, had been carved all around it and was bordered with an iron handrail. Though he felt uncomfortably conspicuous, Jagger began to climb the stairs, working his way around the stone column as naturally as he possibly could.

About halfway up he met a fuelition guard who was on his way down. The guard stopped and jabbed Jagger in the chest with a finger.

"You," he said. "Where do you think you're going?"

"Message for the cage masters," replied Jagger, bowing his head and being careful not to meet the guard's eyes. "Job placement for new slave recruits."

The guard eyed him suspiciously for a moment then said, "All right, on your way."

Jagger moved past the guard as quickly as possible and continued his climb. When he finally reached the slave cage level he breathed a sigh of relief and stepped out onto the platform. He eyed up the situation and counted four fuelition guards in total. If he was going to immobilize them without being discovered he was going to have to do it quietly.

Now, one thing that should be mentioned about Jagger Nazz is that he is an avid clotchee drinker. He finds it very difficult to make it through a day without consuming a minimum of ten cups a day. The only problem is that he can't stand black clotchee. He requires four heaping teaspoons of sugar and a healthy dose of cream to add to his favourite drink. To avoid being caught without his condiments, Jagger always carries a canister of both sugar and powdered cream with him everywhere he goes.

Though he desperately desired a clotchee fix, he set aside his craving and reached into his backpack, pulled out the canister of sugar, and loosened the top. He concealed it beneath his clothing and began to cross the platform slowly, so as not to alarm the guards. The fuelition closest to him looked up and held a hand out like a stop sign.

"Hold up there, slave," said the guard. "State your business."

"Message from down below," said Jagger. "Orders for the new slave recruits."

"All right, you may approach." The guard motioned for Jagger to move in closer.

Jagger slowly unscrewed the cap to the sugar canister and slipped both items into either pocket. As he moved within arms reach, the guard turned and pointed down the line of cages.

"Which ones," he asked.

With the guard's back turned to him Jagger made his move. He grabbed hold of the guard and reached around to cover the fuelition's mouth.

"Oww," hollered the guard.

Jagger cursed silently to himself and moved his hand off the guard's eye and slid up to the forehead to cover the mouth. The guard struggled to break free as Jagger reached around with his other hand and unscrewed the fuel cap in the fuelition's stomach. He reached back into his own pocket and pulled out the lidless canister of sugar. He swung it around the front of his struggling captive and drained a portion of its contents into the guard's fuel tank. He quickly shoved the canister back into his pocket and grabbed the fuel cap, which was dangling on a chain, and screwed it back into place.

The fuelition began to convulse, immediately reacting to the sugar that had just been dumped into his fuel tank. Within seconds he had completely seized up and fallen to the floor, unconscious. The second guard ran up to investigate and one by one Jagger managed to fool all four guards. Soon, they were all lying in a heap at his feet. He pulled the set of master keys loose from the first guard's belt and began moving down the platform in search of Sirian adults.

"What's goin' on," said Seth, as he and the others watched the guards jog past their cell.

"Some sort of problem with that slave over there," said Chucklee.

"You recognize him, Chuck?" asked Boognerp.

"Never seen him before."

"There's something oddly familiar about his face," noted Jethro.

"You're right," said Quasar. "Really familiar."

The slave had soon immobilized all four guards and was moving down the platform toward their cages. It was apparent that he was looking for something or someone in particular due to the fact that he was looking, intently, into each cage he passed. When he finally reached them, he stopped and stared at them.

"You're kids," he said.

"No kidding," said Val.

The slave shook his head. "You're supposed to be adults."

"Who are you?" demanded Quasar.

"The name's Jagger Nazz. I'm here to rescue some Sirian rock stars but they're supposed to be adults. You are Sirian aren't you?"

"Ya," said Jethro, "but I don't understand. Who sent you?"

"A couple of kids I encountered on Fuelitia. Their parents were sold into slavery and I agreed to help find them but, apparently you're not them."

"Were their names Bobbee and Bettee Draicon?" asked Quasar, suddenly.

"Whose names?"

"The kids you agreed to help."

"Oh, oh ya. Bobbee and Bettee. Ya that's them, why...hey, wait a minute. You guys must be their missing friends."

"That's us," confirmed Quasar.

Jagger jammed a key into the lock and swung the door open. "Well, come on then, let's go. You're not exactly what I planned on, but you're a pleasant bonus and I'm sure your young friends will be happy to see you."

As the young Sirians filed out of the cage, they introduced themselves one at a time. Jethro was the last to exit and he stopped before stepping out. He looked over into the adjacent cage.

"What about Chuck and Boog," he said.

"Go on," said Chucklee. "Get out of here. I'll just slow you down. Take Boog with you. He'll fit right in your pocket.'

"I'm not leaving without you," insisted Boognerp. "We didn't come this far together to just split up."

"Come on Chucklee," said Jethro, "this is your chance to make a difference."

"I'm needed here Jethro. What'll these slaves do without me?"

Jethro looked down into the ominous cavern at all the suffering slaves. He looked long and hard, creating an uncomfortable tension amongst his friends, who wanted to escape the mining colony as quickly as possible.

"This is wrong," he finally said.

"What's wrong," said Seth, tugging on his friend's arm. "C'mon Jethro, we gotta get out of here."

Jethro didn't move though. He stood and stared silently at the thousands of working slaves.

"What if our parents are here?" he said.

"They're supposed to be," said Jagger. He turned and looked at Chucklee and then unlocked the slave veteran's cage. "What about you? Have you seen or heard anything about these kids' parents?"

Chucklee sat and thought for a moment. "You know, now that you mention it, there was a group of new slaves that came here, but they got moved out right away. I never saw them, but I heard the guards talking about them. Something about overcrowding here and not having enough labour on some other colony. Now, just what was that other colony?" He mumbled the last sentence almost incoherently beneath his breath.

Jagger Nazz sighed impatiently. "Well, we're going to need to hasten our decision. It won't be long before more guards show up."

"The list," hollered Boognerp.

"What list?"

"The guards have a slave registry listing every slave here. I've seen them with it. It should be down at the other end. It'll tell us whether the kids' parents are here or not."

"Is there an exit on the other side?" asked Jagger.

"Nope. Only way outta here is down the stairs or down in the cages."

"Okay, everyone wait here. I'll check this list and be right back."

Jagger ran off down the platform barely even glancing at the other slaves that filled the rest of the cages. They called out to him begging to be freed. Without even thinking he tossed the keys into one cage as he jogged past. The slave snatched them up and quickly freed himself, then proceeded to unlock the remainder of the cells.

Jagger found the registry on a desk at the end of the platform and began running his finger down the directory. Within a moment he realized that it was alphabetized and he quickly skipped to the

S's. He found the name 'Ozzbourn Sirius' within seconds and, sure enough, he'd been moved to the Sibiliant Canyons of Graico 6K48582, an asteroid mining colony on the other side of the galaxy.

Running back down the platform wasn't quite as easy as running up it. All the slaves that had now broken free of their cells were fighting their way toward the stairs. Jagger pushed his way through the bodies until he reached the Sirians. They were waiting patiently with Chucklee and Boognerp next to their cells.

"Did you let all of these slaves out?" demanded Chucklee.

"Guess I did," replied Jagger.

"Why?"

"Seemed like the right thing to do."

"Well they're blocking your escape route now." Chucklee pointed toward the stairs where the slaves had begun moving down and around the stone column in a thick congregation of bodies. The commotion had drawn the attention of a large number of guards down below, who were now moving up the stairs to meet the slaves halfway.

"Now what are we gonna do," demanded Val.

"Get in the cages," ordered Jagger. "All of you."

"I just got out of that stinky prison," said Val. "I'm not about to get back in."

Quasar shoved Val into the cage and jumped in after her and was soon followed by Jethro and Seth. Jagger shot a glance at Chucklee and Boognerp.

"Get in," he said.

"I can't," insisted Chucklee. "They need me here."

"Chuck, how long have you been here?"

"I don't know. A little over ten years, maybe."

"Then you've done your time here. You're not helping anyone. You're simply a counselor. These slaves don't need therapy. What they need is a leader. Someone who's not afraid to lead them to freedom. Come with us. I belong to the Anti Slavery Coalition and I'm telling you that you'll be far more helpful on the outside than the inside. Now stop trying to play the martyr and get in the cage."

"Come on Chucklee," said Jethro.

Chucklee looked at the kids in the cage, then turned and looked toward the stairs. A battle had broken out halfway down as the guards and slaves fought for control while at the same time, trying to prevent themselves from toppling over the edge of the railing.

"The clock is ticking, Chuck," said Jagger.

Chucklee finally made up his mind and jumped into the cage.

"Let's do it," he said.

The kids cheered him on as Jagger shut them all into the cage with a loud clang.

"What are you doin', Jagger?" asked Seth.

"Saving our butts. Now hold on. This is gonna be one fast ride."

Standing on the outside of the cage, he dropped his pack to the floor and pulled out the device he'd used to escape the eleventh floor of the G.M.C. headquarters back on Fuelitia. He attached a new circular coil to it and shot the end into the platform on which he stood. He attached the device itself to the side of the cage and grabbed his pack and slipped it back over his shoulders.

"Okay guys, this device is the difference between life and death. Just before you're about to crash into the ground below, you need to hit this button here. It stops the cable release and will prevent you from turning into pancakes. The chain release is way over by the first cage so I won't be able to release the chain and be in the cage at the same time. But don't worry about me. I'll get down on my own."

"Why not just lower us down on the chain then. It'll be much safer," said Chucklee.

"Because the cage will take two minutes to get to the bottom that way and we've only got about thirty seconds before the guards reach us."

"What are you talking about? The guards are all still stuck in battle on the stairs."

"Not those guards. Those ones!" Jagger pointed straight above them and about a hundred feet up, another platform was covered with guards who were attaching repelling ropes to the railings and throwing them over the edge. Black, snake like ropes fell all around Jagger as he made a run for the chain release.

The guards had slid, gracefully, about halfway down their ropes when he reached the controls. Unfortunately none of the chains were labeled so he began randomly slamming the release levers all the way up. Spherical cells began dropping through the air like giant iron raindrops and crashed to the floor below. The first guard's feet hit the floor followed by another twenty or so. Half of them ran for the cage and half ran toward Jagger, who was still in the process of trying to locate the correct lever. He looked over at the guards approaching him then looked toward the stairs. A group of guards had broken through the battle and had reached the top of the stairs. He was trapped, with barely any time to lose.

The first guard reached the cage, grabbed hold of the door and was about to swing it open when Jagger located the chain release lever he was looking for. He slammed it up as far as it would go and the cage dropped suddenly, pulling the guard along with it.

Jagger was flanked on both sides by menacing looking guards, who all knew he had nowhere to go. The noble thief knew differently though and ran toward the edge of the platform and jumped.

Meanwhile, the falling cage's door had swung open and the guard dangled from the edge of it holding on with an iron-like grip as the sphere plummeted toward the ground below at an unbelievable speed. Just before the cage met it's destination, Chucklee hit the cable release button on the device, causing the cage to come to a sudden halt one foot above the ground. The sudden stop caused the guard to let go of the cell door and he slammed noisily into the ground and fell silent. The cage swung like a pendulum on the end of the cable.

Jethro looked up at the chain, which lay loosely on top of the cell, having been completely released. Looking through the bars of the cell, he noticed a figure dropping out of the sky, a large parachute open above it. It was Jagger Nazz and he soon landed on the ground safely and detached himself from his chute. He ran up to the cage and grabbed hold of it to stop it from swinging.

"Come on, there's no time to lose," he said.

The former prisoners all leapt from the cell and followed Jagger as he led them through the colony.

Slaves eyed them suspiciously as they weaved their way through the walls of stone. Jagger was attempting to lead them back to the tunnel from which he'd come through in the first place. Unfortunately, being discreet about his movement wasn't going to be quite as easy as it had been when he'd come through the first time. The entire guard population was now alerted to the escape attempt and was on the lookout for the prisoners.

"Keep moving," said Jagger over his shoulder as they passed a guard on their right who had his back turned to them.

A few close calls and narrow escapes from being sighted later, and they reached the entrance to the tunnel that led to the parked burrower. The only problem was that, standing directly in front of the entrance were two rather alert looking space goblins: Helgump and Hildump.

The escapees hid behind a mound of broken rock and discussed what their next plan of action should be.

"That's the way I came in," whispered Jagger. "My vehicle is a short ways down that tunnel and if we can get to it, then we can get back to the kids' tour bus."

"Unfortunately, the goblin sisters aren't about to just let us stroll through the entrance," said Chucklee.

"Isn't there another way out," asked Seth.

"There is, but most of them are far too conspicuous for us. The entire colony has been alerted to our escape and every way in or out is going to be heavily guarded."

Quasar turned to Chucklee. "What about that train?'

"What about it?"

"Where does it lead to?"

"Well, it leads to the shipping cavern, where they export all the mined materials."

"So, there's ships there, then."

"Ya, lots of 'em but, like I said, they'll be guarded."

"Okay, let's not get carried away here," said Jagger. "The burrower is parked in the middle of a whole fleet of ships. Getting a ship is not the issue here. Getting off this colony undetected is."

Just then, an open-air mining vehicle pulled up in front of the goblin sisters. It was full of fuelition guards. One guard in particular hopped out and approached the goblins.

"Any sign of them?" he asked.

"Nothin'," said Helgump, "but if they try and get through here, we'll know."

"Good. These slaves need to be taught a lesson. They're setting a bad example and we need to show the rest of the slave population what happens when they try to escape."

"You can count on us, sir," said Hildump.

"All right, every one out," said the guard, motioning for the rest to get out of the vehicle. "Let's cover this entire area and flush 'em out."

The guards climbed down out of the vehicle and began fanning out into the immediate area. Jagger cursed silently to himself as a guard approached the mound of rocks.

"What now," hissed Val.

Jagger looked over at Chucklee. "Any suggestions?"

"I'm thinking," came the reply.

"We don't have time to think. We're about to get busted and I, for one, don't want to be taught a lesson by these guys," said Val.

Just as the guard was about to come around the rock mound and surely discover them, a beautiful singing voice broke out suddenly from about fifty feet away from them. It caused the guard to stop and change direction.

"Where's that singing coming from," said Jethro.

"I don't know," replied Jagger, "but it seems to have temporarily distracted the guards. Now's our chance."

The guard vehicle had been parked directly between the rock mound and the goblin sisters, allowing the group of escapees to approach the vehicle on their hands and knees, undetected. When they reached their destination, Jagger urged them all to climb aboard.

"Keep your heads down," he whispered.

Once they were all safely concealed in the vehicle, Jagger climbed into the driver's seat and turned the key in the ignition. The vehicle rumbled to life and immediately drew the attention of the goblin sisters.

Hildump put an alarm whistle to her lips and blew hard. The sound alerted every guard in the immediate vicinity and they were soon all making their way back toward the vehicle.

Helgump, in the meantime, made a leap for the vehicle just as Jagger shifted it into gear and hit the gas. The sudden movement caused the tires to dig into the ground and spray the pursuing guards with a screen of dirt and gravel. Helgump managed to catch the side of the vehicle with her fat fingers and began to work her way inside. Her feet dragged in the dirt as Jagger steered the speeding vehicle through the labyrinth-like colony rock walls.

The space goblin now had both elbows inside and was in the process of pushing the rest of her large mass up and into the moving transport. She would have made it, too, if it hadn't been for Val, who ran up and slammed her elbow into Helgump's nose. The space goblin fell back and was now holding on with only one hand, the rest of her body now dragging through the dirt. She was about to grab on with her other hand when Boognerp sunk his teeth deeply into the only hand that attached Helgump to the vehicle. She let out a howl of pain and let go. The escapees watched as she rolled through the dirt like a giant bowling ball, knocking down a group of ten guards.

Jethro worked his way to the front of the vehicle and climbed into the seat beside Jagger.

"Where are we going?" he demanded.

"First place that'll take us off this rock," Jagger hollered, cranking the wheel to the right and narrowly missing a group of slaves.

"And where's that?"

Jagger pointed directly in front of them. They came around a corner and the train they'd seen earlier loomed up in front of them. It was just pulling out and heading toward the tunnel that would lead it to the shipping cavern. Jagger steered the guard transport vehicle behind the train and followed it into the tunnel.

The train soon disappeared ahead of them, but Jagger stayed the course. It was a rough ride and the vehicle bumped almost uncontrollably along the tracks.

"Hold on," screamed Jagger.

Everyone held on, exactly as ordered, when a curious thing occurred. The sound of the train had grown quieter as it pulled further away from them but, for some strange reason, it grew louder again.

"Uh, oh," said Jagger.

"What," demanded Jethro.

Jagger stopped the vehicle, shifted it into reverse, and began backing up.

"What are you doing," hollered Val from the back, huddled in closely next to Seth.

Jagger didn't need to answer for, within a few short seconds, the train appeared in front of them forcing them back from where they'd come. As Jagger pushed his foot down on the gas, the vehicle felt as if it might flip over on the tracks, it was bouncing up and down so erratically. Just when they all figured they were about to be run down by the train, they burst through the tunnel entrance, traveled a short distance, and came to a sudden stop as they cleared the end of the tracks. The train stopped and Jagger quickly looked around for an escape route, but there were none visible. They were completely surrounded by guards.

CHAPTER 18

CLOSE ENCOUNTERS WITH THE BIG BOSS – FOR THE THIRD TIME

"Sorry kids," said Jagger as the guards slowly approached the vehicle.

"It's not your fault Jagger," said Quasar. "You did the best you could."

"Anyone got any suggestions?" asked Jethro.

"I'm sorry to say it, but I think this is it guys," said Val, grabbing hold of Seth's hand and squeezing it tightly.

Jagger and Jethro had climbed into the back with the others and they huddled in the middle of the vehicle as the guards began climbing up the sides. The first guard stood on the edge and reached for Quasar's antenna when a loud explosion sounded in the distance. The noise distracted the guard long enough for Quasar to jump up and kick him in the stomach, sending him over backwards. He fell to the ground with a thump just as another explosion went off.

The guards all mumbled nervously amongst themselves and a few broke off from the group to go and investigate the explosions. It didn't take them long to locate the source of the disturbance, because it soon flew out of the train tunnel and into the main mining cavern. A familiar looking spacecraft slowly lowered itself to the cavern floor and guards had to move out of the way to avoid getting squashed. The door slowly opened and the landing platform extended forth. A set of feet stepped out and slowly walked down its length. As the rest of the figure came into view the Sirians, as well as Jagger, let out a series of gasps.

"Vack?" said Jagger.

"Jag?" said Vack.

Jethro looked at Jagger. "You two know each other?"

"Of course we know each other," said Jagger. "We're brothers."

Bobbee and Bettee Draicon sat in the cockpit of the tour bus, impatiently awaiting the return of Jagger Nazz and, hopefully, their parents. He'd been gone quite a long time and they were beginning to get a little nervous.

"I wish he'd hurry up," said Bobbee. "I'm starting to get worried."

Bettee nodded his agreement followed by some hand gestures.

Bobbee shook her head. "No, I don't think that's a good idea. Jagger told us to stay put until he gets back and that if he doesn't return within twenty four hours that we're supposed to contact the A.S.C. and ask for help."

Bettee shrugged and spun around repeatedly in the swivel chair he was sitting in.

"You're gonna get sick if you keep doing that," said Bobbee.

Bettee ignored her and kept doing it.

"Oh, children," said Libby suddenly. "I hate to interrupt your playtime, but we've got an intruder alert on level three."

"What do you mean, intruder alert?" said Bobbee.

"Someone just broke into the bus," said Miron.

"Libby I thought you were supposed to let us know before anyone got on the bus, not after."

"I know, I'm so sorry, but Miron and I were playing cards and I was winning for once. Sorry, I wasn't paying attention."

"What kind of computer are you anyways?"

"Look, there's no need to get snarky with her," said Miron. "You know, she is entitled to a little bit of 'Libby time' every now and then."

"Ya, but not when someone's breaking into the bus. I mean, c'mon, we've been sitting here for five hours. She's had plenty of time for 'Libby time' if you ask me...."

"Uh Bobbee," said Miron.

"...and I don't see why a super computer like Libby can't even take a few moments out of her time to..."

"Uh, Bobbee," Miron repeated.

"...on the outside perimeter to see if there's anyone sneaking around..."

Bobbee's last sentence was cut off as one of the drive lifter doors suddenly opened up. A figure stepped through and blasted both Bobbee and Bettee with a beam of blue electricity.

"What do you mean you're brothers," demanded Jethro.

King Rubb, Geeno, and a handful of other scary looking monsturds had walked down the landing platform and now stood with Vack. They all carried weapons and brandished them menacingly, pointing them at the fuelition guards, who were in the process of backing away from the space craft, apparently not too interested in losing their lives over a few insignificant and easily replaceable slaves.

"No time to explain," said Jagger, jumping down out of the vehicle. "C'mon kids."

The Sirians all jumped out of the vehicle one at a time and were followed by Chucklee. Boognerp had, once again, settled down in his partner's pocket. Jagger led them quickly toward Geeno's vessel and ran up the ramp to meet his brother.

"So. We meet again," said Jagger.

"No time to reminisce," replied Vack. "Get these kids in the ship."

Vack put his hand out and stopped Chucklee.

"Who're you," he asked.

Jethro spun around and answered for his newfound friend. "He's with us Vack. It's okay."

Vack eyed Chucklee suspiciously, then let him pass. He began to walk up the ramp when the entire cavern began to rumble and vibrate. Vack looked up toward the cavern ceiling and what he saw caused worry lines to stick out of his face.

Cracks began to open in the rock that made up the ceiling and small chunks of stone were dislodging themselves from the collective whole and dropping to the ground, hundreds of feet below. Fuelition guards and slaves ran in every direction, seeking a safe place to hide.

Meanwhile, above the surface of the mining colony, a lone, un-piloted pod had come shooting through space and collided with the mined meteor, digging itself deep into the surface of the rock. Moments later, a space dawg named Day-zee launched herself into the meteor in pursuit of the pod and began digging her gigantic, scrap metal paws into the surface of the meteor.

Inside the cavern, Dayzee's unrelenting digging frenzy was causing a hailstorm of rock and debris. Vack crawled up the ramp and into the ship. Geeno was in the process of powering up the vessel when Chucklee spoke.

"Let me out." he said.

Jagger rolled his eyes. "Oh, come on. Not this again."

Chucklee pointed out the window at the endangered slaves. "I can't just leave them here. If they don't get crushed by rock, they'll suffocate when the artificial atmosphere gets sucked through the cracks in the ceiling."

"Chucklee, are you sure this is what you wanna do?" said Seth.

"Of course I'm sure. Open the door and let me out. Boognerp, you with me?"

"Always," replied his slug-like friend.

"All right," said Vack and led them to the door. "Good luck."

"Thanks," Chucklee turned and looked at the Sirians, who had followed him. "Take care kids. Perhaps we'll meet again someday."

The kids smiled and waved goodbye as Chucklee ran through the open door and down the ramp. The door closed and Vack led the kids back to the cockpit.

"Can we get out of here now," he said.

"Geeno, take us out," said King Rubb.

Geeno's craft slowly cut through the interior of the mining cavern. The ship's exterior had already been damaged by falling debris, but Geeno still did his best to avoid the falling boulders.

"Just a little bit further," said Geeno, slamming the controls to the right and just barely missing a large cylindrical rock. They soon reached a hole in the cavern wall large enough to accommodate the monsturd craft.

King Rubb pointed at it. "Get us outta here."

The small ship careened down the short tunnel and burst into the shipyard where Jagger had originally entered the colony in the burrower. As they approached the end of the yard Geeno hovered his thumb above the button that would ignite the blasters. The hangar doors were still closed and he had no other way of opening them. Jagger realized what the pilot was about to do and stopped him by holding up his remote control and giving it a simple click. The hangar doors opened up and Geeno's craft shot out into the mountainous regions of the meteor. The ship careened through the rocky hills until it was a safe distance away from the colony center.

The tour bus was parked behind a large mushroom shaped boulder and Geeno set his ship down gently beside it. Inside, the young Sirians were thanking their unlikely group of saviours.

"So whatchoo gonna do next, kids," asked King Rubb.

"Find our parents, I guess," replied Jethro.

Jagger stepped up and placed his hand on Jethro's shoulder.

"I'll help you find your parents, kids," he said. "Freeing slaves throughout the galaxy is what I do and Graico 6K48582 is only about three days journey. We'll find your parents."

"I'm coming too," added Vack. "There's no way I'm letting you take all the credit."

"Gee, Vack, I kind of always thought that you and all your collecting cohorts were part of the problem."

"Don't start with me, Jagger."

"Hey, I'm not the one who 'started' it in the first place. Do you have any idea how many people have been sold into slavery because of collectors."

"Look, I said 'don't start with me'."

"Or what? Whatcha gonna do Vack? Pull my hair?"

"Shut up."

"Ah. Resort to witty comebacks. I see. Nothing ever changes, eh Vack."

"Jagger, why do you always..."

"Hey, I hate to break up this heartfelt reunion," said Jethro, "but I think we need to get a move on. I don't exactly want to just sit around here arguing and waiting for more trouble to arrive, as it seems to always want to do."

"Da' kid's right," said King Rubb. "You two should save yer fightin' fer anudder time. Git dese kids ta' dere bus."

King Rubb and Geeno approached the children and shook their hands.

"Nice knowin' 'ya, kids," said Geeno.

"Thanks for coming to get us, Geeno," replied Seth.

"No problem kid. My pleasure."

"You kids ever need us for anytin, you don hesitate to call us."

"Thanks King Rubb," said Jethro.

"My friends call me Rubby. You kids call me Rubby."

All their goodbyes having been said, Geeno and King Rubb led them down to the docking tube. Geeno punched a few commands into the controls and a large tunnel-like cylinder extended from the side of his ship and attached itself noisily to the side of the tour bus. He quickly applied the vacuum sealer, making the air breathable, and opened the door.

"Well, dis is it. Good luck," he said.

"Thanks again for everything," said Jethro, as he stepped into the tunnel.

King Rubb called out to him once more. "Hey, kid"

Jethro turned. "Ya?"

"Don't forget to send me a CD."

"Ah, just download it Rubby, everyone else does." He turned and entered the tube to the sound of King Rubb's thick laughter ringing in his ears.

Vack stopped before stepping through. "Ya, thanks for saving me from becoming that giant's lunch."

"No problem," said Geeno. "Robly woulda chewed you up and spat choo out anyway."

"Well, that's reassuring." Vack smiled and stepped into the tube.

The door closed behind them as they boarded the tour bus. While listening to the sound of the monsturd ship taking off, Val got down on her hands and knees and kissed the floor.

"So good to be home," she said.

The others laughed and got down and did the same. Vack and Jagger stood beside them and shook their heads.

"Do you have any idea how dirty that floor is," said Vack.

"Hey, I'm actually looking forward to seeing my parents again, Vack," said Jethro. "Please don't say things that remind me of how annoying they actually can be."

Vack shrugged. "What? Is commenting on a floor's obvious lack of cleanliness a parent-like thing to say?"

The kids all exchanged looks and shared a good laugh.

"C'mon," said Seth. "Let's go see Bobbee and Bettee."

They all marched down to the drive lift doors and began their ascent back up to the cockpit. The doors opened and they stepped through, half expecting the two siblings to run up and hug them. Instead, they were shocked to see the two youngsters hanging upside down in the middle of the cockpit. Blue electricity, shaped like rope, was wrapped around their ankles and extended up into the ceiling. Bossentical Distort stood between them, grinning fiercely and showing off a psychotic glint in his eye.

"Thought you'd get away from me eh?" he growled, while brandishing a dangerous looking weapon.

Jagger made a reach for his backpack, but the Big Boss was too quick and fired his weapon. A dazzling tangle of blue electricity shot towards Jagger and wrapped around him like neon netting. A strand of electricity attached itself to the ceiling and Jagger was picked up off the floor and left, swinging, in his electrical net, about a foot off the ground.

Bossentical never gave Vack a chance to react and fired a second shot at him. Vack soon joined his brother in a similar predicament. The kids all huddled together.

"Well that makes it easier," said Bossentical, firing a shot at them.

A net wrapped itself around all four of them and soon they were swinging between Jagger and Vack.

Bossentical approached the nets. "I warned you, Mr. Sirius. Your talent will be mine. It was all just a matter of rhyme before I caught up with you again. As I'm sure you've all discovered, I am full of surprises."

"Not to mention, full of a bunch of annoying anecdotes that you're always getting wrong, you idiot," snarled Jethro.

"Oh, come now. Let's not get ourselves into an insult war Mr. Sirius. I assure you my ego is quite large and not easily bruised."

He raised a small communicator device to his mouth and spoke into it. "All right, Marion. Everything is good to go. Plot a course for 'P' station. It's not far from here and I've got a fully functional talent sucker on board there."

"Not a problem," came the reply from the communicator.

"Libby," hollered Seth, suddenly.

"Don't bother, you slime. If you're trying to communicate with your central computer, it won't work. I've already dismantled her and her annoying cheese ball of a friend."

Vack continued to struggle, although it was clear that his efforts were in vain. He sneered at the Big Boss. "How did you escape the monsturds?"

Bossentical grinned and laughed his ear-piercing laugh. "I thought I made myself clear when I told you that no one outsmarts the Big Boss. I have my ways, and your monsturd friends are going to have a big surprise waiting for them when they get home, but that's a tale for another day. All you need to know is that you have lost, and I have won."

Marion, on board her own vessel, engaged the tow beam and lifted off, towing the tour bus behind her. Within minutes they had left the atmosphere of the meteorite, mining colony and charged on toward 'P' Station.

Chucklee moved with surprising agility through the torrential downpour of rock. Boognerp bounced comfortably in his pocket.

"Where we goin' Chuck?" He asked.

"The train," replied Chucklee. "The shipping caverns have a slave transport that's big enough to accommodate us all. We need to spread the word fast. Everyone meet by the train. Throw your voice in every direction possible."

Not only was Boognerp a phenomenal singer but a remarkable voice-thrower, as well. He was the one responsible for distracting the guards earlier when they'd almost been discovered hiding behind the mound of rocks. He began using his talent once again, throwing his voice in every direction. "Spread the word, meet by the train. Spread the word, meet by the train."

Once he felt they'd spread an adequate amount of the word, Chucklee began making his way back to the train. One thing he didn't find all that surprising was the fact that most of the guards had disappeared; run off to save themselves.

They reached the train just in time. It was already pulling out and Chucklee had to make a giant leap in order to grab hold of it. He struggled his way up the back and through the door. Only one fuelition guard sat in the back compartment and he turned around, startled by the presence of Chucklee.

"Get off the train, slave," he snarled.

"Or what," asked Chucklee, moving toward the guard. "You'll gnaw me to death with your forehead?"

"I'm warning you. Don't come any closer."

Chucklee ignored the guard's threats and continued to approach him. The fuelition was unarmed and they both knew it. The moment Chucklee was within striking distance the guard took a swing at him. Chucklee ducked and at the same time, thrust his gnarled fist into groin of his attacker. The guard let out a long slow moan and dropped to the floor. Chucklee dragged the groaning guard to the back of the train and tossed him out.

The train itself hadn't picked up much speed, but Chucklee sprinted through the compartments like a hurricane, leaving a jumble of groaning fuelition guards in his wake.

It didn't take him long to reach the engine and the driver was more than a little surprised to see him. The thump he received on the top of his head reminded him why. Chucklee grabbed hold of the controls and slowed the train to a stop, then slammed it into reverse. Once again it began moving backward. It moved along the tracks speedily and burst through the tunnel and back into the main mining cavern.

Boognerp's call must have worked because a few hundred slaves were waiting for the train to return when it arrived. Chucklee hung his head out the window and pulled the whistle cord.

"Allllll Aboooarrrdd," he called out to his slave compatriots.

This time there were no guards to push, poke and prod them forward and they all took a great deal of pride in climbing about freely. It didn't take long for them to fill the train up and Chucklee performed a quick runaround to make sure everyone had made it. When he was satisfied that most had, he made his way back to the engine, climbed in, and punched the train into gear. He could hear loud cheers emanating from the train as the entire slave population indulged in their long awaited cries of freedom.

The train sped through the tunnel and hummed along the tracks almost noiselessly. It burst through into the shipping caverns in no time at all and came to a complete stop. As the slaves began pouring out, Chucklee jumped down and scanned the cavern for the slave transport. He located it almost immediately.

It was a massive ship designed to hold nearly a thousand slaves. The few hundred that were there gathered around it. Chucklee motioned for silence and soon the large group of excited voices died down to a quiet murmur.

"Everyone, can I have your attention," Chucklee hollered. "It's very important that everyone listen to me. We're taking this transport to a slave free zone and I'm going to need everyone's cooperation. Please, is there anyone who can fly this beast?"

"I can fly it," came a voice from amidst the crowd.

"Who said that," Chucklee demanded.

"I did."

A tall, beautiful Butterflynerian moved through the crowd. Years of slavery had caused her wings to hang from her back like tattered rags, but she walked proud.

"I may not be able to fly myself anymore, but you put me behind any ship and I can fly it."

"What's your name, again?"

"Mona Ark." She reached out, grabbed Chucklee's hand, raised it to her lips, and planted a gentle kiss upon it. She then leaned forward and kissed his cheek.

"I thank you Chucklee for endowing us with freedom. It is clear to me that your spirit is beautiful."

At this point, Boognerp popped his head out of Chucklee's shirt pocket.

"I helped too 'ya know," he said.

Mona leaned over, once more, and planted a kiss as best she could on Boognerp's tiny head.

"I'm sure the entire slave population thanks both of you."

She turned to the crowd, stretched out her wings and raised her hands in the air.

"Let's hear it for Chucklee and..." She turned and stared at Chucklee's shirt pocket. "What's your name?"

"Boognerp."

"Chucklee and Boognerp, saviours of the Y2K50-90210 Asteroid Slave Colony."

A few hundred voices rose together in cheers. After a moment, Mona raised her hand to silence them.

"Now let's get outta here," she said, turning toward the ship.

Within no time at all, the entire slave population had boarded the ship. Years of whips upon their backs had taught them how to move fast when needed. Mona headed straight for the cockpit and powered up. Chucklee was the last to enter the ship, as he wanted to make sure everyone made it safely on board. He was just walking up the landing platform when a familiar voice stopped him.

"Not so fast, blubber boy."

He turned around. Helgump and Hildump were standing ten feet away, blasters pointed directly at him.

"Just where do you think you're going," demanded Hildump.

Chucklee flashed them a smile. "Just going out for an evening-cruise."

"Ya right," said Helgump. "You ain't goin' nowhere Chubby Chuck."

The two goblin sisters approached Chucklee slowly, keeping their weapons pointed directly at him. Helgump was looking worse for wear. She looked like she'd gone a few rounds with a Bultonian Boxer; her face puffed up and looking like a rotten melon.

"C'mon you two," pleaded Chucklee. "What's the point? The colony's been destroyed and they can't be paying you that much."

"They're payin' us enough," said Hildump. "Besides, this ain't just about gettin' paid. It's about pay back. Pay back for what you did to my sister."

"Oh, come on. You're not still mad about that are you?"

"Take a close look at her face and ask me that question again."

Chucklee raised his hands, palms forward, and said, "Isn't there something we can work out?"

"Nothin'," said Helgump. "We're marchin' on board and then we're all marchin' off. Now turn around and move."

Chucklee, completely dismayed and mind racing, turned and began heading up the ramp. At that very moment a strong wind picked up and began tugging at the back of his head. Helgump and Hildump felt it too and turned around, looking back down the train tunnel. Chucklee suddenly realized what was happening and grabbed hold of the ramp stabilizer as tightly as he could. Helgump and Hildump were too busy trying to figure out why the wind was pulling at them rather than pushing them. As the suction got stronger and they suddenly realized that they might be in trouble, they turned and reached for the landing platform, but their effort was a few moments too late. Both were suddenly pulled off their feet and slammed into the ground, stomach first. Chucklee took the opportunity to pull himself up the ramp. The goblin sisters had no such luck and dug their fingers into the ground. It was no use though, and the suction eventually took them over, pulled them up into the air and sucked them back down through the train tunnel.

Chucklee listened to their disappearing screams as he reached the top of the ramp and closed the door. He ran for the cockpit as fast as he could and burst in, panting and gasping for breath.

Mona spun around and looked at him. "You okay?'

"I'm...fine...now...get us...outta here," he panted.

Mona didn't need to be told twice and soon the slave freighter was rising up and out of the shipping caverns. They rose past both sets of air lock doors, breached the surface and began moving towards the mountainous regions of the asteroid. Mona looked down at the surface and was astounded by what she saw.

"Look at that," she said.

"Wow. That's somethin' else, ain't it?" said Chucklee.

Looking down they saw a giant mechanical dawg digging in the rock. It had pawed its way through to the mining cavern below causing the interior atmosphere to be sucked out through the hole. A huge stream of rock, mining supplies, cages, and two space goblins were shooting out of the hole in a constant geyser of mining excrement. A bus pod shot past the space dawg's mouth, only this time, was snatched between the robotic canine's teeth and crushed to smithereens. Day-zee wagged her massive, metallic tail, spun around, and dog paddled back into space, finally content that she had won her game of fetch. Mona steered around the obstruction and sped off above the asteroid surface.

Movement off to the right of the ship suddenly caught Chucklee's eye and he looked to see two ships taking off from the asteroid surface. Closer inspection revealed that it was one ship taking off while dragging the other one behind it. Mona was about to turn the freighter off in another direction when Chucklee stopped her.

"Mona wait," he said.

"What is it?"

"Those two ships over there."

"What about them?"

"We gotta follow them."

"What do you mean?"

"The ones on board that bus being dragged are the reason we're all free. We have to save them. I owe them. We all owe them."

"All right. If you say so."

"Just keep your distance."

Mona put a lock on Marion's ship just before Marion made the leap into hyperspace. She waited a moment before following, then made the leap herself.

CHAPTER 19

THE BIG BOSS FINALLY GETS HIS TALENT

Marion's ship pulled in to 'P' Station within the hour and she was glad of it. Though the Big Boss had offered her an exorbitant amount of money for this one last job, she really didn't like the pink little creature and just wanted to get home and cuddle up on the couch with Merp and a decent size bag of popcorn.

She knew they'd been followed. She knew and didn't care. She'd been paid to get them to 'P' Station. Whatever happened after that was entirely not her problem as far as she was concerned. She docked the ship and waited for further instruction from the Big Boss.

Back on the bus, Jethro and his friends were all still caught up in the netting of blue electricity. The curious thing about the net is that it didn't hurt to touch. There was some sort of insulation around it, which prevented it from electrocuting them.

Bossentical pointed his weapon at them and fired it once more, only this time nothing came out of it. Instead, the net was sucked back into it, causing the kids to fall to the floor. The Big Boss continued to wave his gun at them.

"Don't even think about trying to escape," he said. "Harmless, electrical netting isn't the only thing this weapon shoots. Now move. We have some unfinished business to attend to."

Vack and Jagger, however, continued to struggle in their respective nets.

"Let them go, you scumbag," cried Vack. "They're just kids."

Bossentical turned toward Vack. "Oh, and you'd like me to believe that wouldn't you. I may be stupid but I'm not gullible...wait..I mean...I mean, I may be gullible but I'm not stupid...no, no, no. I may be..."

"Why don't we just leave it at stupid," said Jagger.

Bossentical spun around, ran over to Jagger, and cracked him over the head with his weapon. Jagger fell unconscious almost immediately.

"You little freak," hollered Vack. "When I get my hands on you..."

"What? What are you going to do, collector? I'll suck the talent out of you so quickly you won't even know what hit you."

Bossentical delivered Vack one last triumphant sneer, then turned his weapon back on the Sirians. They had managed to move all the way to the drive lift doors in the hope that they might escape.

"And just where, exactly, do you think you're going?" The Big Boss moved toward them. "A curious place, 'P' Station. When I had it built I wanted it to be different from all my other, previous stations. It was the sixteenth one in the series and I insisted the architects use their creativity. You see, 'P' Station is one giant labyrinth. Once you get in, you'll never find your way out. Only I, and a select few hold the map to the maze, and I assure you, it'll never lay before your eyes. Now move. We've got some talent suckin' to attend to."

Bossentical urged them through the drive lift doors as Vack continued to struggle. Soon they were out of the bus and moving across the hangar bay. Bossentical raised his communication device to his mouth.

"Marion. Wait here until I return. I may need a ride."

"You never said anything about a ride. I thought my job was done," replied Marion.

"Your job is done when I say it's done. If you want to get paid, you'll sit tight and wait for my return." He shut the device off and forced the kids through a doorway.

The young Sirians soon realized that the Big Boss hadn't been lying. 'P' Station really was one big maze. Within five minutes they had taken so many twists and turns that the kids were beginning to feel dizzy. When they finally arrived at a door, Jethro felt like he was going to fall over.

"Move it," ordered Bossentical.

The door opened before them and the kids entered a very peculiar room. It wasn't the kind of room you'd expect on a space station. It was a jungle. All around them were trees, vines, streams and grassy mounds. The calls of wild animals rang out as did the sound of rushing water. The Sirians stared, amazed by what they were seeing.

"Pretty impressive eh," said Bossentical. "I sucked the talent out of the top Botanical talent in Botneex and created this place myself. You see over there, across that bridge and amidst the trees." He pointed.

The kids strained to see what he was pointing at. A glint of metal caught their eye.

"What is that," said Jethro.

"That is my pride and joy. That is the Talent Sucker ten thousand, three, six, o, four, mark, five, dash, nine, eight, seven, and let me tell you; she's a beauty."

He urged them forward, over the bridge and into the trees. As they approached the Talent Sucker they soon became aware of how massive it was. It didn't look anything like the previous machine that Jethro had been hooked up to. It was far more sophisticated looking. The wires and tubes wrapped themselves affectionately around trees and roots and the machine itself seemed to grow right out of the ground. The seat looked like a throne fit for a king and the helmet like a crown.

"I'd love to sit and give a history lesson, but I've got things to do and this Sucker takes a while to power up," said Bossentical, pulling back some bark on a tree to reveal a control panel. He punched in some commands and the Talent Sucker came slowly to life.

"Aw, gimmee a break," Marion said to herself as she watched the humongous slave transport pull into the hangar bay. "Merp, we still got work to do."

Merp growled his discontent, but obediently followed Marion off the ship. They stood outside in the open air of the hangar bay waiting patiently for the intruders to exit their ship.

The landing platform of the slave transport extended out and rested on the floor. The door opened and Chucklee walked down the ramp and quickly eyed up his surroundings. He located Marion and Merp and halted, eyeing Merp with a degree of uncertainty.

"Is that what I think it is?" he asked.

"It sure is," replied Marion. "If I were you, I'd turn around, get back on your ship, and get outta here. I don't have time for heroics."

"I'm afraid I can't do that," replied Chucklee, stepping down off the ramp and moving towards the woman and her pet.

"Are you stupid?" said Marion. "Do you have any idea what this thing will do to you?"

Chucklee nodded his head. "I do." He then raised his fingers to his lips and whistled.

One by one, three hundred and forty seven freed slaves marched down the landing platform and filled up half the hangar bay behind Chucklee. He smiled. "And do you have any idea what three hundred and forty seven recently freed slaves with years of pent up frustration are capable of," he asked.

Marion just smiled and bowed. "I can't argue with that kind of logic. What do you think Merp?"

Merp whimpered his response. He possessed only about one hundred and fifty seven tentacles. Not nearly enough to overpower the number of adversaries that stood before him now.

"What do you want?" asked Marion.

"I want the Sirians," replied Chucklee.

"Well you're too late. This whole station is one big maze. By the time you find them, if you find them, he'll be long gone and your little friends will be talentless morons."

She had barely finished her last sentence when they all heard the sound of another approaching ship. They watched as the small vessel cruised into the hangar bay and settled on the ground. It didn't take long for the pilot to come out and he soon joined their numbers.

Marion took one good look at him and said, "I know you."

"I should think so," said the pilot.

"You're the Big Boss's right hand goon."

"The name's Blurtch, actually. Not goon."

"So what are you doin' here Blurtch?"

"I'm here to repair some damage. Now outta my way."

Chucklee ran up and tapped Blurtch on the shoulder. "Hey, hold on a minute. You're a Gulterian aren't you?"

"Ya, so?"

"I spent some time in a cell with some kids who got run down by a Gulterian. You wouldn't happen to be that Gulterian would you?"

"Who wants to know?"

"I wanna know. You see my friends and I are here to rescue them and I'm sorry, but I can't allow you to get in the way."

Blurtch eyed the large crowd of slaves up and down before looking Chucklee in the eye.

"I didn't come here to hurt those kids," he said. "I came here to help them."

"And I'm supposed to believe that?"

"You can believe whatever you want but I'm telling you right now, if you have plans to rescue those kids, you're not gonna be able to do it without my help."

"And why's that?"

Blurtch pointed at the doorway on the other side of the hangar. "Because on the other side of that door is a labyrinth. And I'm not talking about just any old kid's maze. You go in there unprepared and you'll never come out. Besides the Big Boss, me and a couple of others are the only ones who know our way around in there. So you do what you want."

Blurtch turned his back on Chucklee and began moving across the hangar bay floor toward the door on the other side.

"Well, it looks like this job has taken a turn for the worse," said Marion. "I think maybe I'll take off before my conscience goes and gets the better of me too. Does any one have any objections?"

When no one answered her, she turned and walked back into her ship, Merp marching along behind. The door closed behind her and within moments her ship had powered into life and was rising up and moving over the slaves' heads. It no longer towed the Sirian tour bus, and quickly disappeared from view.

One thing's for sure, Marion thought to herself as she cruised off into space, *I'm not taking any more jobs for that lunatic again.*

Chucklee had to run to catch up with Blurtch. He thought about bringing some of the other freed slaves with him, but opted against it. He decided that the element of surprise was important if they were to get the jump on the Big Boss.

It was a good thing that Blurtch had shown up when he did. After only a few minutes of traversing the maze, Chucklee realized that he never would have found his way through the labyrinth. Many twists and turns later, they arrived at a door and stopped.

"This is it," said Blurtch.

"What's in there," asked Chucklee.

Blurtch raised his finger to his lips. "Shhh." He keyed in the access code and stepped through to the other side, Chucklee following close behind.

They heard Bossentical's voice right away. It was a difficult one to miss. Hysterical ravings interspersed with insane laughter conducted auditory dances among the trees. Blurtch led the way, his footsteps surprisingly light despite his massive size. Chucklee, on the other hand, was not quite as quiet and was having a difficult time avoiding the natural noise makers of the forest: snapping twigs, rustling brush, and crunching leaves. More than once Blurtch had to turn around and shush him.

As they neared their destination, the laughter became louder and the click and the whirr of a large machine could now be heard. Once close enough, they peered through the brush.

They located Jethro right away. He was strapped into the seat of the Talent Sucker and the Big Boss was laughing and dancing around the control panel like a two year old, high on far too much sugar.

"Well, Mr. Sirius," he ranted. "This is the part where I become you and you become nothing but a distant memory."

"Not so fast, Boss," said Blurtch, stepping into the clearing.

"You! What are you doing here?"

"I'm here to stop you. You know, the pay was never really that great and I never liked you anyways."

"What has that got to do with anything? We had a contract."

"Ya, so what. I broke the contract and as far as I'm concerned, so did you when you tried to kill me."

The Big Boss smirked. "Oooo, look at the big hero everybody. Suddenly Blurtch has freed himself of the guilt of assisting me to steal the talent of hundreds. Are you forgetting the sucking spree we've been on for the past few years Blurtchy? We actually made a pretty good team, you and I. You shouldered all the guilt and I absorbed all the talent."

Suddenly, a beautiful singing voice rang out in the trees behind the talent sucker. The Big Boss spun around to investigate and Blurtch made his move. He reached up and grabbed a vine that was dangling just off to his right and took a few steps back before lifting his feet off the ground. As he swung toward the Big Boss, Seth, Val, and Quasar ran for Jethro, arms outstretched, eager to free their friend.

Unfortunately, the Big Boss had been far more prepared than they would have guessed. They all slammed into an invisible barrier and bounced back, landing on their bottoms. Even Blurtch, whose outstretched arm had been intended to clothesline the Big Boss, found himself on his back in the dirt. The Big Boss spun around and laughed.

"Did you think I'd be stupid enough to let you get away a second time? Try something like that again and I'll suck so much out of your friend that he'll lose his talent to breath." He looked off into the bush. "And whoever is out there, I suggest you come out where I can see you. That is if you want to see Mr. Sirius alive again."

Chucklee, realizing that there wasn't much they could do to penetrate the invisible barrier that protected the Big Boss, stepped out into the clearing.

"That's better," said Bossentical, a smug, lilting quality attached to his already whiney voice. "And who might you be?"

"Who I am doesn't much matter. I'm just here to inform you that even if you manage to suck that kid's talent, you won't get off this station."

"Oh, and I suppose you're going to stop me."

"Perhaps."

"What I find most curious about you, is your method of distraction."

"What do you mean?"

"Let's just say I have an ear for talent and you, my friend, happen to possess one of the most beautiful singing voices I've ever heard."

"So?"

"So, I'm in the mood for showing off. Seeing as these Sirians have caused me so much trouble, I think a demonstration is in order. How about we up the ante on the fear factor."

The Big Boss reached down, picked up his weapon, and fired it at Chucklee. The blue neon netting wrapped around its victim and dragged Chucklee through the invisible barrier. Bossentical flicked a switch on his weapon and the electric webbing around Chucklee disappeared.

"Don't try anything funny. This weapon is set to kill and, believe me, I won't hesitate to use it. Now up on your feet and go un-strap Mr. Sirius."

"What? Why?"

"Just do it!"

Chucklee slowly got to his feet, walked over to Jethro, and started unstrapping his young friend.

"Chucklee, no," said Jethro.

"It's okay kid. Don't worry about me."

"But it's not fair. You worked so hard to get free. You wouldn't be here if it wasn't for us."

"I wouldn't be free if it wasn't for you, kid. And neither would the rest of the slaves."

"You freed them?"

"I freed them all, kid. I freed them all."

"Oh, enough with the niceties," cut in Bossentical.

Once Jethro was free, the Big Boss shot an electric net around him, then turned the weapon back on Chucklee, whom he approached and began to strap into the machine. When his victim had the sucker crown upon his head, Bossentical walked over to the control panel and flicked a switch.

"Say good bye to that beautiful voice of yours, sucker. Ha, ha, ha, ha, ha!"

The crown upon Chucklee's head suddenly lit up and began making awful sucking noises, and the Sirians looked on, horrified. Blurtch turned his head away. He'd seen this demonstration far too many times to want to see it again. Chucklee had an extreme look of pain on his face as the machine sucked away.

"Can you feel it disappear?" ranted the Big Boss. "All those years of training, gone, in a matter of minutes. Kinda sucks, doesn't it? Ha, ha, ha, ha, ha, ha!"

Chucklee's teeth were clenched tightly together and the veins in his arms were bulging through his skin as he clutched, tightly, to the arms of the throne.

Just as soon as it had begun, it ended. The Big Boss flicked a switch and the sucking ceased. Chucklee's body went into a spasm momentarily, and then stopped. His head drooped as he fell unconscious. The Big Boss approached and unstrapped him. His heavy body fell to the earthen floor and the Big Boss climbed into the chair. He pulled the sucker crown down over his head and looked over at Jethro.

"You are about to witness sacrifice in its purest form Mr. Sirius. You see, in order for me to absorb your friend's talent, I must have all the talent already inside me sucked out and stored in reserve. The more talent I possess, the more painful the process. Only a pure body can absorb fresh talent."

The Big Boss raised a remote control and hit a button. The talent sucker, once again, started up and began sucking away at the Big Boss's brain. He shook uncontrollably, and his eyes looked as if they were about to pop out of his head. Halfway through the process he let out a bloodcurdling shriek that didn't stop until the process was over. He clicked the button and the machine stopped. He hit a few other buttons and turned the machine back on.

"This is my favourite part," he said. "There's nothing better in the universe than the feeling of sucking up raw talent in its purest state."

The Talent Sucker, now working in reverse, began pumping Chucklee's talent into the Big Boss. Normally, he could feel the talent growing in him right away, but this time, judging by the look on his face, something was wrong. Just as he was about to turn the machine off, Chucklee jumped up and snatched the remote control out of Bossentical's hands. He then proceeded to strap the Big Boss into the throne.

"What's going on," screamed Bossentical, who was clearly in pain as the talent sucker continued to pump Chucklee's talent into him.

"You're absorbing my talent," said Chucklee.

"But, it's not supposed to hurt."

"That's because he didn't have any talent," said Boognerp, popping his head out of Chucklee's pocket.

"Who're you," demanded Bossentical.

Boognerp sung a beautiful melody in reply. The Big Boss stared wide-eyed as he realized his mistake.

"You tricked me," he hollered.

"You see," said Chucklee, "right now you're absorbing years of talentless blunder. The look on your face is really quite amusing, actually. I've had the benefit of dealing with my pain over many, many years. You, however, are receiving it all at once."

Bossentical let out one last scream as he absorbed the last drop of Chucklee's talent for being untalented. His chin hit his chest as he fell into unconsciousness. Chucklee reached down and picked up the weapon. He aimed it at Jethro, reset it, and turned it on. It sucked the electric netting off the Sirian and Jethro breathed a long sigh of relief. Chucklee quickly ran over to the control panel and disengaged the invisible force field. Seth, Val and Quasar ran to Jethro and they all embraced in one big group hug. They then all turned and smiled at Chucklee.

"Thanks," they said in unison.

Chucklee returned their smile. "Not a problem, but don't just thank me. If it wasn't for little Boognerp's lovely singing voice, none of this would have fallen into place as easily as it did. Not to mention our Gulterian friend over here. He's the one that led us through the maze. Without him, we probably would never have found you."

Seth was the first to approach the space goblin. He held out his hand and Blurtch accepted it. "Thanks."

"You're welcome. I feel much better now," Blurtch replied, grinning.

"So what are we gonna do with him," said Quasar, pointing at the Big Boss.

"I know what to do with him," said Blurtch. "I've been waiting a long time for this."

He unstrapped Bossentical, who fell to the floor immediately. He then asked Chucklee for the weapon and shot a net around the Big Boss's still form. He then slung the weapon over his shoulder, a thin line of blue electric cord stretching from its tip to the net. He looked over at the others. "You coming?"

They all nodded and fell in line behind the space goblin as he led them out of the jungle chamber and into the corridor on the other side. They followed him through the maze and reached the hangar bay safely. They moved toward their ships and stopped when they reached the congregation of former slaves who were waiting patiently by their transport.

The Sirians were about to say goodbye to the space goblin when Seth suddenly slapped his own forehead. "We forgot about Vack and Jagger and the twins. They're still stuck in electric nets on the bus. Could you do us one more favour Blurtch?"

Within minutes Vack, Jagger and the twins were standing in the hanger bay with their young Sirian friends, listening intently, as all four kids attempted to blurt out the recent chapters of their story all at the same time.

"Well, I hate to cut this reunion short," said Blurtch, "but I've got a lot of talent to restore to its rightful owners."

Bettee disengaged from his friends, walked up to the space goblin and held out his hand. Blurtch obliged the youngster and reached out and shook the Sirian's hand. Bettee smiled and turned to his sister, making some more of his routine hand gestures.

Bobbee translated and said to Blurtch, "My brother says he knew you were good all along. He could sense it when you were chasing him and our friend back on the space station."

Blurtch looked down at Bettee. "Quite a talent you've got there kid. Use it wisely." He looked down at the still unconscious form of the Big Boss.

"You gonna be able to take care of that on your own?" asked Chucklee.

"I got some thugs who owe me a few favours. Shouldn't take me too long." He reattached the weapon to the Big Boss's net and dragged him toward his ship. He turned around before walking up the ramp. "And don't worry about this freak. He won't be bothering anyone for a long time."

The others watched as Blurtch, the Big Boss in tow, disappeared inside the ship. It powered up, lifted into the air and disappeared out of the station.

Vack looked at the Sirians. "Well kids. I guess it's time."

"Are you coming with us Vack," asked Jethro.

"Of course I am. We haven't found your parents yet have we? And after all, I am kind of out of a job."

"After all we've been through, I almost forgot about our parents."

"I suppose that means I ought to come too," said Jagger. "Seeing as I know where they are."

The kids all smiled at the two brothers, then turned to Chucklee.

"So what are you gonna do next?" asked Jethro.

Chucklee grinned. "Take singing lessons, of course. But I suppose I'll help everyone get back to where they belong. They're all going to need to be enrolled in S.I.P."

"What's S.I.P.?" asked Quasar.

"Slave Integration Program. It's a universal social program dedicated to helping freed slaves get integrated back into society."

"Thanks for all your help Chucklee," said Jethro.

"No problem kiddo. Don't ever hesitate to track me down if you ever need my help. I plan on following in the footsteps of our friend Jagger here and joining the ranks of the Anti Slavery Coalition. Contact me through them if you ever need me."

One by one they all shook hands with Chucklee and waved to Boognerp and the others. Chucklee waved one final goodbye from the cockpit as Mona powered up the craft.

As the slave transport cruised out of the hangar bay and out into space, the Jethro Sirius Experiment, along with Jagger and Vack, eagerly boarded the space bus.

"So good to be home," said Val, giving Seth a big hug, causing him to blush.

"I'm going to sleep for an entire day," said Quasar. "Libby, can you get us out of here?"

When she received no answer, Seth suddenly spoke up. “Oh no, I just remembered that the Big Boss said he had dismantled Libby and Miron.”

“I’m pretty good with computers,” said Jagger. “I should be able to get them up and running within no time at all.

Sure enough, within fifteen minutes, Libby and Miron’s voices were soon heard, coming out of the walls.

“Welcome home children,” said Libby.

“I take it you did not find your mothers and fathers,” added Miron.

“No Miron, we didn’t,” said Quasar. “And if you ever want to enjoy intellectual conversation again, you’ll listen to Jagger ‘cause he’s gonna tell you where they are.”

“Dandy,” said Miron.

“Miron,” said Jagger, “plot a course for Graico 6K48582.”

“Well, that’s on the other side of the galaxy,” said Miron.

“Why, yes it is, so you better get a move on.”

“You’re forgetting one thing,” said Libby. “You still have shows to do. We can hit Graico in about five shows. It falls between planets Shlep and Mirror Void.”

“Well, let’s get a move on then,” said Jethro.

As the entire gang reached the cockpit they all slumped into the comfort of swivel chairs.

“I can’t believe, after all that, we didn’t find them,” said Seth.

“We’ll find them Seth. I know we will,” said Val.

“I just hope we find them while we’re still kids. All this adventure stuff is forcing me to grow up way faster than I expected to.”

“Well, look on the bright side you guys,” said Jethro. “At least we’ve got a whole whack of inspiration for writing new songs. Wanna jam?”

EPILOGUE

As the space bus coasted through space and Jethro, Seth, Val, and Quasar jammed on new tunes, and Bobbee and Bettee worked on the lights and sound, a space station shaped like an L in another area of the galaxy welcomed the return of a particular Gulterian space goblin. This particular goblin dragged a pink, furry body behind him and entered a darkened room. Moving past many freeze chambers full of frozen bodies the goblin reached a familiar empty one and stuffed the limp, pink, furry body inside. He pressed a few buttons and the chamber filled up with freezing gel. Kneeling down he read the digital letters on the name panel. They spelled out the name 'Ozzbourn Sirius'. He erased the name one letter at a time and quickly keyed in the new letters, but he did not type in what you might expect. Instead of the name, 'Bossentical Distort', Blurtch had typed in the only name that ever came to mind when he thought of his former boss: *'Jerk Face'*. He smiled contentedly and proceeded to empty the rest of the chambers of their freeze gel, happy that he'd finally found a purpose in his life.